SMALL WORLD

Martin Suter

SMALL WORLD

Translated from the German by
Sandra Harper

THE HARVILL PRESS
LONDON

First published with the title *Small World*
by Diogenes Verlag AG, Zürich, 1997

First published in Great Britain in 2001 by
The Harvill Press
2 Aztec Row, Berners Road
London N1 0PW

www.harvill.com

1 3 5 7 9 8 6 4 2

© Martin Suter and Diogenes Verlag AG
English translation © Sandra Harper

Martin Suter asserts the moral right
to be identified as the author of this work

A CIP catalogue record is available
from the British Library

ISBN 1 86046 927 2 (pbk)
ISBN 1 86046 881 0 (hbk)

Designed and typeset in Fournier
by Libanus Press, Marlborough, Wiltshire

Printed and bound in Great Britain by Butler & Tanner Ltd
Frome, Somerset

For Father

I

WHEN KONRAD LANG CAME BACK EVERYTHING WAS ON
fire apart from the wood in the fireplace.

He lived in the Koch villa on the coast of Corfu, about 40 miles
north of Kerkira. The villa's rooms, gardens, terraces and pools
cascaded down to a sandy bay. Its small beach was accessible only
from the sea or by a sort of funicular railway which ran through
all the levels of the complex.

Strictly speaking, Konrad Lang did not live in the villa itself but
in the caretaker's house, a cold, damp, stone-built annexe higher
up the slope, which stood in the shade of a small pine forest next
to the front gates. Konrad Lang was not one of the villa's guests,
more like its manager. In return for his food, accommodation and
a lump sum he had to make sure that the house was ready at any
time for members of the family and their guests. He had to pay
the staff's wages and the bills of the maintenance men who were
locked in battle with the damp, salty air corroding the structure of
the building.

A tenant took care of the farming side of things: some olive,
almond, fig and orange trees and a small herd of sheep.

The winter months were stormy, rainy and cool, and Konrad had
practically nothing to do, apart from driving to Kassiopi once a day
to meet some of his fellow sufferers who were likewise spending
the winter on the island: a retired antique dealer from England, the
German lady who owned the now rather old-fashioned boutique,

an elderly painter from Austria and a couple from the west of Switzerland who were also keeping an eye on a villa. They would get together for a chat in one of the few tavernas which stayed open out of season and have a few drinks, usually one too many.

The rest of the day he would spend sheltering from the damp and cold that chilled to the marrow. The Koch villa, like many holiday villas on Corfu, was not built for winter weather. The caretaker's house did not even have a fireplace, just two electric heaters which he couldn't have on at the same time or the fuse would blow.

And so, on particularly cold days, and sometimes at night too, he would use the guest wing on the lower level. He liked it there. At the front window he felt as if he were a captain on the bridge of a luxury liner: a turquoise-blue pool beneath him, ahead of him nothing but the indifferent sea. And there were the bonuses of a very effective fireplace and a telephone. The caretaker's annexe had originally housed the staff for the guest wing below, so he could transfer calls down to the guest rooms and pretend he was where he was supposed to be. Elvira Senn, the owner of the villa, had issued instructions that the rooms of the main building were out of bounds for Konrad.

It was February. A stormy east wind had ruffled the palm trees all afternoon and driven wisps of grey cloud across the sun. Konrad decided to tuck himself away with a few piano concertos in the guests' living room at the bottom. He loaded some wood and a can of petrol on to the funicular railway and went down.

He needed the petrol to help light the wood. Two weeks ago he had ordered a load of almond wood, which burned for a long time and gave off a good heat when it was dry. But the new delivery was damp. There was no other way of lighting it except with petrol: not very elegant but effective. Konrad had done it like this dozens of times.

He built up a few sticks of firewood, poured petrol over them and lit a match. Then he went up on the railway to fetch two bottles

2

of wine, a half-full bottle of ouzo, olives, bread and cheese from his little kitchen.

On the way back from his house he bumped into the tenant farmer, who wanted to show him a place on the wall where the saltpetre had eaten away the plaster.

As the railway car started back down the slope Konrad Lang could already smell the smoke. He put it down to the wind, which was blowing from an unusual angle off the sea and into the chimney, and thought no more about it.

When the railway car stopped at the guest wing, everything was on fire apart from the wood in the fireplace. It was one of those mishaps that happen to a person when he is lost in thought: he had piled up the firewood in the fireplace but then set light to the stack of wood at the side of the fireplace. In the time he had been away the flames had spread to the Indonesian rattan seats and from there to the ikat fabrics on the walls.

The fire might still have been tamed had the open petrol can not exploded at the very moment when Konrad Lang was getting out of the car. Konrad did the only sensible thing: he pressed the top button.

As the car crept upwards, the shaft filled with acrid smoke. Between the two upper levels the car hesitated, shuddered violently, and then stuck fast.

Konrad Lang held his sweater over his mouth and looked at the smoke, which was growing blacker and ever more dense. He levered the handle of the car door in a panic, managed to break it open somehow, held his breath and crawled up the steps at the side of the track. After only a few metres he reached the top level and emerged coughing and spluttering into the open air.

Not long before the fire, the Koch villa on Corfu had been completely refurbished by an interior designer from Holland. It was bursting at the seams with Indonesian and Moroccan antiques, exotic textiles and ethnic kitsch. The whole lot went up like a tinder-box.

The wind fanned the flames up through the railway shaft into the living rooms on every floor and from there into the bedrooms and adjoining rooms.

By the time the fire engine arrived the fire had finished with the house and, chased by the wind over the palm trees and bougain-villea, was heading for the pine forest. The firemen confined themselves to preventing the flames spreading to the pines and surrounding olive trees. There had been surprisingly little rain for the time of year.

Konrad took himself off to the caretaker's house with a bottle of ouzo. Not until the king pine in front of the window exploded into a sheet of flames did he stagger out and watch from a distance as the fire destroyed the little white house with all his possessions.

Two days later Schöller was on the scene. He was taken round by Apostolos Ioannis, the manager of the Greek subsidiary of Koch Engineering. He poked around in the charred rubble with the toe of his shoe. He soon put his notebook away. The villa had been gutted.

Schöller was Elvira Senn's personal assistant. A thin, neat man in his mid-fifties. He fulfilled no official function in the firm – his name did not appear in the commercial register – but he was Elvira's right-hand man and as such feared even by people at the very top of the company.

Until now Konrad Lang had concealed his fear of Schöller by treating him with the condescension of a person more highly born. Although it was Schöller who gave the instructions, Konrad had managed to accept them as if they merely confirmed the result of his earlier confidential consultation with Elvira. Even though Schöller knew perfectly well that all communication between Elvira Senn and Konrad Lang went through him, he personally held it against the arrogant old man that the *grande dame* of Swiss high finance was always pulling strings for Lang, always finding him a place in life as a companion, caretaker or general dogsbody

4

somewhere in her broad empire and her international circle of acquaintances. Simply because he had spent a part of his youth with her stepson Thomas Koch, she felt duty-bound to keep his head above water, albeit at a distance.

For Schöller, Lang was one of his most tiresome duties. He hoped that the fire would enable him to cross "dear Koni" off his To Do list for good.

For hours Konrad Lang stood amidst the commotion of the fire-fighting teams, transfixed by the flames. He only moved to swig from the bottle or to duck as the fire plane roared low over the pine trees to drop another load of water. At some point the tenant farmer arrived with two men who wanted to question him about the incident. When they noticed that Konrad was not in a fit state to be interviewed, they took him to Kassiopi where he spent the night in a police cell.

The following morning when he was being questioned he said he could not explain how the fire had started. And he was not lying.

His memories about the cause of the fire only re-surfaced in little snippets during the course of the day. But by then he had already indignantly rejected any feelings of guilt and desperately stuck to his story. Perhaps he would have got away with it if the tenant had not stated that he had seen Konrad Lang that afternoon on his way to the guest wing with a petrol can.

As a result Lang was taken to police headquarters in Kerkira on suspicion of wilful arson pending clarification of the matter. He was still there as Schöller, in his room in the Corfu Hilton International, washed off the soot, changed and took a tonic water from the minibar.

An hour later Lang was led out of his cell into the bare room where Schöller was waiting for him. He had spent more than 50 hours in police custody, long enough to shed all his arrogance. The man who took care to be correctly dressed and clean-shaven for every situation was now wearing soot-stained cords, filthy shoes, a dirty shirt, a crumpled tie and the once-yellow cashmere sweater that he had used as a smoke filter. His short clipped moustache merged into his stubble, strands of grey hair straggled over his face and the bags under his eyes were darker and heavier than usual. He was shaky, from agitation certainly, but mainly from the sudden withdrawal of alcohol. Lang was just past 63, but that afternoon he looked 75. Schöller ignored the hand he was offered.

Konrad Lang sat down and waited for Schöller to speak. But Schöller said nothing. He only shook his head. And when Lang shrugged his shoulders helplessly he continued to shake it.

"What now?" Konrad asked at last.

Schöller was still shaking his head.

"The almond wood. It doesn't burn when it's damp. It was an accident."

Schöller folded his arms and waited.

"You've no idea how cold it can get here in winter."

Schöller looked towards the window. A glorious day was drawing to a close outside.

"That's rare for this time of year."

Schöller nodded.

Lang turned to the officer: "Tell him a day like today is very rare for this time of year."

The officer shrugged. Schöller looked at the clock.

"Tell them I'm not an arsonist. They're going to keep me here."

Schöller stood up.

"Tell them I'm an old friend of the family."

Schöller looked down at Konrad Lang and shook his head again.

"Did you explain to Elvira that it was an accident?"

"I shall be speaking to Frau Senn tomorrow." Schöller moved towards the door.

"What will you say to her?"

"I shall advise her to start legal proceedings."

"It was an accident," Lang stammered again, as Schöller walked out of the room.

The following day Schöller took the only plane that flew from Ioannis-Kapodistrias airport to Athens out of season. He had a reasonable connection back to Switzerland and by late afternoon was in Elvira's study in the "Stöckli". This was the name the Kochs gave to the bungalow of glass, steel and exposed concrete that a famous Spanish architect had designed for Elvira as a retirement home in the grounds of the Villa Rhododendron. It was set in over two acres of gently sloping land with little paths winding through a great range of rhododendrons, azaleas and old trees. The study, like all the rooms, faced west and had a magnificent view across the lake to a range of hills beyond and, on clear days, the Alps.

Elvira Senn had come, aged 19, to work as a nanny for Wilhelm Koch, the widowed founder of the Koch empire. His wife had died not long after the birth of her only child. Elvira soon advanced from being child minder to wife. Two years after Wilhelm's untimely death she married again; this time the managing director of the Koch Works, Edgar Senn. He was a competent man who, during the war years, had brought prosperity to the works – an engineering factory which was solid rather than innovative. He manufactured unavailable spare parts for German, English, French and American cars, engines and machines. After the war Senn made use of this experience and manufactured many of the same products under licence. He invested in property on a grand scale using the profits from the years of the economic miracle, sold at the right moment and thus created the means for wide diversification. Thanks to him, Koch Industries survived the recession. Not unscathed, but well enough.

It was generally believed that his shrewd hand was guided by the even shrewder hand of his wife. When Edgar Senn died of a heart attack at 60 in 1965 and the enterprise continued to thrive without a hitch, many people were confirmed in their suspicions.

Koch Industries were now a well-balanced mix of companies, in several sectors: engineering, textiles, electronics, chemicals, energy. Even green technology.

Ten years ago, when Elvira announced that it was time to make room for the younger generation, she had moved into the Stöckli. But she contrived to keep a tight hold of the reins which, according to the press releases, she had handed over to her 53-year-old stepson Thomas. Although she did not remain on the board, the decisions taken at the regular meetings at her home were more far-reaching and binding than anything decided by the directors. And she wanted it to stay that way until Thomas's son Urs was ready to take over her role. She intended to miss Thomas out, for reasons to do with his character.

She received the news of the disaster in Corfu with her usual composure. She had been there only once in her life – more than 20 years ago.

"How will it look if I put him in prison?"

"You won't be putting him in prison. The courts will. They lock up arsonists, especially in Greece."

"Konrad Lang isn't an arsonist. He's just getting on a bit."

"If you want them to call it causing fire by negligence we'll have to testify in his favour."

"And what will they do with him then?"

"He'll be fined. If he can pay he won't have to go to prison."

"I don't need to ask you what you would do in my place."

"No."

Elvira thought it over. The idea of knowing that Konrad Lang was safely behind bars 1,500 kilometres to the south was not entirely unattractive to her. "What are Greek prisons like?"

"Ioannis tells me everything can be made quite bearable with a few drachmas."

Elvira smiled. She was an old woman although you would not have thought so to look at her. All her life she had spent time, trouble and money on not becoming old. From the age of 40 she

8

had begun to undergo minor corrective cosmetic surgery at regular intervals, especially to her face. True, this had endowed her for a while with a rather prematurely well-preserved look, but now that she was 78, on good days she could pass for 60. This was not only due to money and surgery; nature had been kind to her too. She had a round baby-doll face and so, unlike other women, she had never had to choose between face and figure. She could afford to stay slim. She was healthy apart from diabetes (her GP had been discourteous enough to call it "old-age diabetes"), and because of this for several years now she had had to inject herself twice a day with delayed-effect insulin, using a syringe that looked like a fountain pen. She kept strictly to her diet, swam every day, went for massages and lymphatic drainage, spent three weeks in a clinic on Ischia twice a year and tried not to become irritated, something which was not easy for her.

The ball was still in Schöller's court. "No one can reproach you after all you've done for him. After this incident there's nowhere else you can put him. Or can you still take responsibility for him even now?"

"People will say I've put him in prison."

"Far from it. They will think well of you not suing him for damages. No one will expect you to get a man who set fire to a five-million-franc villa out of prison."

"Five million?"

"The insurance value is about four."

"How much did it cost us?"

"About two. Plus about one and a half which Herr Koch invested in it last year."

"In the interior designer, that Dutchwoman?"

Schöller nodded. "There'll never be a more convenient way of getting rid of him."

"What do I have to do?"

"That's the nice thing about it: nothing."

"Then that's what I'll do."

Elvira put on her reading glasses and turned towards a sheet of paper on the desk in front of her. Schöller stood up.

"And Thomas," she said, without looking up. "There's no need to rub Thomas's nose in every aspect of the story."

"Herr Koch will not learn anything from me."

Before Schöller had reached the door, there was a knock and Thomas Koch strode into the room.

"Koni's burnt down Corfu." He failed to notice the look that passed between Elvira and Schöller.

"Trix van Dijk has just phoned. The villa looks as if a bomb's hit it." Then he grinned. "She was there with a team from *The World of Interiors*. They wanted to do a front-page story and make a big splash about it. But there weren't any interiors any more. She says she'll kill Koni. The way she was talking, I believe her."

Koch was bald except for a tonsure of black hair; the sun broke through the clouds and shone briefly into the room, making it gleam unnaturally. His face seemed too small for the polished expanse above it, even when Thomas was grinning broadly, as at this moment.

"I think you should go and see everything's all right in Corfu, Schöller. Deal with the formalities, and for God's sake keep that van Dijk woman away from me." Koch turned back to the door.

"Oh, and get Koni out of prison. Explain to them that he's a boozer, not an arsonist."

As Thomas Koch closed the door behind him, they could still hear him chuckling: "*The World of Interiors!*"

Three weeks later Lang and Schöller met again. Apostolos Ioannis had been commissioned by Koch Industries to arrange bail and to provide Konrad Lang with temporary papers, essential clothing, some pocket money and his second-class steamer and train tickets.

Konrad Lang had spent eight rough hours on the ferry-crossing to Brindisi and then hung around the station for another three. He arrived the next day, at a quarter past five on the dot, at the address that Ioannis had given him. It was already dark.

Tannenstrasse 134 was a block of flats on a very busy street in which, despite its name, there was not a fir tree to be seen. It was in a working-class district of the town. Konrad Lang hesitated for a moment at the entrance to the flats. His slip of paper gave no indication of the floor. He studied the black name plates neatly set into an aluminium frame. "Konrad Lang" was already engraved alongside a bell for the third floor. He pressed the button and moments later the buzzer sounded. Three floors up, Schöller was waiting for him in the doorway of a flat. "Welcome home," he grinned.

Lang's journey had lasted 33 hours. He looked almost as bad as he had at their meeting in the police headquarters in Kerkira.

Schöller showed him around the small one-bedroom flat. It was simply furnished. The kitchen cupboards and drawers contained the bare necessities of crockery and cutlery, a few pots and pans and some basic stores. There were bedclothes and towels in the bedroom cupboards and a television in the living room. Everything was new, including the fitted carpets and the paint on the walls. Just like a brand-new holiday flat, Konrad Lang thought. Apart from the noise of trams and car horns. He sat down on the reclining chair.

"The agreement goes like this," Schöller said, sitting down on the little sofa next to him, and putting a piece of paper on the coffee table. "Frau Senn will pay for the flat. If you want to add to the furniture, you can make a list of what you would like. I have the authority to comply with your requests within reason. Insurance, health care, dentist are all taken care of. Clothing likewise. One of my female colleagues will report to you tomorrow and will accompany you and advise you on the purchase of your wardrobe. The advice will mainly be of a financial nature. She has only a modest budget."

Schöller turned the sheet of paper over. "Diagonally opposite is the Café Delphin, a very pleasant tearoom where you can have breakfast. For your other meals we have spoken to the Blaues Kreuz, a very respectable alcohol-free restaurant four tram-stops away. Do you know it?"

Konrad Lang shook his head.

"You will have an account at both establishments which will be paid by Frau Senn. For any expenses outside this arrangement you will have 300 francs a week pocket money which you can draw every Monday from the manager of the Rosenplatz branch of the Kreditbank. He has instructions not to give you an advance. Frau Senn has asked me to tell you that she does not expect or want anything in return for all this. But if I may add a personal piece of advice: you should avoid playing with fire from now on."

Schöller pushed the sheet of paper over the little table towards Konrad Lang and took a biro from his breast pocket. "Read that through carefully and sign both copies."

Lang took the biro and signed. He was too tired for reading. Schöller picked up his copy, stood up and went out. At the door of the flat he turned round and came back again. He had to say it. "If it had been up to me, you would have stayed in Corfu. Frau Senn is much too generous."

No reply. Konrad Lang had fallen asleep in the reclining chair.

2

I HOPE URS ISN'T AT HOME, KONRAD LANG THOUGHT, AND rang the bell. In the past, Lang would have been able to hear it ringing far away in the Villa or even, when the wrought-iron bellpull was still working, clattering under the porch above the main door. But now he was almost 65 and his hearing was not what it used to be.

For the same reason, he also didn't hear the footsteps of a couple who had just got out of a four-wheel drive and were now approaching him. They were both wearing jodhpurs, riding jackets and muddy boots. The man was in his late twenties, tall and handsome, if you disregarded his receding chin.

The woman was younger, not much over 20, with brown hair, and pretty rather than beautiful. She looked inquiringly at her companion. He was holding his index finger to his lips.

They walked quietly up to the old man standing waiting at the garden gate. He was wearing a Burberry and a green felt hat that from a distance gave him the air of a country squire.

One of the family's many friends, the young woman presumed, and played along with it. They crept up to him on tiptoe.

Konrad Lang put his ear to the gate and listened carefully. Was that footsteps?

The couple had reached him now and the man struck the metal gate hard with the palm of his hand.

"Hello, Koni! Are you after some money?" he shouted.

Konrad Lang felt as if something had exploded in his head. He pressed his hands to his ears. His face looked strained as if he expected another blow. He recognised the young man now.

"Urs," he said quietly, "you gave me a fright."

He noticed the young woman standing next to Urs, who was looking quite taken aback. He raised his hat and ran his fingers through his grey hair, which was combed back from his high forehead. He looked distinguished, albeit in a rather down-at-heel way.

"Konrad Lang." He held out his hand to her.

She shook it sympathetically. "Simone Hauser."

"Urs and I are old friends. He doesn't mean it like that."

In the meantime Urs had opened the gate. The intercom crackled. "Yes?" said a woman's voice with an accent. "Who is it?"

"No one, Candelaria," Urs Koch replied. He held the gate open for Simone and rummaged in the pocket of his jodhpurs. Simone turned round just in time to see Urs slipping a crumpled note to the old man before slamming the gate in his face.

The clash with Urs had its good side. He was better off by a 100 francs. Perhaps because Urs regretted his ill-mannered attack, or perhaps because he wanted to impress his new girlfriend, or perhaps simply because it was the only note he could find in a hurry. At any rate a 100-franc note was a good haul. He would normally have gone away empty-handed from Urs Koch.

Probably from Tomi, too. Unless he had caught him in one of his sentimental moods. But these had become less frequent of late. Or Konrad's timing had got worse. More often than not Thomas Koch was irritated whenever Konrad turned up. He pretended not to be there or sent him packing over the intercom or, worse still, dismissed him to his face at the gate.

Normally one of the members of staff opened it for him. If he was lucky it was Candelaria, who would sometimes lend him 20 or 50 francs. He owed her a few hundred by now. He paid her back some smaller notes from time to time out of his pocket money, as a gesture of good will and for tactical reasons, for the next time.

Undoubtedly, a 100 francs does not go very far in the bar of the Grand Hotel des Alpes. But they treat you like a human being there and Konrad Lang needed that at the moment. The barmaid on duty in the afternoon was called Charlotte and she addressed him as Koni, like an old friend. She was old enough to have known him from the days when he sometimes occupied the tower suite in the hotel. Tomi and he, that is. Tomi in the tower suite, and Konrad in the room directly underneath it. But in those days, she told him, she had had no need to work. So she was like him, not rich but independent.

"Your good health, Koni," she said as she brought him his Negroni.

A Negroni is the ideal afternoon drink, Koni always maintained. It looks like an aperitif but has the effect of a cocktail.

This one she was bringing him now was only the second. There would be enough for three, if you counted in Charlotte's flutes of champagne which she poured for herself each time he gave a sign and which she placed behind the bar alongside the ashtray where her Stella Filter was smoking.

"Health and happiness," Konrad said, raising his glass to his lips. His right ear was still ringing from Urs's thump on the iron gate and his hand was trembling more than usual for this time of day.

The bar was nearly empty, as it tended to be in the late afternoon. Charlotte was putting dainty silver dishes of salted nuts on the little tables. A dim light came through the curtains. Behind the bar next to the till a lamp was already on; blue smoke from Charlotte's forgotten cigarette curled upwards in its light. Roger Whittaker sang "Smile, though your heart is aching", and from the little table next to the piano came the rattle of teacups from the two Hurni sisters, waiting in silence for the pianist, as always.

The Hurni sisters were well over 80 and had moved into the Grand Hotel des Alpes a few years ago, in the same way as other people who have not inherited twelve per cent of a brewery move into an old people's home. Both of them were thin and frail right down to their unshapely legs in flesh-coloured support stockings, peeping out like sausages from under their large floral-patterned dresses. Each time they went solemnly up to the bar Konrad Lang felt he was being reminded of something from the distant past. It was so far back that it did not recall any image, but rather an intimate, long-forgotten feeling that he could not describe. It made him smile warmly at the sisters, but they always ignored him indignantly.

Konrad Lang took a little sip and put the glass back down on the table. The Negroni had to last him until the pianist arrived. Then he would order another. And a glass for Charlotte, "with a beer for the man at the piano". Then he would have to decide whether he should invest the remaining francs in a taxi or take the tram and have a few ordinary schnapps with Barbara in the Rosenhof.

It did not happen often that one of Urs Koch's girlfriends was introduced to Elvira Senn. They were all the same type and he changed them so frequently that Elvira could not tell them apart. But recently she had made inquiries about "this Simone". A sign that it would suit her plans if Urs entered into a more permanent relationship.

Elvira had chosen afternoon tea in the Villa's small drawing room for the presentation. Intimate enough to form a first impression but not so familiar as lunch, nor so official as dinner.

Urs and Simone, no longer in their riding gear, sat holding hands on a leather Breuer sofa. Thomas Koch poured champagne into four glasses.

"When we say 'for tea' it's the setting we mean, not the drink," he said, laughing. He put the bottle back into the ice bucket, gave everyone a full glass, took one for himself and raised it. "What shall we drink to?"

"To us," Elvira said, pre-empting Thomas, who was about to say something hasty. This was obviously not his first drink today and he was feeling rather euphoric about his potential daughter-in-law. As he did about all pretty young women.

In order to relieve the awkwardness of the silence that followed the toast, Urs said, "When we got back from our ride Koni was standing at the door."

"What did he want?" his father asked.

"No idea. Probably the west wing, a chauffeur-driven Bentley and an unlimited allowance. I gave him 100 francs."

"Perhaps it wasn't money he wanted. Perhaps he just wanted to pay us a visit."

"He didn't complain about it, anyway." They both laughed.

Elvira shook her head and sighed. "You shouldn't give him money. You know why."

"Simone would think me inhuman," Urs smiled.

Simone felt she had to say something. "You have to feel a bit sorry for him."

"Koni's a tragic case," Thomas Koch confirmed, pouring out champagne.

"Has Urs told you about Herr Lang?" Elvira wanted to know.

"Please don't get me wrong, I think it's wonderful what you've done for this man. And still are doing, after what happened."

"He's my grandmother's little mascot."

Thomas Koch nearly choked. "I thought mascots were supposed to be lucky charms."

"She keeps an unlucky one. She always was a little eccentric." The way Elvira looked at him caused Urs to stand up and give her a conciliatory kiss on the forehead.

Thomas Koch leant over towards Simone. "Koni's all right, he just drinks too much."

"He simply can't get it into his head that he isn't a member of the family. That's his problem," Urs added. "He doesn't know where to draw the line. You daren't give him an inch: he's just one of those types. So it's better to keep your distance."

"Which is not always easy, as you probably saw today, Simone."

Thomas picked up a little silver bell and rang it. "But will you have some more tea?"

"I don't know," she answered, looking uncertainly at Urs. When he nodded, she nodded too.

As Thomas was opening the second bottle of champagne, Simone said, "It's very sad when a person loses his dignity."

Thomas pretended he had misunderstood her. "Don't worry, my dear. It will take more than three glasses of champagne for me to do that."

Father and son laughed. Simone blushed. The perfect woman for someone as self-centred as Urs, Elvira Senn thought. Perhaps a little too much make-up for the middle of the afternoon, but nice, straightforward and easy-going.

The bar at the Grand Hotel des Alpes was filling up. The lamps over the tables were on now, Charlotte was taking orders and the pianist was playing his cocktail repertoire. The Hurni sisters were lost in thoughts of another age with the same tunes. Konrad Lang was imagining that he was the one playing.

In the summer of 1946 he had resolved to become a famous pianist. Elvira had removed Tomi from the private grammar school that spring after the school had gently brought it to her attention that her stepson would be better off at a less academic school. She had put him into an expensive boarding school on Lake Geneva and Thomas had insisted that Konrad should accompany him. Konrad, for whom the grammar school presented no difficulties, reluctantly went with him.

A large proportion of the children of those whom the war had made rich, or at least not poor, were assembled at St Pierre's in those days. The new and the old money from what remained of Europe sent their sons to the 17th-century manor to prepare them for the burden of being the future elite. Konrad lived amongst boys whose names he had previously known only as cars, banks, stock cubes, companies, and dynasties.

There were four boys to a room at St Pierre's. Thomas and Konrad's room-mates were Jean Luc de Rivière, junior member of an old banking family and Peter Court, an English boy. That was Court as in the Court Gas Mask, which had been adopted under licence by virtually all the allies. His father held the patent.

"Of Koch Industries?" Jean Luc asked of Thomas, as they shook hands amongst their suitcases.

Thomas nodded. "Of the bank?"

Jean Luc nodded. Then he offered his hand to Konrad and looked inquiringly at him and then, when he hesitated, at Thomas.

Thomas was a loyal friend provided that he was alone with Konrad. But as soon as someone else turned up whom he wanted to impress he was quick to change sides.

"He's the son of a former employee of ours," Thomas explained. "My mother's helping him."

This also settled the question as to who was given the bed by the door.

From then on Konrad was treated with patronizing politeness by all the schoolboys. Never once – in the whole of his time at St Pierre's – was he involved in any of their many intrigues and never once was he the victim of their cruel pranks. They could not have made it any clearer to him that they did not regard him as their equal.

Konrad tried everything. He surpassed the most nonchalant in nonchalance, the coolest in cool, the most insolent in insolence. He made himself look ridiculous simply to make them laugh and he invited punishment simply to impress them. He climbed over the wall and bought wine in the village. He obtained cigarettes and porn magazines. He kept watch for his fellow schoolboys during their rendezvous with Geneviève, the head gardener's daughter.

But in this schooling for life as a rich man, Konrad forever remained the one who had forgotten to bring the most important prerequisite: money.

At the farewell party before the summer holidays of 1946 –

19

St Pierre's, as an international institution, began its school year in the autumn – Konrad decided to become a pianist.

It was a sultry day in June. The gates of St Pierre's were standing wide open, and the limousines were lined up nose to tail on the large gravel square in front of the main building. On the lawn at the lakeside they had set up seating in front of a small stage with a grand piano and alongside it, under a canopy, a cold buffet. Parents, brothers and sisters, old boys, teachers and pupils stood holding glasses and plates, chatting in small groups and looking with increasing concern at the sky. Heavy clouds were gathering.

Konrad stood with Thomas Koch and Elvira Senn. She was holding a conversation in French with Jean Luc de Rivière's mother. Like all the pupils, Konrad was wearing a school blazer with the gold embroidered emblem of a cross, anchor and bishop's crosier, and a green, blue and gold striped school tie. The mothers had put their hair up and were wearing silk floral-patterned summer dresses, the few fathers who had taken time off to collect their sons were wearing dark lightweight suits, white shirts and ties, here and there in the St Pierre colours.

In the midst of this elegant, self-assured society, unnoticed by the smiling groups that casually broke up and re-formed again, stood a small, pale, stooping man in a badly fitting morning suit, sipping at his empty glass. As Konrad was watching him, the man caught his eye and gave him a smile.

Konrad almost smiled back but then he remembered how the others had all been avoiding the little man and, so as not to make a blunder, let his gaze wander coolly away.

The first thunder rolled over the lake and heavy raindrops began to spot the summer outfits of the guests. In no time at all the lawn was empty, the grand piano covered and the group reassembled, laughing and gasping, in the gym where the senior teachers had prepared a second grand piano and everything else necessary in the event of bad weather.

During the headmaster's speech and the solemn goodbyes of

those who had done their final exams Konrad searched in vain along the rows for the inconspicuous little man whose melancholy smile he had not returned. Not until the headmaster announced the musical part of the ceremony, a piano recital by the pianist Jósef Wojciechowski, did he see him again. Suddenly there he was standing on the stage, bowing and sitting down at the piano, waiting with his smile until the noise had died down in the audience who would much rather have moved on to the informal part of the celebrations.

When everything had gone silent Wojciechowski let his hands sink on to the keyboard.

He caressed four quiet Chopin nocturnes out of the piano. There was no coughing, no blowing of noses, only occasionally the dull rumble of the storm that had long since abated. After 20 minutes he stood up, bowed and would have gone had the thunderous applause not forced him into playing two encores.

Later, over the farewell drinks in the large dining hall, Konrad saw the man again, surrounded, harassed and fêted by those same people for whom an hour earlier he had not existed. A Polish émigré, they said, an internee, with whom a teacher at St Pierre's had become acquainted in the war whilst a guard in a camp in the east of Switzerland. A nobody therefore.

Konrad Lang plumped for the taxi. He sat in the back and let himself be driven down the winding road into the town. Dusk was setting over the roofs. He could have taken the tram and with the meagre 20 francs looked in on Barbara at the Rosenhof. But he was too depressed. Piano music when he was in the wrong mood could depress him just as much as it could cheer him in the right one. Today it had depressed him because he had heard it after being humiliated. It made old, deeper and long-suppressed humiliations come to the surface again. Humiliations that he might have been able to spare himself – of this he was quite certain – had he been able to play the piano.

During the summer holidays of 1946, which they spent in the Koch villa in St Tropez, he had convinced Thomas of the advantages of being able to play the piano. Girls, who were beginning to be of some interest at this time, adored pianists, he maintained. So Thomas had surprised his stepmother by announcing that he wanted to take piano lessons at school the following year. Which automatically held good for Konrad too.

Konrad was a keen pupil, quite the opposite of Thomas. His teacher, Jacques Latour, was thrilled by so much enthusiasm and, as he was soon to notice, talent. Konrad could play a tune by ear after hearing it only once. Jacques Latour gave him private tuition in reading music and very soon he could sight-read. Right from the start he possessed an impeccable arm and hand position and quickly acquired a very promising touch. In less than two months Thomas had become disheartened by Konrad's fluent runs.

Konrad was given free access to the music room. He practised whenever he had time: theme and inversion of the left and right hands separately, then together, then consecutively with the right, then consecutively with the left. Monsieur Latour corrected him less and less often, more and more he simply listened to him, moved by the certainty of having a great talent, perhaps even a little genius, before him.

Until the "Mosquitoes' Wedding".

In the "Mosquitoes' Wedding" the hands worked independently. The right hand played its melody. The left accompanied it, but not simply like a shadow: it stopped, paused for a few bars, brought in the right hand again, picked up the melody from it, continued alone, then threw the melody back to the right hand. In short, it behaved like a being with a will of its own.

Until the "Mosquitoes' Wedding" it had seemed to Konrad that his hands were like two circus horses perfectly in tune with each other. One trotted when the other trotted, reared up when the other reared up, and shook its mane when the other shook its mane. Konrad's hands received commands from his brain together and carried them out together, sometimes in parallel and sometimes in opposition, but always in step.

"It'll come," Monsieur Latour said. "It's like that for everyone at the beginning." But no matter how persistently Konrad practised, his hands continued to be two puppets hanging on the same strings. The "Mosquitoes' Wedding", a humorous song from Bohemia, marked the end of his career as a pianist.

Six months after the first lesson Latour gave up on his best pupil. He had been trying for a long time to persuade him to play another instrument. But the piano, and only the piano, was Konrad's instrument. He still practised in secret for a few months on a keyboard drawn on a roll of material. He could play the most difficult runs up and down in his sleep. But as soon as he ordered a hand to act independently the other one followed it like a little dog.

Konrad Lang knew the scores of every Chopin waltz and nocturne off by heart and the piano parts of all the important piano concertos. After a few bars he recognised the most famous pianists from their touch. Even if he did not gain much recognition in the circles in which he moved he could nevertheless impress people from time to time with a few virtuoso one-handed or consecutive runs late at night in a piano bar where the pianist still did not know him.

Thomas Koch developed into an average uninspired pianist.

The taxi stopped in front of the Rosenhof. Konrad had decided that he was not in the right frame of mind to sit in his flat alone and broke. He paid, giving the driver his last coins as a tip: 1 franc 20, an amount that shamed him rather. Like all people who are dependent on the generosity of others, he hated meanness.

He walked up the three steps to the entrance of the Rosenhof. As he pushed aside the heavy vinyl-edged covering of the inner doors he was met by a smell of smoke, beer fumes and cooking oil and the steady hubbub of men talking, grabbing half an hour's freedom between work and home. He hung his coat on the overloaded coatstand, put his hat on the empty hatrack and went over to join the regulars.

The men moved up. One stood and fetched him a chair. Konrad Lang was highly respected in the Rosenhof. He was the only person who always wore a tie, the only one who spoke five languages (plus beginner's Greek) and the only one who stood up when a lady came to the table, which did not happen often. Koni was elegant, educated and had perfect manners, yet never stood on ceremony, as they said in the Rosenhof. It did not bother him in the slightest if he drank beer and ate cold pasties with joiners, railway workers, street-cleaners, storemen and the unemployed.

The first few times Konrad Lang turned up in the Rosenhof he was cold-shouldered by the customers. But the more his life story leaked out, the more they treated him as their equal. Many of the regulars worked at the nearby Koch assembly shop No. 3 or had been victims of the closure of the gas turbine division.

It was not that Koni complained. If he was halfway sober, he did not allow a bad word to be said about the Kochs. And when he was drunk he broke off every sentence and put his finger to his lips – ssh! Whether out of discretion or because he could no longer speak was hard to say. Between these two stages, however, there were also spells when he spoke his mind.

Konrad Lang was the illegitimate child of one of the Kochs' maids. When Herr Koch senior died she looked after his young widow, Thomas Koch's stepmother. The two were friends. They travelled around the world – London, Cairo, New York, Nice, Lisbon – until shortly before the war. Thomas's stepmother went back to Switzerland, Koni's mother stayed in London. She had fallen in love with a German diplomat, from whom she concealed Koni's existence.

"What do you mean concealed?" one of the regulars asked when Koni told the story for the first time.

"She went to Switzerland with me, left me with a farmer in the

Emmental valley and was never seen again."

"How old were you then?"

"Six!"

"That's a bloody disgrace."

"I had to work for the farmer for five years. It was tough. You know what people in the Emmental are like."

A few of them nodded.

"And when the money stopped coming from Germany, the farmer dragged Elvira's name out of me. He took me with him to see her to get her to pay up. She knew nothing about it and took me in."

"That was decent of her."

"From then on I grew up as Thomas Koch's brother, more or less."

"So why are you sitting here now having to put it on the slate?"

"I'm wondering that myself, too."

For the regulars of the Rosenhof Konrad Lang was their only direct link to high society. What he had to say about it confirmed their opinion.

There was one more reason for Konrad Lang's special status in the Rosenhof: his relationship with Barbara, the waitress. He was the only customer who was allowed credit. Strictly speaking he was slightly over 1,600 francs in the red. Even if you ignored what she had not put through the till, his debt was still approaching 700 francs. On Mondays when he received his pocket money he sometimes repaid her 50 or 100 francs. But recently he had been drinking more and repaying less.

Barbara herself wondered about her generosity. She was not the type to give things away. She had turned 40 this year and no one had ever given her anything. When she looked at herself in the mirror, rather too slim for her build and rather too thin-lipped for her age, she had little hope that there were any great changes ahead.

But she had a soft spot for Konrad Lang. There was something distinguished about him, it was the only way she could put it. The way he dressed, how he behaved even when he was blind drunk, how he spoke and above all how he treated her. She had been reminded of "Milord", by Edith Piaf (whom she could never stand) when, on his third visit to the Rosenhof, Konrad Lang's eyes had suddenly filled with tears. "Mais vous pleurez, Milord," she had thought and sat with him when it had grown quieter.

Barbara was a great advocate of Konrad's cause. When someone in the Rosenhof suggested that there were sadder fates than his, she could get quite worked up. "Playing Thomas's stooge all his life? When Thomas was kicked out of the grammar school, Koni had to change schools with him. When he didn't sit the school-leaving exam Koni wasn't allowed to do it either. And when Thomas Koch was 30 he married and was given a job in the company. And Koni just stood there looking stupid."

When her only friend Doris Maag, the traffic warden, remarked that people could train for things, even at 30, Barbara had defended him saying, "He tried to. It's true he hadn't studied for anything but he had good manners. And plenty of connections from the days with Thomas. He was in a private bank and in the property business. But when things began to work out for him, Tomi was always just around the corner. A marital crisis, summer ski-trips, divorce, a driving disqualification, a Mediterranean cruise."

"And what did he live on the rest of the time?"

"Loans from Tomi's friends at first. And when they got so out of hand that he never paid them back, he did jobs for them. Keeping an eye on the yacht out of season, keeping an old mother company, managing the holiday villa, things like that."

And why had he put up with it all? Barbara was ready with an answer: out of gratitude. Because Thomas Koch had persuaded his mother to take Konrad in. Because without Thomas Koch he would have grown up as something like a slave, on a farm in the Emmental.

26

When Doris Maag asked, "And what is he today?" Barbara thought about it for a moment. "You should hear him play the piano," she replied.

Barbara was in the thick of it, serving glasses of beer, clearing away the empties, taking orders and swiping money into the large purse under her waitress's apron. When she saw Konrad, she brought him a beer in a tall glass into which she had first poured some clear liquid out of a bottle.

Towards seven o'clock the Rosenhof was empty apart from a few determined drinkers and Konrad Lang in front of his third glass of fortified beer.

Barbara took a bottle of white wine out of the chiller cabinet, poured herself a glass and sat down with it next to Konrad.

"Any success?" she asked.

Konrad shook his head. "Urs."

"Shall I put it on the slate then?"

"Is that all right?"

Barbara shrugged her shoulders.

The evening after the clash with Urs Koch, Barbara took Konrad home with her. She had sometimes taken him with her before, if she felt sorry for him or if she was lonely, or wanted to make Kurt, her married sporadic lover jealous.

On the first occasion, Konrad made advances as she was turning down the bed, more out of a sense of duty than desire, and because a gentleman ought to have an affair from time to time, if only so that he can hush it up. She laughed and shook her head, which was all that was required to deter him. They went to bed, Barbara in baggy faded cotton pyjamas, Konrad in his underclothes, and Konrad told her about his life. Stories and anecdotes from the great world of the rich and the beautiful in which he had spent much of his life that were amusing at first and then became increasingly boring.

"Gloria von Thurn und Taxis had a birthday cake made for the Prince on his sixtieth birthday with 60 marzipan penises," he told her that evening, when he had got his breath back. (Barbara lived on the fourth floor of a block of flats with no lift.)

"I know," Barbara answered, helping him out of his coat.

"The prince was queer of course."

"I know," Barbara answered, walking into the kitchen.

"But only a chosen few knew," he shouted after her.

"I know," Barbara said, coming from the kitchen with a glass of mineral water.

"Have I told you that before?"

"Often enough."

Barbara could have kicked herself, as Konrad's eyes immediately filled with tears. She knew how over-sensitive he was when drunk. But she was tired and cross. Cross with him because he let himself be treated like that and with herself because she had brought him back.

"Sorry," Konrad said. She didn't know whether he was sorry for the repetition or the tears.

"Don't apologise. Stand up for yourself," she snapped and handed him the glass.

"What's that?"

"Drink it."

Konrad drained his glass obediently. Barbara watched him and shook her head.

"Why do you do everything everyone tells you to? Say, no, I don't want any mineral water, I want a beer with schnapps, drink your mineral water yourself. For heaven's sake, stand up for yourself!"

Konrad shrugged his shoulders and made an attempt to smile. Barbara stroked his hair.

"Sorry."

"You're quite right."

"I don't know. Come to bed."

"But I don't want to go to bed, I want a beer with schnapps. Go to bed yourself," Konrad answered.

"Forget it," Barbara said.

Konrad Lang had a dream that night. He was playing croquet in the grounds at the Villa Rhododendron. Tomi was there and Elvira and his mother, Anna Lang. It was a balmy summer's day. The women were wearing white dresses. Tomi had short trousers on and was very small. Then Konrad noticed that he himself was not any taller.

They were being boisterous and laughing a lot. Tomi had the ball with the blue stripe, he had the one with the red. It was his turn. He hit the ball, it rolled through the gate and on and on. Koni ran after it as it disappeared over a bank. He followed it into the shrubbery. By the time he found it, he was lost. As he strayed deeper and deeper into the bushes, the undergrowth grew thicker and thicker. Finally he stepped out into the open. The Villa had disappeared. No sign of the others anywhere. He began to sob loudly. Someone took him into their arms and said, "You have to change your life, or you'll go to pieces." It was Barbara. Outside it was getting light.

After breakfast in the Café Delphin he went to his flat and wrote a letter to Elvira Senn.

Dear Elvira,

Yesterday I had a dream. You, Anna, Tomi and I were playing croquet in front of the veranda on the lawn which the gardener (was he called Herr Buchli?) always had to mow, especially before a match. We were so happy and carefree. Tomi always had the blue ball and I had the red. You were wearing the white linen dress that Tomi had spoilt picking cherries, but in my dream it was still pure white. When I woke up all my memories came flooding back. It seems as if it all happened yesterday and I am wondering why things have turned out this way. Why have you cast me off? We were like

a family at one time. Why can't it be like that again? Why do
I have to spend my old age alone with my memories? Why
do I have to share them with complete strangers who have no
idea what I'm talking about?

  Please don't misunderstand me. I don't want to appear
ungrateful. I appreciate your generosity. But I can't put up
with this way of life any more. Please, Elvira, cast me off
completely or forgive me and take me back into the family
again.

  Yours in desperation,
  Koni Lang

He read the letter through a few times and could not make up his
mind whether to send it. He slipped it into an envelope with the
address on it and put it into his breast pocket without sealing it.
Over coffee in the Blaues Kreuz he read it through again and
decided not to send it. Far too whining. He put it away and forgot
about it until he was drinking his aperitif in the Rosenhof. Barbara
greeted him with the question, "Well? What plans have you made
to change your life?"

"I've written Elvira Senn a letter." He felt in his jacket and
showed her the envelope.

"And why haven't you posted it?"

"No stamps."

"Shall I post it for you?"

Konrad Lang could not think of an answer and so allowed the
envelope to be taken from him. When the early evening rush died
down Barbara stuck a stamp on it, put on her coat and walked
the few steps to the post box round the corner. Never put off until
tomorrow . . .

Unaware of this, Konrad thought about the letter over a few
glasses of beer and came to the conclusion that it was not whining,
it was pathetic. And that in fact it was not a letter, it was an
appeal. Appeals have to be pathetic or else they don't work.

The postman had long since emptied the box when Konrad decided to let Barbara post the letter. The next morning, when he might have gone back on his decision, he had forgotten all about it.

Elvira Senn was sitting in her breakfast room in the Stöckli. It was still early in the day. The fabric slats of the blinds, which turned the glare of the morning sun into a flattering milky light, were still half closed. Frau Senn drank freshly squeezed orange juice and tried to forget the letter that lay open on top of the pile of post.

She finished her glass. She was no longer thinking about the letter being an impertinence. It was not the first time that Konrad Lang had allowed himself to be impertinent. What unsettled her were the detailed memories. The gardener's name had in fact been Buchli, and – what was much worse – he had died when Koni was not quite six years old. Tomi really had always insisted on the blue ball and Koni, whose favourite colour had also been blue, had always had to accept the red uncomplainingly. What had confused her most were the stains on the white linen dress. When she used to play croquet with Anna, Tomi and Koni she no longer had it. He was right: she had thrown it away because it was covered in cherry stains. But it had not been Tomi who had stained it. The idea that the old drunk's memory stretched so far back worried her.

There was not much in Elvira Senn's life that she regretted. But she cursed herself for what she failed to do that warm Sunday in May 1943, when she could have made a financial arrangement with a certain farmer and sent Konrad back to the Emmental.

It was the first day they were able to eat outside. The very early rhododendrons were in bloom. She was sitting with Thomas under the striped awning on the large sun terrace drinking coffee, which even for Elvira Senn was not an everyday occurrence during the war.

One of the maids announced visitors, a man with a young boy – a friend, the man claimed, a surprise. Elvira was curious and said she would see them.

She watched them both as they drew nearer. A rough-looking man with a young boy carrying a small suitcase. Thomas jumped up suddenly from the table and ran towards them both. Then she knew she had made a mistake.

"Koni! Koni!" Thomas called.

The young boy answered, "Hi, Tomi."

Elvira had no idea that Konrad was in Switzerland. The last time she had seen him had been five years before, in Dover shortly before the outbreak of war: the day when she had come back with Thomas, and Anna had stayed in London with Konrad on account of her German diplomat. They had written to each other from time to time; there had been a marriage announcement from London and a postcard from Paris. Then nothing more.

Now this farmer was telling her in a dialect which was very difficult to understand that Anna Lang had also travelled to Switzerland shortly after her and had put the then six-year-old child in his care. A hundred and fifty francs had been transferred from a Swiss bank every month until three months ago. And since then nothing. Nowt.

He couldn't feed the lad, he said. His name was Zellweger, not Pestalozzi. And now he thought that perhaps she might be able to help. She was an aunt of Koni's, so it seemed. There was obviously money around, he added, looking about him.

If Thomas had not put so much pressure on her, "Please, Mama, can Koni stay, please, please?", she would at least have insisted on some time to think about it. But Thomas was so happy and Konrad so meek and the farmer so unpleasant that she did something rash – a rare occurrence – and nodded.

She gave Zellweger 450 francs for the outstanding three months and twelve francs for his travelling expenses. Then she stood there with the awkward-looking child and had the uneasy feeling that she would never be free of him for the rest of her life.

At first there were no problems. Konrad was an unassuming little boy and a good companion for Thomas. She sent them to the same school, they played together and did their homework together. Konrad exercised a positive influence on Thomas, who was incapable of being by himself and tended to dominate those around him. Konrad was patient and right from the start accepted Thomas as number one.

The problems came only later. Thomas developed into a moody young man who could not stand being in the same place for long. Elvira had other interests at the time and tolerated his playboy lifestyle out of sheer laziness. She not only watched his escapades, she even gave them generous financial support. Koni, whom he dropped and picked up according to his whim, was just one of his escapades. When Thomas was 30 she decided to call a halt to *la dolce vita*. There were a few financial obligations outstanding on the international circuit – and Konrad Lang.

A further 35 years on he had still not disappeared from her life. And he was still being impertinent.

On Konrad Lang's first visit to the Blaues Kreuz he thought the smell was coming from all the old women. Only when they brought him his food did he realise that it was the dish of the day which was producing the smell. Cauliflower, spinach, carrots, fried potatoes.

"Is it vegetarian here as well?" he asked. He received the sharp reply: "You ordered the gardener's plate, didn't you?"

Since then, he had grown accustomed to it. He had his own little table and the elderly waitress treated him like one of the family. "The Cordon Bleu's good, Herr Lang, but the steamed chicory's bitter. I'll give you some kohlrabi instead."

Konrad Lang sat in front of the cup of milky coffee they brought to him after his meal, reading the paper on its wooden pole. He was slightly uneasy; last night Barbara had asked him if he had received a reply to the letter yet.

"What letter?" he had asked.

"The letter to Elvira Senn, which I posted for you. The letter which is supposed to change your life."

33

"Oh right, that letter. No, still no reply," he had stammered. He had been racking his brains ever since about what he might have written. But he could only come up with some vague memory of a rather insistent tone.

"Is this free?"

Konrad looked up. In front of him stood a woman of about 50, good-looking, a rust-coloured cashmere twin set, a double string of pearls, fine wool trousers. One of us, he thought. He stood up.

"Is this seat free?" she inquired again.

"Of course," Konrad replied in some surprise and pulled the second chair out from under the table. The restaurant was practically empty.

As she sat down the door opened. In came a younger man who looked around, saw her and came up to the table. When he had nearly reached it the woman grabbed hold of Konrad's hand, pulled it towards her and asked, "Have you been waiting long, darling?"

Konrad Lang sensed that the man was now standing right by the table. He looked deep into the woman's eyes, put his left hand over her right and answered, "Almost a lifetime, darling."

The man stood at the table and waited. But when neither Konrad nor the unknown woman looked up he turned and stalked out of the restaurant.

"Thank you," the woman said. She sighed with relief. "You've just saved my life."

"I'd call it a good deed," Konrad Lang said in reply. "May I buy you a cup of coffee?"

The woman's name was Rosemarie Haug, her maiden name, which she had adopted again after her divorce four years ago. She accepted his offer and was pleased that Konrad Lang made no reference to the incident. A real gentleman of the old school, she thought.

Dr Peter Stäubli was a general practitioner and had recently given up his practice in the vicinity of the Villa Rhododendron. He now looked after only a handful of patients whom he had known for a long time. He was Elvira Senn's GP and personal physician. He visited her twice a week after breakfast to check her blood sugar level. She could of course easily inject the insulin herself but she could not bring herself to extract even one drop of blood. Elvira Senn could not stand the sight of blood.

This morning while she was waiting until the drop of blood could be smeared on to the test strip, Elvira asked, "How old are you now, Doctor?"

"Sixty-six."

"How far back can you remember?"

Stäubli wiped the test strip and put it into the meter. "I remember the time Fritz our dachshund was found stone-dead on the garden path one morning. I must have been about six at the time."

"Is it possible for people to remember things further back than that?"

"The central nervous system is still not fully formed at birth. The memory of small children can't retain anything from the first two years of their lives. It has to learn how to learn at first and then to recall what it has learnt."

"So theoretically one could remember events which happened at three years old?"

"My youngest grandson is ten now. When he was four I took him to a restaurant which had a Russian week. Anyone who drank a vodka after the meal was allowed to throw the glass at a specially made wall afterwards. I had to drink about five vodkas so that the little one could throw the glasses at the wall. It made such a big impression on him that he used to talk about it every time he visited us. He's ten now and he can still remember it. And the chances are that when he's 80 he'll still be able to remember it."

As he was speaking Dr Stäubli noted down the blood sugar levels. Then he put on the blood pressure cuff.

"And his other memories of that time have gone?"

"Not gone. They aren't accessible any more."

Stäubli put his stethoscope in his ears and took her blood pressure. "You'll live to 100," he said as he wrote down the two readings.

"And it's totally impossible ever to gain access to them again?"

"Not totally impossible. There is a form of hypnosis that brings back early childhood memories. Recovered memories. In the United States respectable fathers are taken to court on the basis of it by their grown-up daughters who say they were abused as children."

Dr Stäubli picked up his doctor's bag. "And it can sometimes happen that people with senile dementia, because they lose the ability to learn new things, delve deep back into their early memory and recall something right at the limit of their early childhood memories." He shook his patient's hand. "The older a person gets, the nearer the past becomes, Frau Senn, isn't that right? Friday at the same time?"

Elvira Senn nodded.

They met again the following day for dinner. It was the day on which Konrad Lang had drawn his pocket money. He could afford a restaurant that was not exactly the "in" place but was also not so intimate that an invitation there might have seemed improper.

Konrad arrived reasonably sober and behaved well all evening. Rosemarie told him about her life before the divorce, something she never normally talked about. She had been married for the second time to a surgeon nearly ten years younger than herself. She had financed his studies out of her first husband's money. Her first husband had died young and left her half a textile business. She had sold it to her brother-in-law at the right moment before the business went into receivership in the seventies.

"Röbi Fries was your first husband?" Konrad asked in surprise. "I was at St Pierre's with him, you know?"

"You were at St Pierre's? Röbi told me a lot about St Pierre's."

All evening they exchanged names of mutual acquaintances and places where they must already have met.

In the taxi Rosemarie said, "Don't you want to know who you saved me from in the Blaues Kreuz?"

"Is he important to you?"

Rosemarie shook her head.

"Then let's forget him."

Rosemarie lived in a penthouse flat in a four-storey building next to a lake in a small park. Konrad asked the taxi to wait, accompanied her to the door and said goodbye. He was about to turn round when she opened the door again and said,

"Are you free on Saturday evening? I could cook us something."

The restaurant of the Grand Hotel des Alpes was called Carême after the great 19th-century French chef. It was proud of its *ancienne cuisine*. Elvira Senn loved the restaurant for other reasons. It was close to the Villa, celebrity guests were not stared at, she had her own table out of earshot of the other guests and the kitchen staff would cater to her special dietary requirements.

She ate in the Carême every Thursday evening. More often than not, she used the evening meal for informal but important business meetings.

This evening she had asked her grandson Urs Koch to accompany her. During the meal she revealed to him that she was seriously considering handing over the management of Koch Electronics to him. Over the dessert (an apple for her, a crème brûlée for him) she turned the conversation round to Simone. When she was sure that he had understood that the two subjects went hand in hand for her, she came to the subject of Konrad Lang.

"He worries me," she confided to him.

"You're worried about Koni?"

"Not for him. Because of him. I don't want him to do us any harm."

"How could someone like Koni harm us?"

"By gossip. Skeletons in the cupboard."

"Are there skeletons in the cupboard then?"

"He could invent some."

Urs shrugged his shoulders. "The show goes on."

Elvira smiled. "With Urs directing it." She raised her glass of mineral water. Urs poured himself the rest of the Burgundy. They clinked glasses.

"Besides, he'll drink himself to death soon enough anyway."

"His pocket money won't stretch to that," Elvira Senn replied.

The following morning she instructed Schöller to raise Konrad Lang's weekly allowance. From 300 to 2,000.

On the first evening Konrad and Rosemarie had shown off a bit, as people do on their first date. They had shown each other their good sides, spoken of their successes and omitted their failures.

On their second evening, it was different. Rosemarie welcomed him casually and put him to work straightaway setting the table. She was amazed at how much skill and artistry he displayed. She poured out two glasses of Meursault and they took them out on to the terrace. It was a mild evening, spring was in the air, and the lights of the village opposite danced on the lake. Piano music drifted up from the window below.

"Chopin, Nocturne Number 1 in B minor, Opus 9," Konrad said. Rosemarie shot him a sidelong glance.

They ate wild rice which was rather too soft and salmon which was rather too dry. With the white wine, Konrad forgot his reserve. He told her the unvarnished truth about his life.

She understood his story well enough. Her first husband's circle of friends had tolerated her only as an appendage to her wealthy spouse.

Shortly before midnight Konrad revealed one of his best-kept secrets to Rosemarie. He sat down at the piano in her living room and played the right hand of the nocturne they had heard a few hours earlier on the terrace. Then he played the left.

"And now together," Rosemarie smiled.

Konrad told her about his failure as a pianist.

At one o'clock in the morning she sat down next to him and played the left-hand part of "Für Élise" while he played the right. Not quite without mistakes, but enough to tempt Konrad to reveal his last-remaining secret to her: the truth about his situation. His dependency on the Kochs. The whole damn business.

The next morning Konrad Lang woke up in Rosemarie Haug's bed and could remember nothing.

Konrad would have liked to ask Rosemarie what had happened the night before. But he didn't want to sound like a schoolboy asking "How was I?" after the first time.

So he went away feeling a little uneasy, but reassured to some extent by the fact that she had invited him round again for dinner that evening.

He spent the day in his flat searching his brain for any memory of the night before.

He arrived at her flat on the dot, holding a long-stemmed rose. She greeted him with a kiss, took the flower, went into the kitchen with it and filled a small vase with water.

"There's white wine in the fridge, or would you prefer red?" she called over her shoulder.

"Do you have any mineral water?" Konrad asked on impulse.

"In the fridge." Rosemarie dried off the vase and took it into the living room. "If you're having water, I'll join you," she said as she walked past. She put the rose on the dining table. Konrad came in with a bottle of mineral water and poured two glasses.

"Your very good health!" he said, passing her a glass.

"Hence the water?"

They both drank.

"No, for my memory. More for my memory." He paused to find his resolve. "I can't remember last night."

Rosemarie looked him in the eye and smiled.

"What a pity."

*

39

The next morning Konrad Lang walked back into town along the lakeside. A fresh morning. There were light green shoots on the chestnut trees and the crocuses were already clustering around their trunks.

Konrad had not drunk a drop all evening and his memory of the last few hours was, as far as he could judge, absolutely perfect. He had seldom felt so fantastic. Maybe just the once, in 1960 on Capri. But then he had been young and in love.

They had been cruising the Mediterranean on the *Tesoro*, the Piedrinis' old-fashioned motor yacht. They were an international set of rich young people who felt, and were, decadent. Fellini's *La Dolce Vita* had been released that year and had had a long-lasting and not exactly deterrent effect on them all.

They docked in Capri because they wanted to have a party in the exact spot where Tiberius had pushed young boys over the cliffs during his orgies, and to hold a picnic on the dizzy heights of the Villa Lysis's gardens, which Baron Fersen had dedicated to young lovers.

During their stay on land Thomas stayed in the Quisisana with the others. He had suggested that Konrad should keep an eye on the yacht, a totally unnecessary measure in view of the *Tesoro*'s twelve-man crew. But Thomas was captivated by the Piedrinis' awe-inspiring carelessness and Konrad was in his way again.

Konrad did not know whether to be insulted or relieved to be away from the noisy company for a while. He ate his supper on deck, attentively served by a taciturn steward in white livery, and looked out across the harbour. The coloured lights in the seafront bars twinkled and sad Neapolitan melodies carried over the water to the boat. He was suddenly overcome by the familiar feeling that he was in the wrong place. Couples were dancing, glasses clinking: it was all happening over there. And he was sitting here.

He had himself ferried over to the harbour and stepped on to the short promenade full of expectation. But the harbour bars were packed with German tourists, the music was coming from gramophones and the coloured twinkling lights were shoddily painted electric light bulbs. He continued past the bars to the end of the pier. A young woman was sitting with her arms folded over her knees, looking at the sea. When she heard him coming she looked up.

"Mi scusi," he said.

"Niente Italiano," she answered. "Tedesco."

"I'm sorry, I didn't mean to disturb you," Konrad said, in German.

"You're Swiss?"

"And you?"

"Viennese."

Konrad sat down next to her. They looked at the sea for a while in silence.

"Do you see that yacht out there?"

Konrad nodded.

"With all the lights."

"Yes."

"Sometimes the wind carries the laughter over the water," she said.

"Oh."

"And we're sitting here."

"And we're sitting here," Konrad repeated.

And as if they had decided at that very second, each of them independently, not to allow life to take place without them, they kissed.

Her name was Elisabeth.

They spent three days in her *pensione*. He did not mention that he was from the yacht, for fear of spoiling the magic.

On the fourth day he went to see Thomas in the Quisisana and informed him that he would be making his own way back.

"Because of the blonde?" Thomas asked.

"What blonde?"

"I've seen you in front of the grotto. You only had eyes for her. Understandably, if I may say so."

Thomas wished him all the best and they said goodbye.

The following day Elisabeth came into the room in great excitement. "Do you remember the yacht? The one on our first evening?"

Konrad nodded.

"You'll never believe it. We've been invited over."

Elisabeth became Thomas's first wife. She bore him a son, Urs. Not long afterwards, she followed her restless heart to Rome: a small consolation for Konrad and a hard blow for Thomas, who had never been faithful but had always been vain, and who now remembered his old friend as an ever-present comfort and companion.

Until today, Konrad Lang had never felt the way he felt during those three days on Capri. Perhaps he was in love again. Old and in love.

He decided to give up drinking, at least for a while.

Back home Konrad found a letter from the bank informing him that his weekly allowance would now be 2,000 francs with immediate effect and could be picked up on any weekday he chose.

He wrote a euphoric thank-you letter to Elvira Senn and reserved a table at Chez Stavros. He went to the bank and drew out 1,200 francs. Then he bought some wild salmon, an onion, toast, lemon and capers and four bottles of San Pellegrino and enjoyed a civilised little snack at the open window of his flat, accompanied by a lot of mineral water with lemon and ice.

After the meal he washed up and sat down at his keyboard to mark the occasion.

About two years before in a restaurant in Corfu, he had stood over the shoulder of a pianist who had a little keyboard on his piano and saw that the instrument was playing the left hand by itself. It did sound rather synthetic but it was better than silence.

The very next day he had bought himself a cheap keyboard but

42

this, like all his belongings, had later fallen victim to the fire. To replace it, he put a rather more expensive and sophisticated model on the list of essentials for his flat which he was allowed to request at the Koch's expense. Since then he had occasionally played for himself and sometimes for his rare guests, more often than not for Barbara.

But now when he sat down at the keyboard he could not find the switch. That's odd, he thought, I've turned it on and off thousands of times. He had to search all over the instrument for two or three minutes until he found the switch.

"Love is blind," he muttered.

Doris Maag, the traffic warden, looked tired when she came into the Rosenhof in her uniform straight from work and sat down at Barbara's little table by the bar.

"So what's the panic?"

"Koni's disappeared. Three days ago."

"What do you mean, disappeared?"

"He hasn't shown up here for three days. I phoned him yesterday: no reply. And again today: no reply."

"Perhaps he's changed his pub," Doris suggested.

"I shouldn't think so, seeing as he's bankrupt."

"Perhaps he's found some other idiot who'll put things on the slate."

Barbara stood up. "White wine?"

"Campari."

Barbara went to the bar and came back with a glass of Campari with ice and lemon and a bottle of mineral water. "Say when."

"Fill it up."

Barbara topped up the glass with mineral water. "Cheers," she said out of habit.

Doris took a sip. "Orange, not lemon. It's a slice of orange that goes with Campari, not lemon. Everyone gets it wrong."

"If everyone gets it wrong then it can't be wrong any more."

Barbara sat down again. "He doesn't show up during the day either. And he hasn't been to the Blaues Kreuz."

Doris Maag put on her official voice. "Most missing people turn up again. There's nearly always a perfectly ordinary explanation for their disappearance."

"It's quite out of character."

"They always say that."

"And he owes me 1,645 francs."

"In certain circles that's good enough reason to disappear."

"Not in his."

Barbara stood up and went over to a customer whose waving hand she had been ignoring and who was now tapping insistently on the table with a five-franc coin. When she came back she said, "He's been quite depressed recently. He would burst into tears for nothing."

"The tears of a drunk."

"Well, they're still tears. Most people who kill themselves are drunk."

"He won't kill himself."

"Sometimes you hear of people lying dead in their flats for weeks on end and nobody notices."

"Someone had a stroke in the bath a little while ago and couldn't get out or go to the phone and no one heard him. The only thing he could do was to wait and top it up with hot water now and then and hope that someone would miss him. Then he had the idea of blocking the overflow with his flannel and letting the bath flood until the people underneath informed the caretaker. That worked. But now the insurance company doesn't want to pay for the water damage. Because it was done intentionally."

"Koni's flat only has a shower."

"Well there you are, then."

Tannenstrasse 134 was only five minutes' walk from the Rosenhof. Barbara had pestered Doris to go with her. It would look more official with her uniform if they had to ask the caretaker to open the door.

"I'm in the road traffic department, not the CID," Doris had protested but had gone with her nevertheless.

They had phoned from the Rosenhof five minutes before and no one had answered. Konrad's third-floor flat was dark. The only light was behind a little frosted-glass window.

"The bathroom!" Barbara rang the bell against the name "O. Bruhin, caretaker".

She had to ring three times until a light went on in the stairwell. "You do the talking," Barbara hissed at Doris when a bad-tempered, unkempt man with a bloated face opened the door.

"Folks like us have to get up at half past five in the morning," he growled. When he saw Doris's uniform he became slightly more affable. He listened to her and agreed to have a look. He took them up to the third floor and told them to wait there. After a while he came back with the master key and put it in the lock.

"It won't go in. There's a key on the inside.

"Then we'll have to force the door open," Barbara insisted.

The caretaker turned to the traffic warden. "I'll need to see your identity card for that."

While Doris Maag was getting out her identity card the key turned in the lock inside the flat. The door opened a crack and Konrad Lang's surprised face appeared.

"Koni, are you OK?" Barbara asked.

"And how," he answered.

Konrad Lang had just put his first week without alcohol behind him. The itching and scratching were easing off. He was beginning to sleep through the night without sweating. He got up feeling rested and raring to go and the moments when he thought about alcohol – the "ache" he called it – were becoming less frequent.

He was well-practised in giving it up. He was familiar with each stage of the process up to the second month. He remembered the euphoria which came over him each time from the third day. But he had never felt the indescribable delirium that he was experiencing now. It could not be coming from the few glasses he had gone without. Nor from the unexpected improvement in his finances. There was another reason: Rosemarie Haug.

Since the "night of oblivion" as they now called it, they had spent every day and every night together.

They had travelled as the only passengers on the only steamer that sailed at this time of year right to the end of the misty lake and back.

They had been to the zoo and watched the monkeys in the company of an old lady who addressed her chimpanzee by name and was recognised by him.

They had walked up to the observation tower along the path with the old gas lamps, eaten apple-cake and drunk coffee with the pensioners in the old-fashioned tourists' restaurant.

"Just like old folk," Rosemarie had said.

"Well, I am an old man."

"It doesn't seem like that to me," she had said with a smile.

It didn't seem like it to Konrad Lang, either.

The previous evening they had gone to a concert. A Schumann evening. Once, when Rosemarie gave Konrad a sidelong glance, he had had tears in his eyes. She had taken his hand and given it a squeeze.

When Konrad looked in the mirror today he could already notice a change. He thought his blood vessels had become slightly finer, his cheeks a little less red, and the small burst veins a little less visible. His tear ducts were also not so swollen. His whole face looked firmer and his whole person much more full of go. And, as he thought, younger.

Perhaps this is the start of my lucky streak, Konrad Lang thought.

He was in this mood when Barbara, along with the traffic warden and the caretaker, was about to break into his flat. He had not been to the flat for two days and was going to collect some clean underwear, some clothes and a few other things, when he heard the voices outside the door of the flat.

The caretaker and the traffic warden said a quick goodbye. Barbara stayed. She considered he owed her an explanation.

Konrad was happy to give her one. He enthusiastically told the ever more silent Barbara about the great and happy change in his life. When he had finished, he asked her casually, "How much do I owe you?"

"One thousand six hundred and forty-five francs," she replied.

Konrad Lang opened his briefcase and counted out 1,800 francs for her.

"I don't take interest," she said, giving him the change out of her waitress's purse.

"Aren't you pleased for me?" Konrad asked.

"Yes, of course," Barbara answered. It was true, too: she wasn't jealous. But she was not happy to be losing the only person whom she did not mind taking advantage of her.

Konrad Lang ordered a taxi, took his little suitcase and dropped Barbara off outside her flat.

At the door he gave her a fatherly kiss. "Take care. And thank you for everything."

"You take care, too," Barbara replied.

3

NEWLY WASHED CARS, NONE OF THEM COSTING LESS THAN 100,000 francs, were parked on both sides of the street in front of the Villa Rhododendron. The local police were directing the guests as they arrived and guiding the other traffic through the narrow space between the parked cars. "As if we had nothing better to do than play at parking attendants for multi-millionaires," the officer on duty had grumbled when he had been given the task by his superior. The latter had shrugged his shoulders helplessly and pointed upwards.

In front of the iron gate two uniformed men from a private security firm were comparing the invitations against the guest list and keeping an eye on the photographers waiting for an opportunity to slip inside.

"When people like this celebrate a wedding, even the weather plays along with it," the reporter from the tabloid newspaper commented to the reporter from the local rag. "It pissed it down at ours."

It really was an unashamedly beautiful summer's day. A few fine clouds hovered in the deep blue sky, a breath of wind ensured that the brilliant June sun was not too hot, and the scent of linden blossom and of the dog roses on the perimeter walls was already in the air.

The grounds around the villa looked like the headquarters of an army camp during the Napoleonic Wars. There were tents everywhere, decorated with the pennants and flags of nations that existed only in the imagination of the event organiser.

In tents open on all four sides the guests sat in armchairs at flower-strewn tables laid with white cloths. Or on long benches at festively decorated wooden tables under the old trees. Or in groups artistically arranged on picnic rugs on the closely cropped lawn.

String quartets, country and western bands, dance orchestras and folk groups took their turn to play at various locations around the grounds.

A fitting wedding for the heir to the Koch empire.

Urs Koch welcomed the guests. Everywhere he appeared with his sweet bride people clapped, kissed the couple and congratulated them both on each other, on the successful occasion and on the glorious weather.

Thomas Koch's third wife Elli stood at the balustrade on the balcony, surveying proceedings.

When Thomas had met her at the beginning of the seventies Karl Lagerfeld had just taken over the management of Chanel. Elli Friedrichsen had been one of his top models. A year later she had married Thomas Koch. Ten years later she lived her own life as far away from Thomas as possible.

Next to her was Inga Bauer, a Swedish woman much younger than Elli who, at the age of 25, had married an industrialist from Thomas Koch's circle of acquaintances.

The two women had quickly become friends. Elli had become Inga's only support in the strange mix of rectitude and decadence that characterised the social scene of Swiss high finance. What Elli liked about Inga was that she had not allowed herself to be disillusioned by ten years of the Bauer clan. She had kept her ideals as well as she could and had a refreshing way of making known her opinions about right and wrong.

"If I'd realised Koni hadn't been invited, I wouldn't have come."

"A big sacrifice for an old bore."

Inga pointed to the wedding guests. "Do you find this lot any more amusing?"

Elli bestowed her Chanel smile on a couple strolling past on the terrace.

"No, they're no more amusing. But more important. We have enough bores to contend with as it is. Why should we have to put up with the unimportant ones too?"

"Is that what you think?"

"That's what Thomas thinks."

"What about you?"

Elli took a sip from her champagne glass. "Me? I'm getting divorced."

This came as a surprise. Inga had not regarded Elli's marriage as something for which it was worth going to the trouble of a divorce.

"But you've been unofficially divorced for a long time."

"In future I'd like it to be official."

"But why?"

Elli smiled. "There's someone who would appreciate it."

Inga grinned. "So there's no age limit, then?"

"You'll have to ask Elvira. I'm only 46."

The folk band by the group of spruce trees was playing "For He's a Jolly Good Fellow", and the guests nearby were joining in. They rose to their feet and toasted Urs and his bride.

"Poor girl."

"If that's the woman he's been looking for all this time," Inga said in surprise, "then he could have married any of the others before her."

Elli looked at her mockingly. "Simone was the one within range when Elvira decided that the time was right. Just as Urs's mother just happened to be the one within range when Elvira decided that the time was right for Thomas."

"It sounds like the 19th century," Inga laughed.

"Take a look around," Elli replied. "It *is* the 19th century."

*

Elvira Senn was holding court in the bride's tent, looking as if there was no upper age limit on love. She beamed with happiness and sparkled with jewels; she was quick-witted and charming and always kept a hand's breadth between the back of the upholstered chair and her own straight back.

Thomas sat opposite her and was less relaxed. Elli's behaviour was irritating him. Usually on social occasions they pretended to be the happy couple whose recipe for the perfect marriage was "to each his own space". But today she was really keeping him at a distance. She had refused to circulate with him as substitute mother to the groom and she had exchanged no more than a few words with the bride's parents. (Although Thomas had to admit that they were a rather overdressed couple, who were finding it difficult to hide their pleasure at their daughter having married so far above her station.) She was quite blatantly staying out of his way.

He could not get used to his new role as number two. Up until now he had always been the centre of attention on these occasions. Or if his wife or Urs had been the focus then it was always because he had wanted it that way. This time, Urs was being toasted as the man of the future. Thomas was not ready for that yet.

But what was really upsetting him was Koni Lang. In the old days, he would have turned up, with or without an invitation. He would have been stopped at the door, it is true, but Koni could always muster enough gravitas to make someone from the security firm come to fetch Thomas: "There's a man outside. Says he's your oldest friend and has left the invitation at home."

But Koni would not be appearing today. He was in Italy. He had had a very formal greetings card delivered to Urs and Simone and a beautiful bouquet from "Blossoms", the most sensational florist in town. He had sent a personal letter to Thomas.

Dear Tomi,

A new phase in your life will be starting for you in a few days time. Your son will be getting married and with that you will have finished handing over the reins. You can soon step back into the ranks with the confidence that your work and Elvira's is in good hands.

My life, too, has seen dramatic changes. Just imagine, in my old age I have met the woman of my life. I am in love just like a schoolboy and have given up drinking. Life, which has recently been playing so many tricks on me (and so on you too), suddenly appears to be turning out well for me.

Isn't it strange how time and time again we have reached a turning point in our lives at the same time but in quite different places? Don't you sometimes feel that our fates are closely bound together whether we like it or not?

We are here on a little sentimental journey through Italy. When we were eating our lunch under the arcades in St Mark's Square I suddenly saw us as small boys again with Elvira and Anna taking it in turns to take photographs of us. Do you remember? You were trying to catch a pigeon and you fell and made your knee bleed. Anna washed it for you in the restaurant where we used to eat and bandaged it up with a damask napkin. Elvira felt sick because of the blood.

How long ago was that? Sixty years or six days?

Next week we shall be back in Switzerland again. You will have a surprise when you meet Rosemarie.

I wish you all the best from the bottom of my heart.

Your old friend,

Koni

Thomas Koch couldn't remember having been in Venice as a child with Koni.

"Shall we take a little walk?" Elvira asked. The gentlemen at the table stood up. Thomas offered her his arm. They strolled through the festively decorated grounds.

"What's depressing you?"

"Nothing. Why?"

"You're brooding."

"When your only child gets married."

Elvira smiled. "It only hurts the first time."

Thomas smiled now too. They sat down on a seat away from all the festivities.

"Were we ever in Venice when we were children, Koni, me, you and Anna?"

Elvira stared at him. "Why do you ask?"

"I had a letter from Koni in Venice. He remembers me falling chasing after a pigeon in St Mark's Square and making my knee bleed. Anna bandaged it up and you felt sick."

"What rubbish," Elvira answered.

The wedding celebrations lasted well into the night. When it was dark they lit Chinese lanterns and torches in the garden. The Pasadena Roof Orchestra played English waltzes and foxtrots, and the couples danced on the large terrace. Someone who sounded like Donovan and actually was Donovan sang and played guitar in the little pavilion amongst the rhododendrons and, in the big tent, George Baile sat at the grand piano playing tunes from *The American Songbook*.

At eleven o'clock there was a large firework display which the people in the pavement cafés in the town below applauded. After that the first guests started to leave.

Urs circulated until after midnight and became visibly more drunk. Simone tried to hide her disappointment and Elvira's discreet but forceful intervention was required to avoid a scene before the bridal couple finally climbed into their waiting limousine. "Just married!"

Shortly before two, Thomas Koch, listing heavily, sat down at the piano with George Baile and began to play "Oh, When the

53

Saints Go Marching In", good-humouredly assisted by the pianist (whose fee of 8,000 francs compensated, though only just, for such antics from his client) and enthusiastically applauded by the hard core of the guests.

The last guest left at three. The exhausted staff extinguished the lanterns and any torches which were still burning.

Thomas Koch took a beer into the bedroom with him. As he sat down on the bed with it he saw a note in his wife's handwriting.

Can I speak to you tomorrow? I suggest after lunch in the library. Elli.

The following afternoon Elvira Senn could bear it no longer. She had to see Konrad's letter. She walked up the path from the Stöckli to the Villa. The tents had been dismantled, all traces of the celebrations had gone.

Thomas occupied a wing of the Villa, Elli another, Urs the tower. The large reception rooms were used by all of them as required.

As Elvira came into the hall, Elli was just emerging from the library; she waved at her and walked up the broad open staircase to the first floor.

Thomas appeared in the library doorway. "Elli!" He noticed his stepmother. "She wants a divorce. I can't understand it. Can you?"

Elvira shrugged her shoulders. She did not understand how people could get divorced but it did not surprise her. She knew that Thomas was difficult to live with and that his wife, once she had decided on a divorce, would get justice in court. It was a question of damage limitation. Elvira had the best lawyers at her disposal and she knew Elli to be a sensible and realistic woman who would listen to reason. The divorce would be easy to handle. The real difficulty was Thomas's injured pride.

She went with him into his gentleman's study, listened to his moans and groans, shared his indignation and confirmed his opinion of Elli for as long as her quickly exhausted patience

54

allowed. Then she came to Konrad Lang's letter. Thomas could not remember what he had done with it; he only knew that he had still had it before lunch. It was Elvira who finally found it crumpled up in his dressing gown pocket.

She smoothed it out and read it through carefully. Then she screwed it up again. "He's imagining things."

"He's given up drinking, he says."

"And you believe that?"

"But he's right, unfortunately, about the turning point."

Elvira put the crumpled letter in the large crystal ash-tray on the occasional table next to her armchair. "Why don't you go off somewhere with him? It'll give you something else to think about."

"But I shan't be able to part him from his beloved now."

"They'll be able to manage without one another for a few weeks."

"I don't know. Things seem to be going so well for him."

"And not so well for you. I think he owes you."

"Do you think so?"

"If only for Corfu."

Elvira picked up a lighter and set fire to Koni's letter.

Thomas Koch's appearance caused quite a stir on Tannenstrasse. His chauffeur drove the midnight blue Mercedes 600 SEL up on to the pavement and helped Thomas out. His assistance was more than ritual subservience: the boss was not quite steady on his feet today. And it was still early in the day.

A few Turkish children with coloured satchels on their backs stood watching the car. A tram slowed down slightly and the faces at the windows turned towards the limousine. "Must be one of those property sharks who rents out dives to tarts at exorbitant prices," a young man explained to his girlfriend.

An old woman was leaning out of her first-floor window. She had put a cushion on the window sill and was resting her heavy forearms on it.

"Who do you want?" she shouted to Thomas Koch when she saw him ringing for the second time.

"Lang."

"We hardly see him here any more. Only to pick up the post now and then."

"Do you know where I can find him?"

"Perhaps the caretaker knows."

Thomas Koch rang the bell and waited.

"You'll have to ring for a long time. He's on night shift."

After a while a curtain twitched on the second floor. Shortly afterwards the door buzzer sounded. Koch went inside.

Othmar Bruhin, who drove a fork-lift truck in an assembly shop at one of the Koch factories and was the caretaker for this property which belonged to the Koch Industries pension fund, was to re-tell countless times the story of how he opened the door straight out of bed, unshaven and in his tracksuit and there stood "Koch himself, I nearly died," wanting the address of a tenant. "And, if you ask me, you could smell the drink on him too."

When Thomas Koch was helped into the car again by the chauffeur he gave Rosemarie Haug's address.

Konrad was playing backgammon with Rosemarie on the terrace when the doorbell rang. He had taught her the game on their Italian trip and they had played it passionately ever since, partly because of Rosemarie's ambition, for she had still not been able to beat him, partly out of sentimental reasons, for it kept alive the memories of their first holiday together.

Rosemarie stood up and went to the intercom. When she came back she was amazed.

"Thomas Koch, asking if you're here."

"What did you tell him?"

"Yes. He's coming up."

For almost all of Konrad's life, Thomas Koch had been the most important person in it. But recently he had receded more and more into the background. He had thought of him in Venice, it's true. But he had followed the reports of Urs's wedding with surprisingly little interest. Now, however, with Thomas just about to walk through the door, he was nervous. He felt the same way he always felt when Thomas was around: like a recruit waiting for the commandant's inspection.

Rosemarie noticed the change. "Should I have told him you weren't here?" she inquired, only half joking.

"No, of course not."

They went to the door of the flat. They could hear the lift outside. Then footsteps in the corridor.

"What can he want?" Konrad mumbled. More to himself than to Rosemarie.

When the bell rang he winced. Rosemarie opened the door.

Thomas Koch had a delicate finely shaped nose, which looked a little out of place in his fleshy face. He was wearing a blazer and a polo-neck sweater in burgundy cashmere, which made his short neck appear even thicker. He had bright close-set eyes and smelt of alcohol. He nodded to her curtly and turned directly to Konrad.

"Can I have a word with you?"

"Of course. Come in."

"In private."

Konrad looked at Rosemarie.

"You can go into the living room," she said.

"I would rather we went somewhere else." Thomas left no doubt that this was not to be taken as a request.

Konrad looked to Rosemarie for help. She frowned in irritation. Thomas waited.

"I'll just go and put my jacket on."

Konrad disappeared into the bedroom. Rosemarie shook hands with Thomas. "I'm Rosemarie Haug."

"Thomas Koch, pleased to meet you."

Then they waited in silence until Konrad came back out of the bedroom. He had put a tie on and was wearing a linen jacket that matched his trousers.

"Let's go," he said and followed Thomas to the lift.

"Ciao," Rosemarie called after him, perhaps a little sharply.

"Oh, yes. Ciao!" Konrad stopped, seemed to want to come back again to say goodbye properly, noticed that Thomas was already by the lift and went after him.

Rosemarie saw him opening the lift door for Thomas, letting him in first and then pressing the button like a bell-boy. The lift door closed before Konrad had time to look back at her again.

Thomas raised his eyebrows in amusement when Konrad ordered a Perrier water with ice and lemon. He himself ordered a double Tullamore Dew, without ice and without water, his depression drink.

Charlotte had received Konrad with a slightly reproachful "back in the country again?" but had understood immediately when he ordered something non-alcoholic. She had seen a lot of people give up. It soon passed.

The bar of the Des Alpes (for old times' sake and because it was handy for Thomas at any rate) was empty apart from the Hurni sisters. Roger Whittaker was singing "Don't Cry, Young Lovers, Whatever You Do". At a table in the corner Tomi was delivering his monologue; Koni was listening.

"You know when they have someone else, they suddenly look better."

Koni nodded.

"I don't have any objection if she has a little fling with someone now and then. You know me, I'm not exactly . . ."

Koni nodded.

"Treats me like the last arsehole. Calls me into the library. Tells me she wants a divorce."

Koni nodded.

"Doesn't just tell me, *notifies* me."

Koni nodded.

"Doesn't say she wants a divorce. Says she is getting a divorce. Full stop."

Thomas Koch finished his glass and held it up. "What's her name?" he asked.

"Charlotte," Koni whispered.

"Charlotte!" Tomi called.

"So that I won't hear it from her lawyer first. Charlotte!"

The barmaid came with another glass. Tomi held the empty one out to her without looking up.

"Would you put up with that?"

Koni shook his head.

"Do you know what she spends on clothes every month? Just on clothes?"

Koni shook his head.

Tomi took a gulp. "Neither do I. But I'll tell you this, it's a hell of a lot. You only have to look at her."

Koni nodded.

"When they have someone else they look even better. On purpose. To get back at you."

Koni nodded.

"I'll get my own back on her. She'll be surprised at what life costs."

Konrad Lang, the only one in the conversation who had some idea what life cost, nodded.

"I'll get my own back." Tomi made a sign with his empty glass in the direction of the bar.

When Charlotte had brought the whisky he asked, "Do you still go skiing?"

"Not really. I stopped after Aspen."

In 1971, during the crisis of his second divorce, Thomas had taken Koni out of storage, jetted off to Aspen with him, bought him new clothes and kitted him out. They had both had lessons before with the same ski instructor in St Moritz and Konrad had developed into a reasonable skier (and nervous bob-sleigh driver) over the course of four winter seasons. He had cut a fine dash in Aspen, too, after a few days. But that was a quarter of a century ago.

"You never forget it, it's like riding a bike," Tomi continued. "And the equipment has improved so much that you'll be better than ever."

Tomi downed his whisky. "We're going to Bariloche," he decided. "It'll give us something else to think about."

Koni didn't nod.

"We'll get the things you need when we get there. Check that your passport's still valid. We fly on Sunday."

Koni didn't nod.

Tomi held his empty glass up. When Charlotte came he said, "Bring one for him, too."

"I'd rather not," Koni said, but not loud enough for Charlotte, who was already on her way back to the bar.

"She seems familiar to me somehow."

"Charlotte?"

"No, the woman you're living with. Should I know her?"

"She's Röbi Fries's widow."

"Röbi Fries's widow? Then she's probably on the wrong side of 50. At least."

"I haven't asked her."

"But still quite attractive."

Koni nodded.

"Is that the reason you aren't drinking?"

"Part of it."

Charlotte brought the two whiskies. Tomi raised his glass.

"To Bariloche."

Koni nodded.

Shortly before midnight, when Konrad Lang had still not appeared, Rosemarie Haug threw away her pride and dialled his number. Engaged.

Shortly after midnight she tried again. Still engaged.

When it was still engaged at one o'clock she called the fault line and was told that the subscriber had not hung up properly.

If he had not wanted me to phone him he would have disconnected it, Rosemarie said to herself and ordered a taxi.

It was the third time that Othmar Bruhin had had his sleep disturbed because of Konrad Lang. This time he was on early shift and the alarm clock was due to ring in an hour and a half. When he saw the time, he knew that it was too early to get up and too late to go back to sleep.

He was in this sort of mood when he opened the door below.

The woman standing in front of him was the type his father used to call "a lady"; he could see that even in the dim light of the stairwell. She was somewhat embarrassed but not as much as the situation demanded. She asked quite firmly to be taken to Lang's door. She had rung the bell a few times already but he was not answering, she said.

"Perhaps he isn't at home," Bruhin grunted.

"The light's on."

"Perhaps he left it on. Perhaps he's asleep."

"He's left his phone off the hook."

"Perhaps he doesn't want to be disturbed," Bruhin suggested. "It does happen, you know." Something about the woman irritated him.

"Listen, I'm worried that something's gone wrong. If you don't open up for me and something has happened, I shall hold you personally responsible."

Bruhin let her in and took her up to the third floor.

They rang and knocked, banged and shouted until half the block had crowded round. No response from Konrad Lang. Bruhin would have sent everyone back to bed again had it not been for the piano music. Because of that he finally allowed himself to be persuaded to fetch the master key.

There was no key in the lock. Bruhin and Rosemarie went inside and were horrified at what they found: Konrad Lang was lying half naked on the living room floor, one leg over an armchair, his mouth and eyes half open. On the table was a half-empty bottle of whisky alongside a keyboard which was beating out the bass line of a steady waltz. One, two, three, one, two, three . . . The room reeked of alcohol and vomit.

Rosemarie knelt down beside him. "Koni," she whispered, "Koni," and felt his pulse.

Konrad Lang groaned. Then he put his forefinger to his lips. Ssh.

"If you ask me, he's pissed," Bruhin declared and walked out.

He calmed down the occupants of the block who were waiting by the door. "Everything's OK. Pissed."

When Konrad Lang woke up he was lying in his own bed; he knew without opening his eyes. He recognised the traffic noise: the cars stopping at the lights, waiting and moving off again, the trams ringing their bells at the tram-stops.

His head was hurting, his eyelids were sore, his mouth was dry and his arm felt as if he had been lying on it awkwardly. He had an uneasy feeling that he was about to regret something but he could not remember what.

He opened his eyes slowly. The window was open but the curtains were closed. It was daylight. He had a hangover. What else?

"But I'm not drinking," he thought suddenly. He closed his eyes again. What else?

Tomi! What else?

A sound came from the kitchen. Then he heard footsteps. And then a voice.

"Would some Alka Seltzer help?"

"Rosemarie!"

He opened his eyes. Rosemarie was standing by the bed with a glass of something foaming.

Konrad cleared his throat. "Three. Three would help a bit."

"There are three in here." Rosemarie held out the glass to him. He propped himself up on his elbow and gulped it down in one go.

Bariloche!

"I'm going home now. If you like you can come when you're feeling better." She stopped at the door. "No. Please come, as soon as you're feeling better."

When Konrad Lang left the flat in the afternoon Bruhin was just returning from his early shift. "What women see in you," he said in the stairwell.

"What do you mean?"

"Completely pissed and covered in sick, and they still fancy you."

"Covered in sick?" Konrad had seen no trace of it.

"From head to toe. Not a pretty sight."

Konrad stopped the taxi at a florist's and bought a large bouquet of garden roses which smelt almost too strong for his still rather fragile stomach.

Rosemarie smiled when she saw him standing at the door with the roses. "We're neither of us afraid of clichés, are we?"

She made him some consommé with an egg, sat at the table next to him and watched him spooning it into his mouth with his trembling hand. When he had finished, she took his cup away and came back with a bottle of Bordeaux and two glasses. "Or do you need a beer?"

Konrad shook his head. Rosemarie poured two full glasses and they clinked them together.

"What the hell!" he said.

"What the hell!" she answered. Then they both took a sip.

Afterwards Konrad told her the story of Bariloche.

By now they were on the third glass.

"Just for ten days," he said.

"And if he wants to go to Acapulco after that, you'll say no."

"Of course."

"You won't. I saw you when he came here. You'll never say no to him. Not ever."

Konrad made no reply.

"You must know that."

Konrad twirled his glass round by the stem.

"It's your life."

He looked up now. "For a while I thought it was our life."

Rosemarie banged the table with the palm of her hand. He flinched. "And don't you think I did?" she shouted at him.

Konrad's eyes filled with tears. Rosemarie put her arms round him. He leaned his head on her shoulder and wept uncontrollably.

"I'm sorry," he sobbed repeatedly. "An old man and crying like a child."

When he had calmed down she said, "Tell him no."

"I live off him."

Rosemarie filled up his glass. "Then live off me."

Konrad made no reply.

"The money's there."

He took a sip.

"You mustn't be embarrassed about money."

"I never have been embarrassed about it. Unfortunately."

"Everything's OK then."

"Yes. But what should I say to him?"

"Piss off."

Thomas Koch was sitting in his bedroom amongst half-packed suitcases and bags, knocking back a cold beer. On the telephone table was a tray with further two bottles of beer. He was in a foul temper. Koni had phoned a while ago and informed him that he was not going to Argentina with him.

"What do you mean, you're not coming?" he had asked in an amused voice.

Konrad Lang did not answer immediately. Thomas heard him take a deep breath. "I don't want to come. Count me out."

64

"You've been invited."

Another pause. "I know. I'm declining the invitation. Thank you very much."

Thomas was slowly becoming more annoyed. "You've got to be joking."

"I'm a free person. I've the right to decline an invitation," Koni said. But he was already sounding less convinced.

Tomi laughed. "Don't joke. Tomorrow at nine. I'll send the chauffeur. We'll go to the airport together from here."

There was silence for a moment. Then Koni said, "Piss off!" and hung up.

Thomas rang back immediately. Röbi Fries's widow answered. "Get me Koni," he ordered.

"Lang," Koni announced when he picked up the phone.

"People don't hang up on me," Thomas bellowed.

"Piss off," Konrad answered and hung up.

Thomas Koch poured himself another beer and tipped it down his throat. He dialled Elvira's internal number.

"He's refused."

Elvira knew immediately who he meant. "But he can't really afford to do that."

"He can't. But Röbi Fries's widow can. She's supporting him."

"You know that for certain?"

"I was in her flat. He's living with her, too."

"And it's true that he isn't drinking any more?"

"Before I arrived he wasn't." Thomas laughed. "When I left, he was as pissed as ever."

"And he refused anyway?"

"That woman's behind it all."

"So what are you going to do now?"

"I'm flying out on my own."

"Fancy him leaving you in the lurch after all we've done for him. Still are doing for him."

"How much is it costing?"

"Schöller has the figures. Do you want him to give them to you?"

"Better not. I'll only get annoyed."

Ten minutes later Schöller rang. "Do you want it broken down or the overall sum?"

"The overall sum."

"About 150,600 francs a year."

"How much?"

"Do you want the monthly breakdown?"

"I do now, yes."

"Food: 1,800, accommodation: 1,150, insurance and health care: 600, clothes: 500, sundries: 500, pocket money: 8,000. Rounded up and on average."

"Eight thousand pocket money?" Thomas yelled.

"Frau Senn raised it in March. It used to be 1,200."

"Did she mention why?"

"No, she didn't."

Thomas hung up and poured another beer. Someone knocked at the door.

"Yes?" he called out crossly. Urs came in.

"I hear you're going away."

"Have you any idea why Elvira raised Koni's pocket money from 300 to 2,000 a week in March?"

"Did she?"

"Schöller just told me."

"Two thousand! That'd buy a few schnapps!"

"You could drink yourself to death on 2,000 a week."

Urs had a sudden thought. He smiled to himself.

"What are you smirking about?"

"Perhaps that's why she raised it."

It took Thomas a moment. "You mean so that . . . ? No. Do you think she would do that?"

"Don't you?"

Thomas thought about it for a moment and then smiled. "Yes, of course I do."

66

Father and son sat amongst the clothes and pieces of luggage, shaking their heads and grinning.

Two hours later Thomas Koch was standing at the door of Rosemarie Haug's penthouse flat.

"Can I have a word with you in private?" he asked Konrad, without even deigning to look at Rosemarie.

"I have no secrets from Frau Haug."

"Are you sure of that?"

"Absolutely."

"Can I come in?"

Konrad looked at Rosemarie. "Can he come in?"

"If he behaves himself."

Konrad took Thomas Koch into the living room. "Can I get you anything, Herr Koch?" Rosemarie asked.

"A beer."

She brought a beer for Koch and a mineral water for the two of them. Then she sat down on the sofa next to Konrad.

Thomas threw her an irritated look. Then he decided to ignore her.

"I think you owe it to me to come with me."

"Why?"

"Because of Corfu, for example."

"I'm sorry about Corfu. But I don't owe you anything."

"And 150,000 a year. Do you call that nothing, 150,000?"

"It's nothing to you. And for me it's not sufficient reason to drop everything whenever you blow the whistle."

"You'll soon see what nothing means."

"I can't stop you."

"And then you'll live off her? Do you think she'll enjoy keeping an old boozer?"

"Rosemarie and I are going to be married."

Koch was speechless for a moment. "Röbi Fries will be turning in his grave," was the answer that finally came to him.

Rosemarie stood up. "I think you had better go now."

He look at her in disbelief. "Are you throwing me out?"

"I'm asking you to leave."

"And if I don't?"

"I'll call the police."

Thomas Koch reached for his beer. "She'll call the police," he laughed. "Did you hear that, Koni? Your future spouse wants to have your oldest friend thrown out of the house by the police. Do you hear that?"

Konrad stood up without saying a word and went up to Rosemarie who was waiting by the open door of the living room.

Tomi slammed the beer glass down on the coffee table, jumped up, rushed to the door and stood up tall in front of Konrad.

"So you're not coming with me. That's your final word?" he shouted at him.

"Yes."

"Because of her?"

"Yes."

"Without me you'd be a farmer's boy: have you forgotten that?"

Suddenly Konrad was filled with a great feeling of peace. He looked Thomas in the eye. "Piss off."

Thomas Koch slapped Konrad hard on the side of his head.

Konrad Lang struck back.

Then he went on to the roof terrace and waited. He saw Koch coming out of the door on to the street. He had a handkerchief in his hand and was blowing his nose.

"Tomi!" Konrad called.

Thomas stopped and looked up. Konrad shrugged his shoulders helplessly. Thomas waited. Konrad shook his head. Thomas turned round and went.

Konrad felt Rosemarie's hand on his shoulder. He smiled at her and put his arm around her. "A sad farewell."

"Isn't it a kind of liberation, too?"

He thought about it. "When a lifer leaves prison, even that's a farewell."

Konrad Lang was quieter than usual all day. In the evening he picked listlessly at the cold meal that Rosemarie served him. Then he put on some Chopin and tried to read. But he was unable to concentrate. Again and again his thoughts strayed to Thomas Koch and the dreadful scene that had brought their volatile and unequal friendship to an end. Around ten o'clock Rosemarie kissed him on the forehead and left him to brood. "I'll be along soon," he promised.

But he wandered around the flat restlessly, went on to the terrace and looked down over the smooth lake and up to the crescent moon above the silent town. Several times he nearly poured himself a stiff drink from Rosemarie's cocktail cabinet.

It was almost two o'clock in the morning when Konrad slipped into bed. Rosemarie pretended to be asleep.

When Konrad Lang opened his eyes the next morning Rosemarie was already up. He opened the curtains. Outside, the sun was high in the deep blue sky: it was almost one o'clock. He hadn't a care in the world and didn't know why.

In the shower he thought about the scene with Thomas again. But the pain that he had felt yesterday had gone. He felt nothing but an extraordinary sense of relief.

He dressed with particular care, took a rose from the bouquet on Rosemarie's dressing table and put it in the buttonhole of his summer jacket.

Rosemarie was sitting on the terrace reading the paper. The pink light of the sun-blind flattered her complexion. She looked up anxiously when she heard Konrad. But when she saw how happy and enthusiastic he was, she smiled. "You slept like a baby."

"I feel like one too."

He ate a light breakfast and they didn't say one word about Thomas Koch. "I'll make us my famous stroganoff today," Konrad said. "To mark the occasion."

Konrad walked to the shopping centre, which was ten minutes away in the centre of the village. As usual, he bought too much.

On the way back he got lost. He was about to ask a passer-by for directions when he realised that he had forgotten Rosemarie's address.

He stood there bewildered, loaded with shopping bags. Everything around him was unfamiliar. Then someone took hold of two of his bags and a man's voice said, "My goodness, you're heavily loaded, Herr Lang. Wait, let me carry these back home for you."

The man was Sven Koller, the lawyer who lived in the flat below Rosemarie.

The flats were barely a hundred yards away.

4

KONRAD LANG STOPPED DRINKING AGAIN. FOR AN ALCOHOLIC this is a full-time project. Amongst other things, he began to play tennis again. Tennis had been part of Tomi's education and so Konrad had learnt it too.

Rosemarie was a member of a club to which she took him as a guest every other day. "Tennis is a sport for life," the club coach said, "and when you get older, the counting is good training for the memory, too."

It was meant as a joke. He was unaware of just how much Konrad's memory needed training.

Since the incident when he had been unable to find Rosemarie's house although he was practically standing in front of it, he had had similar things happen to him. The most stupid was when, in the lift, he had pressed the button for the cellar by mistake, got out and then had found his way back to the lift only by good luck.

The most dangerous was when he had put the kettle on the stove to make tea (in his tireless search for substitute drinks he had hit upon tea, all kinds of tea) and had turned on the wrong ring, the one on which a wooden salad bowl was sitting. When he went into the kitchen half an hour later (to put the kettle on the stove for the tea), the salad bowl was on fire, as was the roll of kitchen towels by the cooker.

He had put out the flames and disposed of the evidence. Up until now he had said nothing to Rosemarie about these lapses. He did

71

not want to alarm her unnecessarily: he did not consider that it was anything serious. He put his blackout that time in Corfu down to his consumption of alcohol. The malfunctioning of his memory and the scatterbrained mishaps over the last weeks were probably a sort of withdrawal symptom. Apart from this, things were going excellently for him.

Rosemarie was the best thing that had happened to him in 65 years. She supported him in his self-prescribed treatment for his alcoholism without assuming the role of a nurse. She was a good listener and an entertaining storyteller. She could be tender and, when they were in the mood, very exciting too.

Konrad Lang and Rosemarie Haug were an attractive couple: a distinguished, mature man with his well-groomed, elegant wife-to-be. They went to the tennis club, to a concert now and then and occasionally to their favourite restaurant. Otherwise they lived a quiet life. Konrad, who had quickly proved himself to be the better cook, prepared lavish evening meals for which now and again, just for fun, they dressed up in evening wear. They played a few games of backgammon almost every evening and from time to time sat down at the piano together.

It may have been Konrad Lang's happiest summer ever. When autumn came he felt neither lonely nor sad, perhaps for the first time in his life.

Elvira Senn was uneasy. When Thomas had returned without success from Konrad, all he had said was, "No more money from now on." Then he had flown off to Argentina without further comment.

She had wanted to give Schöller the necessary instructions immediately but then had hesitated. As long as she did not know what had happened when the two had last met, she did not wish to take any risks. She did not want to drive Konrad into a corner. Who knows how he would react?

Instead, she asked Schöller to find out about Lang's present situation. Schöller duly engaged a firm that he used from time to time for this kind of work.

But before Schöller could pass on his report to Elvira Senn she received a letter from Konrad Lang thanking her very much for all her support and asking her to withdraw it from then on. "My life has taken a turn for the better," he wrote. "I no longer need your financial support and I hope that this will put our long-standing relationship on a new, and very amicable, footing."

As she was to learn from Schöller soon afterwards, the turn for the better was very real. Lang was living a quiet, respectable life with Rosemarie Haug. He really did appear to have given up drinking. On the agency's photographs which Schöller showed her he looked better than he had ever done before.

She instructed Schöller to keep an eye on Koni and to withdraw the financial assistance. Then from an account of which even Schöller was unaware, she made a contribution of 100,000 francs to a children's charity. She named Konrad Lang as the donor. She wrote him a friendly letter, wished him all the best in this new chapter in his life and enclosed a receipt for the donation.

Konrad Lang wrote her an emotional letter in which he swore that he would never forget this noble gesture.

Which was exactly what she had intended.

But as for never forgetting, Konrad had a slight problem.

One unpleasant November day he decided to surprise Rosemarie with a fondue. He went into town by taxi to the only cheese shop which in his opinion had the right mix of cheeses for a fondue, bought enough strong cheese for three (he hated it when there was too little food on the table), chose a suitable wheatmeal loaf in the nearby baker's and got some garlic, cornflour, kirsch and white wine.

At home he saw that Rosemarie had had the same idea. There was a bag of mixed fondue cheeses in the fridge from the same shop next to a bottle of white wine from the same vineyard. On the kitchen dresser was a wheatmeal loaf from the same baker's next to a packet of cornflour and a bottle of the same brand of kirsch.

"Telepathy," he laughed coming into the living room where Rosemarie was sitting.

"What?"

"I thought it was weather for a fondue as well."

"How do you mean, 'as well'?"

Lang's memory might no longer have been on top form. But his reflexes, the reflexes of a man who had been forced all his life to adapt and react, were still in perfect working order.

"Don't say you don't feel like a fondue. I've bought enough for three."

"Of course I feel like fondue," Rosemarie smiled.

"There you are then, if that isn't telepathy."

He went back into the kitchen and dropped a bag of fondue cheeses, a bottle of kirsch, a wheatmeal loaf and a packet of cornflour into the rubbish bin.

Although there had never been anyone else in whom Konrad had such absolute trust as Rosemarie he could not bring himself to tell her about it. In the first place he did not want to worry her about something which he presumed would pass. And in the second place the symptoms looked like a sign of old age. A 65-year-old man does not readily admit to a woman 13 years his junior whom he is about to marry that he is suffering from the onset of senility.

So Konrad Lang developed techniques to conceal his problem. He drew a site plan of the house and the shops in which he normally did his shopping. He drew up a list with names which he often needed and which really ought to be familiar to him. He kept a note of their address in his wallet, his briefcase and his key box. And in case he got confused further afield, he carried a town plan with which he could pretend to be a lost tourist.

But at the end of November something happened that Konrad had not anticipated. He could not find his way out of the supermarket. He wandered up and down the aisles as if he were in a maze. He could not get his bearings at all: he never came to a place which looked as if he had been there before. And it was a small supermarket, too.

Finally he began tailing a young woman with a heavily laden trolley and a whining child. She soon became aware that the old man was following her, moving when she moved and stopping when she stopped. Every time she threw a suspicious look over her shoulder Lang took something off a shelf at random and put it into his trolley. When at last he arrived at the check-out, a much relieved Konrad lifted out on to the belt, alongside some unremarkable vegetables and meats, a series of strange products for the unshockable check-out girl. The most embarrassing being some raspberry-flavoured condoms.

Konrad Lang had a hard time because of these memory lapses, especially since he was completely at their mercy. Sometimes he would have liked to take hold of his brain and give it a helping hand in the way he did with his knee, which sometimes wobbled, or his back, which sometimes ached. On the other hand, he was not someone who liked to face facts. A life such as he had led required that you learnt to push things aside from an early age.

So he did nothing, apart from buying a gingko preparation which he had once heard would improve his memory. "Good for older men with younger women," he joked to Rosemarie when she commented on the bottle, which she had found by his piano music where he had hidden it and forgotten it.

Rosemarie smiled uncertainly.

From her first marriage to Robert Fries, Rosemarie Haug owned a beautiful house at Pontresina in the Engadine. She had stopped visiting it after she discovered that her second husband was using it as a love nest and since her divorce six years ago had often toyed with the idea of selling it. But now, with Konrad Lang, she suddenly felt like spending the holidays there. It seemed to her the time and the man were right.

They travelled by train, because Konrad was of the opinion that the journey would then be the start of the holiday. Rosemarie, who would rather have taken the Audi Quattro which was standing barely used in the garage, soon regretted that she had let herself be persuaded. On the journey Konrad revealed a side of his character that she had never seen before. He was so nervous before their departure that they arrived at the station almost three quarters of an hour early. He looked for the tickets time and time again, never stopped counting the pieces of luggage and during the whole journey in the comfortable first-class compartment and in the nostalgic dining-car, he was so tense and lacking in concentration that she was quite exhausted when they finally arrived.

Frau Candrian, the woman who looked after the house, had gone to a lot of trouble. The rooms were aired and cleaned, the beds made up, the fridge filled. There was an advent wreath on the side-board in the entrance hall and the scent of dried apple peel lying on the warm tiled stove in the pine room.

Rosemarie had been eagerly looking forward to showing Konrad the place which had once meant so much to her and would mean so much again to her with him. But when she took him through the old house he was rather absent-minded and his inattentiveness bordered on rudeness.

They went to bed early. For the first time since they had known each other there were unspoken words between them when they went to sleep.

The following day Rosemarie found Konrad's aide-memoires.

Konrad slept in late, as he had been doing more often recently. Rosemarie made breakfast. As she did so, she found Konrad's briefcase in the fridge.

When she put it on the kitchen table a note fell out. There was writing on both sides. On one side was a diagram showing the position of the butcher's, the baker's, the newsagent's kiosk, the shopping centre and her flat which was labelled "us". On the other side were the names of acquaintances, neighbours and the cleaning lady. Right at the bottom, heavily underlined, it said "Her: Rosemarie!"

Rosemarie put the note back into the briefcase. When Konrad got up she suggested a walk to the Stazersee.

The hustle and bustle of Christmas had still not begun. They met only a few walkers on the newly cleared paths through the woods with their deep covering of snow. Most of the people were, like themselves, well-off older couples who no longer needed to give any thought to school or official holidays. As they approached each other they fell silent, except to say hello or good-morning, so that as they passed, the crunching of four pairs of expensive snow boots could be heard in the firmly trodden new snow and then, in the distance, voices picking up their interrupted conversations.

"But you know how it is; you go into the kitchen because you've forgotten the ladle and then you stand in the kitchen and don't know what you came for."

Rosemarie had taken Konrad's arm. She nodded.

"That's how it is," he continued, "only more extreme. You stand in the bedroom holding the ladle and don't know why you want it. You go into the living room with it, into the bathroom, into the kitchen, into the dining room and you still can't think what you wanted the ladle for."

"And finally you hide it in the linen cupboard," Rosemarie said, finishing off for him.

"Do you do that too?"

"I found it there."

They walked on in silence. Rosemarie had broached the subject half an hour ago. After a long delay – she had prepared a gentle approach which had seemed increasingly silly to her – she had decided to go directly to the point. "I came across your note to help you find our flat and remember my name."

77

"Where?" he had asked.

"In the fridge."

He laughed. This seemed to break the ice. He told her everything. Everything that he could remember.

A couple came towards them, fell silent, said hello and disappeared out of sight. After a while Rosemarie said gently, "That wasn't the first time I've found things in strange places."

"For example?"

"Socks in the oven."

"In the oven. Why didn't you say anything?"

"I didn't think it important. Simple absent-mindedness."

"What else?"

"Oh, nothing."

"You said 'things'."

Rosemarie squeezed his arm. "Condoms in the freezer."

"Condoms?" Konrad laughed in embarrassment.

"Raspberry-flavoured."

He stopped. "Are you sure?"

"That's what it said."

"I mean, are you sure about the freezer?" Konrad now sounded rather irritable. Rosemarie nodded.

"And why didn't you say anything?"

"I didn't want to . . . oh, I don't know."

They walked on slowly. Konrad relaxed. He suddenly burst out laughing. "Raspberry-flavoured."

Rosemarie laughed too. "Perhaps you ought to go to the doctor's."

"Do you think it's that serious?"

"It's better to play safe."

A horse-drawn sleigh rattled behind them. They stepped to the side of the path and let it past. Two small old faces underneath giant fur hats peeped out over a lambskin rug.

They carried on in the warm smell of the horses. When the jingling had died away Konrad said, "It's nice to speak so openly to someone. I can never do that with Rosemarie."

Rosemarie stopped. "But I am Rosemarie."

For a fraction of a second she thought he was going to lose his composure. Then he grinned. "Got you!"

The decision to see a doctor raised Konrad's spirits, as if the determination to investigate his problems would at the same time provide a solution. His memory was no longer playing tricks on him. Rosemarie lost the feeling he would mistake her for someone else.

They spent a harmonious sentimental Christmas Eve with a Christmas tree and sparklers and midnight mass. And a sophisticated New Year with plenty of caviar and no champagne and half an hour at the open window with the sound of distant bells.

They went into the New Year full of confidence.

On the morning of Epiphany Konrad Lang got up quietly at four o'clock, slipped out of the bedroom, pulled two socks over each foot and a raincoat over his pyjamas. He put on Rosemarie's fur hat, opened the heavy front door, stepped out into the starry winter night and walked quickly across the main road towards the edge of the village. There he turned, carefully crossed the railway embankment and stepped out at a fair pace towards the Stazerwald.

It was a cold night and Konrad was pleased to find a pair of pigskin gloves in his coat pocket. He put them on without slackening his pace. If he walked like this he would be there in an hour. That was in plenty of time. He could even afford some delay, because he had got up especially early.

The wood was covered in deep snow. High banks of snow lined the path and swallowed up every sound. There had been no need for him to put on his softest shoes.

Now and then he walked past benches cleared of snow. Next to each one was a rubbish bin on which a sign showed a little black matchstick man on a yellow background throwing something into a matchstick litter bin. But Konrad was not fooled. He didn't throw anything in.

All was going according to plan until he came to a place where the path divided into two. There was a signpost with two yellow signs. On one it said "Pontresina ½ hour", on the other "St Moritz 1¼ hours". He had not expected that.

He stood still and tried to see through the trick. It took him a long time to work it out. They wanted to put him off the trail. He stood there, shook his head and burst out laughing. Put *him* off the trail!

Rosemarie woke up knowing that something was wrong. It was still pitch black and Konrad's place in the bed was empty.

"Konrad?"

She got up, put on the light, slipped into her dressing gown and walked out of the bedroom.

There was a light on in the hall. Konrad's camel-hair coat was hanging on the coat stand and his snow boots were on the shoe rack alongside it. So he must be in the house.

The inside door was closed, but when she went past it she felt a cold draught. She opened it. She was greeted by the icy night air. The main door was standing wide open.

She went back, slipped into her lambskin boots and put on her lined waterproof wool coat. The place where her fur hat should have been was empty.

She walked to the door.

"Konrad?"

Then louder still, "Konrad!"

Not a sound. She walked across the front garden to the open gate. The village street lay before her in silence. The houses were dark.

The clock on the village church struck five.

Rosemarie went back into the house, opened the door into every room and called Konrad's name.

Then she went to the telephone and dialled the police emergency number.

*

Hercli Caprez had been a policeman in Upper Engadine for a long time. He was accustomed to well-off men in the prime of life going missing at night. But he also knew that he had to take such cases very seriously; during high season the place was full of people with influence who could make life difficult for him. His young colleague had not yet learnt the art of deference, but he had enough respect to open his mouth only when spoken to.

Using his most businesslike tone, Caprez immediately passed on a description of Konrad Lang by telephone while Rosemarie watched. "According to our best information to date, the missing person is wearing a raincoat and pyjamas, no shoes and a lady's fur hat."

The policeman at the other end laughed. "He shouldn't be too difficult to find." Caprez replied with a discreet "Thank you".

He hung up, looked Rosemarie in the eye and said, "The search is under way, Frau Haug."

In the grey of the morning, Fausto Bertini was driving his horse-drawn sleigh number one to the workshop of the transport firm for which he worked in the winter. The metal fittings on one of the runners were broken and had to be repaired before the runner came off. It was high season and every sleigh was needed.

Every few metres the broken vehicle lurched and jerked, forcing the mare to break step. Bertini cursed.

At the turn-off to Pontresina the animal came to a complete halt.

"Gee up," Bertini shouted, "gee up!" And when that didn't help "Porca miseria!" and "Vaffanculo!"

The mare didn't budge. Just as Bertini was about to take the whip out of the holder – unusually for him, because, in spite of his language, he was a gentle coachman – he saw a piece of fur moving in the snow by the signpost. The mare shied. Bertini cried, "Whoa there!" and when his horse had calmed down, climbed carefully down from his seat and stepped quietly towards the fur-covered animal.

But it wasn't an animal, it was a fur hat, and it was sitting on the head of an elderly gentleman who was climbing out of a hole in the deep snow.

"I think my feet are frozen," he said.

Konrad Lang's feet were not frozen, but two toes on his left foot and one on his right had to be amputated. Apart from that he was in remarkably good shape. The fact that he had dug himself into the snow had saved his life, the doctors said.

He could remember nothing until the moment when he had heard the jingling of the horse-drawn sleigh. When Bertini had put him into the sleigh he was talking nonsense. In hospital in Samedan, shortly after being admitted, he lost consciousness twice. But now the incident seemed to be putting less of a strain on him than on Rosemarie. His main concern was to get out of hospital.

Since Rosemarie Haug was neither a relative nor his wife she had no rights with regard to Konrad. Fortunately, she was on good terms with the hospital management and asked the senior doctor not to release Konrad until he had been examined by a neurologist.

Felix Wirth was one of the few people from her circle of friends from her second marriage with whom Rosemarie was still in contact. He had studied with her husband and although they had specialised in very different fields, her husband in surgery, Felix in neurology, they had kept in touch.

During their unpleasant divorce battle, Felix Wirth surprisingly took her side. He had testified against her husband in court.

Felix Wirth was always there when she needed him. Why had she not asked for his advice sooner? She could only suggest that she, like Konrad, had closed her eyes to reality. Felix had immediately consented to examine Konrad Lang without mentioning to Konrad that he was doing so at Rosemarie's instigation.

She picked him up at the airport. During the whole of the taxi journey to the hospital Dr Wirth asked Rosemarie questions. Can he shave by himself? Does he participate in what is happening around him? Can he continue a conversation if it is interrupted?

"He isn't senile. He just has these blackouts, as I told you over the phone."

"I'm sorry. I have to ask."

They did not speak until the taxi stopped in front of the hospital. As Dr Wirth opened the door, Rosemarie said, "I'm worried it's Alzheimer's."

Dr Wirth pulled her towards him affectionately, then he got out.

"Are you a brain specialist?" Konrad Lang asked when Dr Wirth had finished the questions about Konrad's previous medical history.

"You could say that."

"And are you bound by the Hippocratic oath?"

"Of course."

"What I'm going to tell you now comes under it: I don't want to worry anyone but I'm afraid I might have Alzheimer's."

"The fact that you're actually suggesting that to me, Herr Lang, makes it an unlikely diagnosis. There are many possible reasons for blackouts like yours."

"Yes. But I would rather you tested me for Alzheimer's. Frau Haug and I are planning to get married."

This news took Dr Wirth aback; he needed a moment to regain his composure. "Unfortunately there is still no reliable test for Alzheimer's disease. The only thing we can do is try to rule out other possibilities. But even if we could exclude them all, we would still not know whether you had Alzheimer's. Not with absolute certainty."

"But with greater probability?"

"Yes, certainly."

"Then let's begin to rule things out."

Dr Wirth sat by the bed, opened his suitcase and took out a few sheets of paper. "I'm now going to ask you 30 questions and give you some exercises."

"A test?"

"A sort of stocktaking."

"Fire away."

"What day of the week is it today?"

"No idea. Tuesday?"

"Thursday." Dr Wirth put a cross on his questionnaire.

"Nineteen hundred and what?"

"Seventy-three?"

Dr Wirth put a cross. "What season is it?"

"I meant ninety-three."

"We're on to seasons."

"Ninety-six? I do know what year we're in."

"Is it spring, summer, autumn or winter?"

"Look outside! Winter!"

"What month?"

"December. No, January. I'll stick with January."

"What date?"

"Next question."

"Where are we?"

"In hospital."

"What floor are we on?"

"I was unconscious when they brought me in."

"In which town?"

"If I knew that I'd know which floor, too."

"Which canton?"

"The Grisons."

"Which country?"

"Greece."

"Repeat after me please: 'lemon'."

"Lemon."

"Key."

"Key."

"Ball."

"Ball."

"And now subtract seven from a hundred."

Konrad repeated, "And now subtract seven from a hundred."

"No, this is an arithmetic test now. Do the calculation, please."

Konrad Lang counted. Dr Wirth waited patiently.

"The change is so sudden."

"That's the intention."

Konrad Lang counted. "Ninety-three."

"And take seven from that again."

Konrad Lang subtracted the number seven from each answer four times. He did not find it easy but he managed it.

"That was very good," Dr Wirth said. "What were the three words which you repeated after me just now?"

"Three words?"

"I asked you to repeat three words after me. Do you remember?"

"If I'd known I had to make a note of them I would be able to remember them now."

Dr Wirth put three crosses and then held up his pencil. "What's that?"

"The test's unfair. If you don't know the rules of the game you've no chance."

Dr Wirth continued to hold his pencil up. "Please, Herr Lang. What is that?"

"For writing."

Dr Wirth put a cross. Then he pointed to his watch. "And that?"

"Lemon. One of them was 'lemon'."

"The three words?"

"One was 'lemon'. Or 'ball'."

"'Ball' or 'lemon'?"

"I can't remember."

Dr Wirth pointed to his watch.

"Eleven?" Konrad Lang guessed.

The doctor put a cross. "Repeat the following sentence after me: *no if and buts, please.*"

"No ifs and buts, please. It's 'ifs', not 'if'."

Dr Wirth gave him a sheet of paper. "Hold this piece of paper in your right hand."

Konrad did so.

"Fold it in the middle."

Lang folded it.

"Drop it on the floor."

Konrad Lang looked at Dr Wirth in surprise, shrugged his shoulders and threw the paper over the edge of the bed. It flew a couple of metres and landed on the polished lino.

The doctor gave him another piece of paper. Written on it was: "Read this: close both your eyes! And do it."

Lang shrugged his shoulders and looked uncomprehendingly at Dr Wirth.

"You're supposed to close both your eyes! Read and do it!"

Lang didn't understand. "Next question."

Dr Wirth gave him another piece of paper. "Write any sentence you like on this sheet of paper."

Konrad Lang wrote, "Which of us two is nuts?" and gave it back to him. Dr Wirth read it, smiled sourly and gave him a clean sheet of paper. There were two pentagons on it, touching on one side. "Draw that please."

Konrad took a long time over this last exercise. But he thought in the end that he had made a decent job of it.

Dr Wirth, on the other hand, gave him zero.

Konrad Lang got 18 out of a possible 30 marks in this test. It was a catastrophic result. Even if Dr Wirth made allowances for the fact that the questions on place and time were difficult to answer in the circumstances, even if he conceded that he had not carried out the examination absolutely fairly for personal reasons, the patient would still not have got the 26 points which a fit person would have to get, at worst.

The doctor recommended Rosemarie Haug to send Konrad Lang to the university hospital for further examination as a matter of urgency.

"If it'll put your mind at rest," Konrad said when Rosemarie proposed it to him.

Three days later Konrad was lying in a private room in the university hospital. He was unaware that he was in the geriatric ward.

Infectious diseases of the brain were ruled out after laboratory tests on his blood and cerebrospinal fluid.

The electroencephalography gave no indication of any other reasons for dementia.

The cerebral blood flow readings ruled out arterio-sclerotic disorders of the blood flow.

The investigation into the cerebral metabolic rate of oxygen and glucose indicated decreased metabolic activity in certain areas of the brain.

Two weeks after he had been found with frozen toes in a snow-hole in the Stazerwald by a sleigh-driver from the Valtellina, Konrad Lang was lying freezing cold in a hospital gown on a vinyl-covered bed.

An auxiliary put a blanket over him and pushed the bed into the circular opening of the CAT scanner. The cylinder began to rotate. Slowly at first then faster, and faster still.

Konrad Lang was lying in a blue hole again. Everything around him was sinking.

From a long way off a voice called, "Herr Lang?"

And again, "Herr Lang?"

They were looking for a Herr Lang.

Someone placed a hand lightly on his brow. He knocked it away and sat up. When he tried to climb off the bed he noticed that his feet were bandaged.

"I want to get out of here," he said to Rosemarie when she came into his room. "They cut your toes off."

She thought he was joking and smiled. But Konrad threw the

cover off and pointed triumphantly to where he had removed his bandages to reveal the barely healed scars on his feet.

"Yesterday there were two," he said. "Today there are three."

Konrad Lang was released from the university hospital that same day. The clinical tests had eliminated most other possible diagnoses.

At Rosemarie's insistence Dr Wirth had agreed to carry out the psychological tests on Konrad as an outpatient.

Elvira Senn was surprised at what Schöller had to report.

"In the geriatric ward?", she asked again.

"They're doing tests on his brain. He's suffering from loss of memory. Dementia."

"Dementia? How old is he? Just under 65?"

"He's helped it along a bit." Schöller tipped up an imaginary glass.

"Can they do anything about it?"

"Not if it's Alzheimer's, for example, no."

"Is that what they think it is?"

"They have to. Over half of the people they examine there have Alzheimer's."

Elvira Senn shook her head thoughtfully. "Keep me up to date on this," she said and then turned to the other items on their agenda.

When Schöller had left her study she stood up and went over to the bookshelves, where she kept a few sentimental photographs. One of them showed her as a young girl with Wilhelm Koch, the founder of the firm, an elderly formal gentleman. On another she could be seen on the arm of Edgar Senn, her second husband. Between them stood Thomas Koch, aged about ten years.

Elvira took a photograph album from the shelf and leafed through it. She paused for a moment over one photograph which showed her with Thomas and Konrad as small boys in St Mark's Square. Only a short while ago Konrad had given her a fright with his sudden accurate recollection of that time in Venice. Was it possible that some lucky fate had now begun to wipe out those memories once and for all?

She put the album back on to the shelf. It had grown dark. She switched on the light and went over to the window. As she closed the curtains she caught sight of her reflection in the glass. It was smiling.

"The lion is eaten by a tiger. Which animal is dead?" Dr Wirth asked him. Now Konrad Lang knew that they were making fun of him.

"The tiger," he answered. Dr Wirth made a note.

"Got you there," Konrad laughed.

"It isn't a game, Herr Lang," Dr Wirth reminded him seriously.

"What else can it be? It's a particularly stupid game in fact. What have a banana and a — thingummy in common, what articles are under this cloth, draw a clock. I'm not a child, you know! I could tell the time before your parents were even born."

"It's important for us to do this test, it helps us with the diagnosis." Dr Wirth held up a small rubber hammer. "What is this hammer called?"

"Don't change the subject now."

"Don't you know?"

"How should I know?"

"Because I told you a few moments ago."

"No idea."

"A reflex hammer," Dr Wirth said, making a note. With relish as it seemed to Konrad.

"Do you really think I don't know what's going on here? You're trying to make me out to be an old fogey in front of her because you've got your eye on her yourself."

"On who?"

"On Elisabeth, of course."

Dr Wirth made a note. "You mean Rosemarie."

89

"That's what I said."

"No, you said Elisabeth."

Konrad made no reply. He took a deep breath and tried to calm himself down. Time and again he had vowed not to let Dr Wirth wind him up. And yet time and again the doctor had succeeded. He knew how to confuse him. Write down what date it is today; what's that; what's it used for; do you recognise the person in this photo? The man was a psychologist, schooled in confusing people like him. And when he had done it once he could catch him out with easy questions. With questions which, under normal circumstances, he could have answered correctly without even thinking. But these were not normal circumstances.

Only because Konrad had promised Rosemarie to see the tests through did he finally say, "Let's carry on."

"We've almost finished," Dr Wirth said. "I'm now going to ask you to explain a proverb to me: 'He who digs a pit for others will fall into it himself.'"

Konrad Lang deliberated for a moment. Then he stood up. "I'm not a five-year-old, you know," he said, walked out of the consulting room, through the anteroom and out into the corridor.

Dr Wirth followed him. "Let me at least order you a taxi," he called after him.

But Konrad Lang was already in the lift and had pressed the button. The door closed automatically and the lift moved off.

Konrad Lang got out on the top floor and could not find the exit.

After a while Dr Wirth arrived, took him back to the lift and went down to the exit with him.

A taxi was waiting in front of the building. Dr Wirth told the driver Konrad's address.

When the taxi arrived at its destination Rosemarie was waiting for him at the garden gate.

In the spring Rosemarie went to Capri with Konrad. She knew that it would be a very strenuous journey. Konrad was becoming noticeably more confused. But recently he had been talking about Capri more and more as if they had already been there together, so she had hit upon the idea of creating some shared memories of Capri.

She hired a large chauffeur-driven Mercedes from a limousine rental company. It was rather ostentatious, she thought, but a tram ride with Konrad was nerve-racking enough; she wanted to spare them both a train journey or a flight.

Konrad enjoyed the journey in the limousine as if he had been travelling by chauffeur-driven car all his life. His only minor panic was when they got into the hydrofoil in Naples and he could no longer see the suitcases.

When the boat reduced speed at the entrance to the harbour and the hydrofoils were back in the water again Konrad put his arm around her shoulders and pulled her close to him several times as if to say, "Do you remember?"

Konrad knew every path and every bay on Capri. He took Rosemarie to the ruins at Monte Tiberio, ate young raw broad beans with her in the garden of a trattoria under lemon trees and walked with her through Fersen's villa, bewildered by its sudden decay.

"Do you remember?" and "Remember this?" he kept on asking her. When she explained that they had never been there together, he would look at her irritably and mumble, "Of course, sorry." And shortly afterwards he would ask her again, "Do you remember?", "Remember this?"

Finally Rosemarie gave up correcting and learnt to indulge in memories which were not her own. They spent some happy days together again, on the island of his first great love.

5

ROSEMARIE HAUG SAT IN THE LIVING ROOM AND READ IN the paper that Urs Koch, 32, had been made a member of the board of directors of the Koch Works and had taken over the management of the electronics sector. Thomas Koch, 66, had stepped down as an executive.

The reporter of the news item described this as the first step in the transfer of power in the company. Not from father to son, as they would have outsiders believe, but from step-grandmother to grandson. Elvira Senn had controlled the works with a firm hand, he wrote, first of all as president of the board of directors and later as a power behind the throne. Fun-loving Thomas Koch's authority over the operational management had remained within boundaries set by Elvira Senn throughout this period. The appointment of the talented and ambitious Urs to manage the electronics division – not the largest sector, but the most prestigious nonetheless – would be recognised by insiders as a sign that the arrangements for the continuation of the company had entered a decisive phase.

Rosemarie put the paper aside. She did not know whether news of the Koch household was something with which she might engage Konrad's interest at the moment. Since their return from Capri she had been visiting an advisory centre for Alzheimer's patients and their relatives, sometimes with him, sometimes on her own. She felt rather out of place amongst all the elderly couples, it is true. It was embarrassing for her to be the only one whose partner mistook her for someone else, even though the remaining symptoms were much further advanced in most of the others. But she did it because she had to do something.

Konrad did exercises in memory training there which she continued with him at home. She followed their other prescriptions religiously, too: kept telling him the date and the day of the week; spoke to him about events of the previous day; encouraged him to tidy his room; listened to music with him; read the paper aloud to him and tried to discover how else she might arouse his interest and maintain his link with reality.

But she found it more and more difficult to assess him. Sometimes he was interested by things to which, in the year and a half since she had known him, he had seemed completely indifferent: football results, local politics, dog shows. Then again, he could stare at nothing for hours and only nod absent-mindedly when she introduced his favourite subjects: Chopin, Capri, the Kochs. Sometimes he could suddenly say: "Gloria von Thurn und Taxis had a birthday cake made for the Prince's sixtieth birthday with 60 marzipan penises. He was queer, you know. But only a chosen few knew."

Shortly after Capri, Konrad had lost to Rosemarie at backgammon for the first time. Not long afterwards he had found it difficult to understand the game. They had not played for a long time now.

He had also stopped cooking. More and more often he had stood at a loss in the kitchen unable to decide in which order to do things so that Rosemarie had to step in and concoct something out of the chaos left behind by the half-prepared ingredients.

They had continued their occasional outings to restaurants for a while. But Konrad found it increasingly difficult to choose from the menu. His slow eating put the kitchen and waiting staff so much out of their stride that they gave up going to restaurants as well.

Neither did they touch the piano any more. "It doesn't mean anything to me now," Konrad insisted when she suggested playing together one of their two-handed pieces from the repertoire of the early days of their friendship.

One day she had arrived home from shopping and heard him desperately trying to play one of his virtuoso one-handed runs. It sounded like a child playing. Since then she had never mentioned playing the piano again.

Meanwhile it was late summer and Konrad Lang was increasingly in need of nursing care. Konrad, who had looked so elegant when they first met and, after he had given up drinking, had always been well-groomed, began to neglect himself. He wore the same things for days until she put them in the wash or took them to the cleaner's. He shaved badly and less and less often. His fingernails grew too long and when she drew his attention to it, no, when she pleaded with him with a hint of annoyance (something that was happening more and more often) to cut his nails, it emerged that he could not do it. He stood there with his nail scissors in his hand and had no idea what he was supposed to do with them.

For a few days she had been finding underclothes in the most unlikely places in the flat. Sometimes they were wet. Felix Wirth had prepared her for this some time ago: "You'll need some domestic help when he starts to wet his trousers," he had said.

She pushed the idea out of her mind at first. She hated the idea of having a stranger in the house. She also knew how difficult it had become for Konrad to get used to someone new. Recently she had begun to think that he did not know who she was. He made mistakes with her name (he called her Elisabeth, or Elvira), and sometimes he seemed to stare at her as if she were a complete stranger.

Konrad used to see himself through situations such as this by offering up one of the meaningless phrases that he had at his fingertips – "At your service, madame" or "Didn't we meet in Biarritz?" or "Small world!" – in the hope that she would help him out. Most of the time she did. She left him in the lurch only now and then when she was tired.

Recently she had sometimes thought that if he saw her as a stranger anyway, some other stranger could clear up his mess.

Rosemarie Haug stood up and went to find Konrad. He had been out of the room for quite a while. Recently it happened more and more frequently that he could not find his way round the flat.

When she went into her bedroom (they had had separate rooms for a little while now, something that Konrad found difficult to understand), she heard him levering the bathroom door handle. The bathroom was accessible both from here and from the corridor. She had begun to lock the bedroom door because Konrad sometimes wandered around the flat during the night and had suddenly appeared by her bed a few times.

"It's locked, Konrad," she called. "Use the other door!"

Instead of answering, Konrad hammered frantically at the door. Rosemarie turned the key and opened it. Konrad, his face bright red, was standing in the bathroom with raised fists. When he saw her he rushed towards her and threw her on to the bed.

"You damned witch," he stammered. "I know exactly who you are."

Then he slapped her face.

"You couldn't be expected to put up with that, even if he were your husband," Felix Wirth said. She had rung him immediately after the incident. He had come straight away and injected Konrad, who was still quite agitated, with a sedative and helped to get him to bed. They were now sitting in the living room.

"He very nearly became my husband. We were going to get married in the summer. But he's forgotten that, too."

"Be thankful for that."

"Nevertheless, I am his wife in a certain way. It seems to me as if we've always known each other."

"He hit you, Rosemarie. And he'll do it again."

"He mistook me for someone else. He's the gentlest man I've ever met."

"He'll mistake you for someone else again. You've come into his life too recently. His memory of you is stored in the part of the brain which goes wrong first. He won't know whether it's summer or winter, day or night, he won't be able to dress or wash himself. He'll have to wear nappies and be fed, he won't recognise anyone any more, he won't know where he is and eventually he won't even know who he is. Let me look for a place in a nursing home for him. Do him and yourself a favour."

"What right do I have? I'm neither a relative nor married to him. I can't just put a responsible adult into a home."

"I can fill in the forms which will certify him as quickly as possible."

They watched the lights on the rooftop terrace for a while in silence. A wind had blown up and was shaking the ornamental vine on the balustrade.

"I've known women – wives – who have lived with their husbands for 30 or 40 years who could never imagine life without them but who have said to me: 'If I don't get him out of the house soon, I shall begin to hate him.'"

Rosemarie said nothing.

"Do you love him?"

Rosemarie thought about it. "I was very much in love for a year."

"That isn't enough for five years of bottom-washing."

The wind was now splattering heavy raindrops on to the terrace window.

"You look terrible."

"Thank you."

"I'm telling you because it isn't unimportant to me how you look."

Rosemarie looked up and smiled. "Perhaps I will get a nurse. At least for nights."

When Konrad Lang woke up it was dark. He was lying in a strange bed. It was narrow and high and Elisabeth wasn't lying next to him. He wanted to get up but it was impossible. There were bars on both sides of the bed.

"Hey!" he called. And then louder: "Hey, hey, hey!"

No one came. Everything stayed dark.

He shook the bars. It made a lot of noise. "Hey, hey, hey!" he shouted to the rhythm of the rattling. And finally, "Help!"

"Help!" – "Hey, hey, hey!" – "Help!"

The door opened and a huge figure stood in the brightly lit rectangle of the door frame. The light in the room went on. "What's wrong, Herr Lang?"

Konrad was kneeling in the bed clinging to the slats of the low rail.

"I'm locked in," he gasped.

The nurse came over to the bed. She was wearing a white apron and her reading glasses dangled on a cord over her huge bosom. She took down the bars.

"You aren't locked in. That's only so that you won't fall out of bed again. You can get out any time." She pointed to the buzzer on the rail above the hospital bed. "All you have to do is to ring here. Then you won't wake Frau Haug."

Konrad didn't know any Frau Haug. He began to climb out of bed.

"Do you need to go to the toilet?"

Konrad didn't answer. He was going to find Elisabeth now. That was nothing to do with this woman.

He stood by the bed and looked around the strange room. They had also got rid of his clothes. But that wasn't going to stop him.

When he tried to go to the door the woman held him back by his arm. He tried to shake her off. But she held on tight.

"Let go," he said very quietly.

"Where do you want to go to, Herr Lang? It's two o'clock in the morning."

"Let go."

"Be a good fellow now, Herr Lang. Go back to sleep again

for two hours and then it'll be light and you can go for a walk."

Konrad tore himself free and ran to the door. The nurse followed him and caught hold of him by the sleeve, which tore with a loud ripping sound. Konrad lashed out and slapped the woman in the face. She slapped him back, twice.

At this point the door opened and Rosemarie was standing in front of them.

"Elisabeth," Konrad said. He began to cry.

This was the second nurse whom Rosemarie dismissed. Admittedly she had not caught the first one hitting Konrad. But one morning Konrad had had bruises on his upper arm and a black eye. The woman had maintained that he had slipped in the bath. Konrad couldn't remember anything.

The manager of the nursing agency refused to send Rosemarie a replacement. Her point of view was that "Herr Lang is an aggressive patient and so someone might very well hit back."

It was Felix Wirth who came to her assistance. He knew a former nurse who had brought up two children and was now thinking about returning to the profession. A well-paid private post as a night nurse would suit her very well.

Her name was Sophie Berger and she was ready to start that same evening on a trial basis.

She was a slim, tall, red-haired woman in her mid-forties. When she arrived Konrad was on his best behaviour: "Small World!" he exclaimed, chatting happily with her and behaving like the confident host he had always been.

When he was going to bed and Sophie Berger explained to him that she would be there all night and that if he needed anything he was to feel free to ring, he winked and said: "You can count on it."

"Personal remarks and familiarity are not normally his style at all," Rosemarie said apologetically when Konrad had gone.

"There's a first time for everything," Sophie Berger laughed.

But however harmonious the evening had been, the night was

a disaster. Rosemarie kept hearing doors banging, the rattling of the bars on the tubular steel bed and Konrad's voice.

Finally she could stand it no longer, got up and went into his room. Konrad was cowering in a corner of his bed holding his hands in front of his face to protect himself. The night nurse was standing at the foot of the bed with tears in her eyes. "I didn't touch him," she said when Rosemarie came into the room, "not a hair on his head."

Konrad kept on repeating, "Mama Anna, go away. Mama Anna, go away."

The following day Konrad Lang disappeared. He ate an unusually hearty breakfast. He did not say one word about the night nurse. Rosemarie helped him to dress and did the things which they had taught her in order to establish his link with reality.

"A really beautiful autumn day, so warm for the end of October," she said. "What is it today, Tuesday or Wednesday?"

He answered as he always had of late, "Every day is Sunday with you."

She read the paper aloud to him and as always at the end, to test his alertness, she opened the stocks and shares pages. "Koch Industries, plus four."

This morning, instead of looking at her in bewilderment, he put on his millionaire look and ordered: "Buy."

They both laughed, and Rosemarie, who had not slept much that night, felt better.

Her sleepless night was to blame for her falling asleep in the armchair after lunch. When she woke up it was three o'clock and Konrad had disappeared.

His coat was gone, his slippers were in the corridor and after she had phoned the police she noticed that his pillow was missing too.

Felix Wirth came as soon as he could get away from the hospital and stayed with her without uttering a word of reproach.

By now it was growing dark and there was still no sign of

Konrad. They made a missing person announcement on the television before the news. When Rosemarie saw Konrad's smiling face on the screen (she had taken the photograph herself on Capri) and heard the voice say that Konrad Lang was confused and that he should be approached gently, her eyes filled with tears.

"I promise you one thing," she said, "if nothing has happened to him, I'll agree to the nursing home."

Konikoni lay in the potting shed, absolutely quiet. It was dark but not cold. He had made himself a bed in the peat under some jute sacks. The sacks had been full of tulip bulbs, which he had emptied into a crate. And he had the pillow.

No one would find him here. He could stay here until winter came. In front of the shed were some plums and nuts. And by the door a tap which sometimes dripped on to a metal watering can. Plop.

There was a lovely smell of peat, bulbs and fertilizer. Sometimes a dog barked, but far away. Sometimes there was a rustling in the leaves outside the door: a mouse, perhaps, or a hedgehog. Otherwise there was silence.

Konikoni closed his eyes. Plop.

She won't find me here.

Rosemarie Haug waited all night in vain for some news. "Please don't ring us again," an irritable policeman implored her at around two in the morning. "We'll get in touch as soon as we hear something."

At around three o'clock Felix Wirth managed to persuade her to take a light sedative. When she had gone to sleep he lay down on the sofa and set the alarm on his wristwatch for six o'clock.

At seven o'clock he took Rosemarie some orange juice and coffee in bed. And the news that nothing had changed. Then he went to the hospital.

Shortly before eight, two policemen rang at the door of the flat.

Rosemarie opened it to them and was alarmed at their serious expression. "Has something happened?"

"We only wanted to inquire whether you had heard anything new."

"Whether *I've* heard anything new?"

"Sometimes missing people turn up and the relatives are so relieved that they forget to inform us."

"If he turns up I'll let you know immediately."

"No offence! We have to cover every eventuality, madam."

"Something definitely must have happened."

"They usually turn up again. Even mentally confused people," the elder officer said consolingly.

"If nothing had happened someone would definitely have found him by now."

"Sometimes they go to strangers' houses. It can be a long time until someone finds them there and phones us."

The younger officer asked, "Cellar, garage, air-raid shelters: they've all been checked?"

Rosemarie nodded.

"Neighbours?"

Rosemarie nodded.

The two policemen said goodbye. "As soon as you hear something, 999," the younger man said before entering the lift.

"You can be sure of that," Rosemarie answered.

"Don't worry, he'll turn up," the elder one shouted as the lift door closed.

"Even if it's in the lake," he said quietly and grinned as the lift moved off.

It was dark under the rhododendrons. Konikoni could see fragments of the hazy October sky through the thick canopy of leaves. The marshy flower bed was damp and cool and smelt of autumn and mustiness. Grey woodlice lived under the stones bordering the granite flagstone path. When he touched them with his finger they rolled themselves up into balls and he could play marbles with them.

An hour earlier the gardener had been raking the leaves barely a yard away from him. Konikoni didn't stir and the gardener moved slowly away.

Later an old lady's legs went by. Shortly afterwards some young ones. Now it was quiet.

A blackbird hopped across the path. At the edge of the flower bed it poked about in the peat for a little while and the end of an earthworm appeared. She pulled at it and stopped suddenly. Her beady eye had spied him. He held his breath.

The blackbird snatched the worm right out of the earth and made off with it.

The wind wafted a smell of burning leaves past him.

If they shout I shan't answer, Konikoni resolved.

When Rosemarie stepped out on to the terrace towards midday she saw a police boat chugging slowly along the bank. She recognised the police in blue overalls by the lake. They were now in two groups walking along the lakeside in opposite directions.

Shortly afterwards she did something she never thought she would do: she phoned Thomas Koch.

Thomas Koch was not easy to contact. "It's private," was not enough to be connected. Neither was "It's an emergency." Only when she said there had been "an accident in the family" did Thomas Koch come to the phone after a short time.

"Konrad Lang is not one of the family," he snapped when she had explained to him why she was calling.

"I didn't know where to turn for help."

"And what do you expect me to do? Go and look for him?"

"I hoped you might be able to use your influence. I don't think that the police are taking the matter very seriously."

"Who says I have any influence with the police?"

"Konrad."

"In that case he must really be very confused."

Rosemarie hung up.

Simone Koch had imagined it would be different. She had been married to Urs Koch now for a year and four months and was already experiencing her sixth marital crisis. She had not set her hopes too high. She knew that Urs was a very dominant personality: she had prepared herself for him having things his own way. And she had anticipated he would often have business or even social engagements where she would not be present. Simone had few interests of her own and so it was not difficult for her to adopt other people's interests. She had become enthusiastic about electronic high-temperature surveillance equipment, rally-driving, the Tokyo stock exchange, pheasant shooting in lower Austria, military riding, golf and even the work of a young woman textile designer — until Simone caught her holding hands with Urs in a restaurant.

Simone had arranged to meet one of her friends there. Urs had said he could not join them because of a business dinner. She was so astonished that she laughed. Then she ran out of the restaurant and bumped into her friend who was just paying for her taxi.

"Come on, let's go somewhere else. It's heaving in there."

They went to a different restaurant and, although Judith was her best friend, Simone did not tell her what had happened. She was too ashamed to admit that her husband was decieving her after only six weeks of marriage.

She reserved her tears for when she got home. Urs stayed out all night. If she had not laughed, he told her later, he would have come home.

That was Simone Koch's first marital crisis.

Sometimes she thought she ought to have made a scene at the time. Then perhaps there might not have been so many more crises.

Urs Koch left her in no doubt that marriage for him did not mean the loss of his personal freedom, as he described his right to little affairs which were completely irrelevant to their relationship.

In many respects Simone had been brought up to be a pragmatic woman. But this was a new experience. Until now, she had been sympathetic when men did not take their fidelity too seriously. But then she had always been the woman with whom they held hands in discreet restaurants.

The fact that a man lost interest in her after such a short time was not only hurtful, it was frightening. Her mother had always said, "You're like me: pretty, not beautiful. Our type have to be married off by 25 at the latest."

She was now 23 and had learnt not to take everything her mother said as gospel. But when she looked in the mirror and imagined her baby face with wrinkles she began to wonder if time was not pressing her to make a fresh start.

So she put up a weak fight, counted her marital crises and became visibly depressed, which didn't make her any prettier.

What made the situation even worse was the fact that she had to live in the Villa Rhododendron. Urs was building a "smart house" close by which, amongst other things, had its windows pointing towards the course of the sun, assessed its own energy sources according to weather and need, and automatically identified its occupants and let them in. Without consulting Simone he had taken up Elvira's offer of the wing which had been empty since Thomas's third wife had left, until this combination of dream villa and showcase for Koch Electronics was completed.

Simone felt even more of an outsider in this large, old house with all its memories which she did not share and all its rituals which she did not know. She had the feeling that everyone was watching how she reacted to Urs's escapades. Urs did not conceal them from members of the family or even from the staff and she was afraid that she would lose what little respect they had shown her at the beginning.

Elvira, Thomas and Urs were all, each in their own way, so preoccupied with themselves that they only noticed Simone's presence when it was socially necessary.

Mostly she was left alone with her depression, which was harder to bear now that autumn was reminding her every day of how quickly time passes and skin wrinkles.

Searching, like all depressives, for a backdrop for her melancholy Simone was wandering through the most remote parts of the grounds when she heard a splashing noise. An elderly man who was obviously having a pee was standing in the middle of the thick rhododendrons bordering the flagstone path.

When he saw her he did up his trousers in embarrassment. Simone turned discreetly away. When she turned round again he had disappeared.

"Hello!" she called. No answer. Only a slight movement of the leaves at the spot where he had been standing.

"Please come out," Simone said in an uncertain voice.

Nothing moved.

"Is anything wrong, Frau Koch?" a voice behind her inquired. It was the gardener, Herr Hügli, who was coming up the path.

"There's someone in the bushes," she answered. "Over there in the rhododendrons, an elderly man."

"Are you sure?"

"I saw him. He's hiding again now. About there."

"Hey you! Come on out!" Herr Hügli called.

Not a sound. He glanced at Simone sceptically.

"I saw him. He had a pee and then disappeared. He must be underneath the branches."

Herr Hügli stepped carefully on to the flower bed and made his way through the shoulder-high rhododendrons. Simone directed him.

"A little more to the right, yes, that's it, you're right there. Careful!"

Herr Hügli stood still, disappeared into the foliage and shortly afterwards re-emerged with the elderly man. "Herr Lang!" he uttered in amazement.

Simone recognised him now: Konrad Lang, the arsonist of Corfu.

Shortly before midday a taxi driver had contacted the police station. He had been called to Rosemarie Haug's address yesterday, he said. An elderly man with a cushion, whom he had driven to Fichtenstrasse 12. He failed to mention that the man had paid him 100 francs instead of 32.

Fichtenstrasse 12 was a late 19th-century villa which had been converted into offices. No one there knew Konrad Lang or had seen an elderly man with a cushion. But because the taxi driver insisted that he had taken him to this address and had seen him going into the grounds Constable Staub asked permission to look around the garden and requested a dog to help him.

The garden behind the villa was gloomy and overgrown. It climbed up a slope in two terraces. On the upper one was a drying area with rusty carpet frames, covered in moss and shaded by a long line of pine trees. A thick thuja hedge immediately behind it formed the boundary with the neighbouring property.

Senta, an Alsatian, led her dog-handler to this hedge. When he set her free she disappeared into the undergrowth. After a while the policemen heard her following the scent in the neighbouring property.

The dog-handler squeezed through the bushes and came across a fence with iron railings which he followed in the direction in which Senta had disappeared. After only a few metres he came to a narrow gate that was half open. Behind it were a few over-grown steps which led into the undergrowth of the neighbouring property.

The Villa Rhododendron.

When the police rang at the iron gate of the Villa Rhododendron a surprised Herr Hügli opened it to them.

"That was quick," he said. It was a minute at most since he had telephoned the police on Thomas Koch's orders.

Constable Staub cleared his throat. "We're looking for a missing person and have reason to believe that he is to be found on this property," he explained.

"He certainly is," Herr Hugli answered and took them into the house.

Elvira and Thomas Koch were standing in the hall of the Villa in front of a carved medieval-style chair the size of a throne. On it sat the pathetic figure of Konrad Lang, dishevelled, unshaven and unconcerned, in a crumpled suit encrusted with earth. Next to him stood Simone Koch who was trying to give him some hot tea.

Thomas Koch went up to the police. "Gentlemen, that *was* quick. Take charge of him, please. They picked him up in the grounds. It's Konrad Lang. He's mentally disturbed."

Constable Staub went up to Konrad's chair. "Herr Lang?" he asked, in a louder voice than necessary. "Are you all right?"

Konrad nodded.

Staub said to Elvira and Thomas rather more quietly, "Missing since yesterday."

And louder again to Konrad: "The things you get up to!"

"No idea how he got in here," Thomas Koch said to Constable Staub.

"I can help you out there: through the little gate over that way, from your neighbour's property."

"A gate?" Thomas Koch asked.

"There's a rusty iron-barred gate down there. It wasn't easy to open: probably not been used for years. Didn't you know about it?"

Elvira answered for him. "I'd forgotten it. A friend of my first husband used to live in that villa. But he moved away when Wilhelm was still alive. The gate hasn't been used since then."

"How long ago is that?"

"Sixty years," Elvira said, more to herself than anyone else.

Thomas shook his head. "I'd no idea about it."

"I would do something about it: anybody can get in," Staub advised him. Then he turned to Konrad again and said in a loud voice, "Come on, we'll take you home now."

Konrad looked at the policeman in bewilderment. "But I am home."

The Kochs and the policemen smiled at each other. "Yes, yes. We'll take you to your other home now."

Konrad thought about it for a moment. "Oh, right," he mumbled finally and stood up. He looked at Thomas Koch. "Don't you remember the gate?"

Thomas shook his head.

Konrad half put his hand over his mouth and whispered, "The pirates' gate." Then he shook Simone's hand. "Thank you."

"Don't mention it," Simone answered.

He looked at her inquiringly for a moment. "Didn't we meet in Biarritz?"

"Quite possibly," Simone replied. The policemen took Konrad outside. Simone went with them.

Thomas Koch shook his head. "The pirates' gate. The pirates' gate. It seems familiar, somehow. Didn't someone say he couldn't remember anything any more?"

Elvira made no reply.

Thomas gazed after the policemen, Konrad Lang and Simone. "Biarritz? They didn't meet in Biarritz, did they?"

Ten days later Schöller informed his boss that Konrad Lang had been admitted to the Sonnengarten old people's home.

"So Konrad Lang is off our hands at last," he added with a thin smile.

Elvira Senn almost answered, "I hope so."

Schöller left very late that evening.

6

THE SONNENGARTEN OLD PEOPLE'S HOME WAS A SIX-STOREY building on the edge of a wood not very far from the Villa Rhododendron and the Grand Hotel des Alpes, where Konrad Lang had drunk so many Negronis, the ideal afternoon drink.

He was now sitting in the day room on the top floor and did not understand what had been taken away from him.

The top floor was the locked ward, where the very advanced cases were accommodated. Or the ones who ran away.

Konrad Lang was not a very advanced case and the doctors would rather have seen him in a different ward where he would have had a better chance of meeting new people. But in the first place a single room had come free in the locked ward; secondly, there was a proven high risk that Konrad Lang would try to run away, and thirdly, it would be only a few months before he would have to be put in the locked ward anyway because of the rapid development of his illness. Nevertheless, for the moment, Konrad Lang looked more like a visitor than a patient in his new surroundings.

When Rosemarie had taken Konrad to the home and helped to carry his belongings into the little room with its hospital bed she had been unable to hold back her tears.

He had taken her into his arms and consoled her. "Don't be sad. It isn't for ever."

Rosemarie's conscience was troubling her. After a sleepless night in which she had planned again and again to get him out, the next morning he behaved like a close friend who was being picked up from a hotel. They went on long walks in the autumn woods around the clinic and occasionally had a drink in the bar of the Grand Hotel des Alpes. Sometimes he greeted Charlotte, the afternoon barmaid, by name and sometimes completely he ignored her.

When Rosemarie took him back to the Sonnengarten to abandon him among those helpless, disoriented, dependent old men and women, it was he who cheered her up, saying, "You have to go now or you'll be late."

He took her to the lift, which could be called and opened only with the ward sister's key, and said goodbye like someone who hoped she would understand that some tiresome commitment was preventing him from accompanying her home in person.

In the early days she tried to make the situation more bearable for him by driving them to her flat and spending the day there together. But it soon emerged that he found the flat strange. Every time they went there he became extremely agitated. He would get up out of the armchair where she had put him while she prepared lunch and then she would find him with his coat and hat on in the corridor, rattling at the locked door.

These were taxing days for Rosemarie. Sometimes she heard him talking in the next room and when she looked in she realised that he was holding a conversation with her. Then when she sat down next to him to continue the conversation his thoughts wandered and his face took on a vacant expression. He was capable of suddenly standing up and saying, "Well, it's time I was off."

He was on the go the whole day yet when it was time to leave he could look at her in bewilderment and say, "I don't want to go out again."

On one such evening, when she had finally enticed him out of the flat and opened the lift door into the day room on the sixth floor of the Sonnengarten and all eyes were turned towards them expectantly, he refused to leave the lift. It needed all her powers of persuasion and the help of a strong nurse to take him to his room.

When she left him later he had tears in his eyes.

The ward doctor said to her the next day that it would be better if she didn't take him home. It was confusing him. He always had difficulty in finding his way about again afterwards. He would have to realise that this was his home here. And so the locked ward of the Sonnengarten old people's home became Konrad Lang's new home.

Frau Spörri, a neat little woman with blue hair, formerly a production manager in a clothing factory, invariably wore a dress and jacket, with a little hat and white gloves. She always had her handbag with her and sometimes — though no one knew what the criteria were — an umbrella. She sat upright on a sofa or a chair, her handbag on her knees, waiting with her dreamy, patient smile for someone to pick her up.

Herr Stohler, a tall man with a stoop in a white casual jacket, a former foreign correspondent on a big newspaper, used to sit motionless at the table, stand up suddenly, walk up to another resident and accost him in a hotchpotch of English, Italian, Spanish, French and Swahili.

Frau Ketterer, a heavy, coarse, former home economics teacher sat with her legs apart at her place waiting for an opportunity to call out to Frau Spörri, "Did you see her gawking like an idiot again?" Or, "Look at her. In her nightie in the restaurant!"

Frau Schwab, housewife and mother, grandmother and great-grandmother, with thin hair and a pointed chin, who had long since abandoned her false teeth, always wore a light-blue, pink and yellow quilted dressing gown or a quilted lime-green one according to which one was not in the wash. She constantly prattled away in baby talk to a naked doll in her high-pitched childish voice.

Herr Kern, a former railway guard, whose appearance gave no clue as to why they had brought him here, kept law and order in the common room. "Shut your stupid mouths," he ordered Frau Schwab and her doll at regular intervals. "For God's sake speak German!" he commanded Herr Stohler when he had hurled another torrent of abuse at someone.

Herr Aeppli, one-time archivist with the municipal authorities, always in a bizarre outfit assembled from the clothes of other residents, went from room to room stocktaking and checking the cupboards.

Herr Huber, a retired Greek and Latin teacher in the local grammar school lay in his wheelchair, mouth wide open, staring at the ceiling.

Herr Klein, a former art-collector and architect of a great many dreary suburban housing estates, was, apart from his dementia, suffering from Parkinson's Disease which caused him to shake violently and made him completely dependent on outside help.

Altogether 34 men and women in various advanced stages of dementia occupied the sixth floor of the Sonnengarten. They sat alone or in the company of bewildered relatives or walked restlessly up and down the corridors, greeting each other like strangers whenever they passed.

For their medical care and therapy they were treated by specialists from Switzerland. And they were cared for, washed, fed and dressed by nurses and care assistants from Eastern Europe, the Balkans and Asia.

Konrad Lang seemed to be unaware that he was in a home. He kept a respectful distance from the residents and the nursing staff and took his meals at a separate little table, with an old newspaper, which well-meaning visitors had left behind in the common room. He behaved like a gentleman in a rather run-down *pension*. Rosemarie only hoped that that was how he felt.

The sole criticism that she sometimes heard from him was: "It stinks in here."

And he was right.

The iron railing fence bordering the neighbouring property was replaced by a security fence. And while he was at it, Urs Koch had the whole boundary of the property modernised. The electronic surveillance was extended to cover the entire perimeter and brought up to the latest technical standards; some additional services were added to the contracts with the security firm.

That, and the certain knowledge that Konrad Lang was in the locked ward on the sixth floor of a home from which no one normally came out alive, ought really to have been sufficient for Elvira Senn to feel safe. But again and again she caught herself thinking about Konrad. She could not get Dr Stäubli's words out of her mind that people with senile dementia sometimes return very dramatically to their early lives and develop precise recall of their earliest memories.

Of course she told herself that no one would take any notice of the senseless chatter of a mentally confused man but it was no real consolation. It made her nervous that Konrad, just at the moment when he appeared to be getting out of control, had removed himself from her sphere of influence. She was a woman unaccustomed to leaving anything to chance.

So she invited Simone, silently suffering in her marriage to Urs, to the Stöckli for tea and found no great difficulty in bringing the conversation round to the old man.

"I wonder what Koni's doing," she said absent-mindedly.

Simone was surprised. "Konrad Lang?"

"Yes. Crouching down there like a little rabbit. You have to feel sorry for him."

"I did feel very sorry for him."

"It's a terrible illness."

Simone said nothing.

"Everything was going so well for him, too. A woman with money and the prospect of spending the rest of his life doing what he liked best – absolutely nothing. And now he's in a home."

"Is he in a home?"

"There are limits to love. The woman's still young."

"I think that's very self-centred."

"It isn't everyone's cup of tea looking after a man with dementia."

"But that's mean, sticking him in a home."

"Perhaps he's all right there. Amongst his own kind."

"I don't believe it."

Elvira sighed. "Nor do I actually." She poured out the tea. "Perhaps you could go and see him sometime."

"Me?"

"See how he is. Whether he has everything he needs; whether we can do anything for him. It would put my mind at rest."

Simone hesitated. "I don't like hospitals."

"It isn't a hospital. It's an old people's home. That isn't so bad."

"Why don't you go?"

"It's impossible."

"Or we could go together?"

"Perhaps you're right. Let's forget it. Let's forget Konrad."

Simone's first sensation was the pungent smell in the lift which increased dramatically when the door opened at the sixth floor.

As she walked out of the lift everything went quiet in the day room. All action was suspended except for Herr Klein's shaking.

She looked about her and discovered Konrad Lang at a little table by the window staring vacantly in front of him.

"Good afternoon, Herr Lang."

Konrad Lang looked up in surprise. Then he rose to his feet, gave Simone his hand and said, "Didn't we meet in Biarritz?"

Simone laughed. "Yes, that's right, Biarritz."

As she sat down next to him the day room reverted to its chattering, stuttering, giggling and bickering.

What Simone had to report about Konrad Lang did nothing to allay Elvira's fears.

"We have to get him out of there, and quickly," she said when she came back from her visit to the Sonnengarten in an agitated state. "Otherwise he'll end up genuinely ill."

He had never seemed like an Alzheimer's patient to her. He recognised her immediately although they had met only twice before and had straightaway opened with his joke about Biarritz and gave her a detailed account of Biarritz after the war as if it had been only yesterday.

He was surrounded by totally demented old people with whom he could not exchange one sensible word, she said. And the best of it was: he could not remember a single visit from Rosemarie Haug.

"The chap is perhaps a bit confused sometimes, but then who isn't? If that man belongs in there then so do a few dozen others out of my circle of friends. He's got to get out of there or it'll kill him."

Elvira had not seen her so enthusiastic since her marriage. Simone was fiercely determined to get Konrad out of that home.

"The poor soul," Elvira remarked. "Were you able to speak to a doctor?"

"I tried. But they won't give me any information because I'm not a relative."

"Perhaps you should take up the matter with that Haug woman."

"I'm going to. But I don't know whether I can stay calm."

"You can count on my full support," Elvira promised.

As Simone left the Stöckli she thought that perhaps Elvira was not after all such a cold old woman.

And so began a short battle for Konrad Lang's release from the Sonnengarten old people's home.

Simone had no success in arranging a meeting with Rosemarie Haug. Finally her caretaker told her that she had gone away for a while.

Typical, Simone thought.

She discovered the name of Konrad's doctor from the home's management and obtained an appointment without delay when she explained that it was about Konrad Lang.

The doctor's name was Dr Wirth and he was not unsympathetic. He received her in his office at the hospital and listened to her patiently as she explained to him that from what she had seen

Konrad Lang should not be in that environment and that she had the feeling that if he was not sick now, then the home would certainly make him sick.

"Do you know Konrad Lang well?" he asked when she had finished.

"No, but my husband's family knows him very well. He practically grew up with my father-in-law."

"Does he agree with your impression?"

Simone was rather embarrassed. "He hasn't been to visit him. He's very busy."

Dr Wirth nodded understandingly.

"They don't have a very good relationship. Some incidents in the past."

"The fire on Corfu."

"Yes, amongst other things. I don't know the exact reasons either. I'm a newcomer to the family."

"You see, Frau Koch, I understand what you have said very well but I can assure you that your impression is wrong. If Herr Lang has given you the idea that he is alert then it's because he can smooth over a great deal with his meaningless phrases and the manners he learnt when he was growing up and because you probably saw him at a good time. Good spells and bad spells are typical of the illness. But we have to cater for the bad ones."

"I look at it a different way. We should be gearing life to the good spells."

"So what do you suggest?"

"That you get him out of there."

"And then who would look after him?"

"We can't count on Frau Haug any more, I suppose?" Simone inquired rather sharply.

Dr Wirth reacted with some irritation. "Frau Haug has done more for Konrad Lang than anyone could expect of a woman after such a short acquaintance. I was the one who persuaded her to take this step."

"I hope she enjoys her new-found freedom."

"Frau Haug is in hospital on Lake Constance suffering from nervous exhaustion and I hope she'll soon be back on her feet. If anyone has neglected their duties towards Herr Lang it's the Koch family, Frau Koch."

Simone was too embarrassed to speak. Then she said with somewhat less self-assurance, "Perhaps it isn't too late to make amends."

"In what way?"

"Private care. I should imagine it would be possible to prepare a suitable private flat and install some private nursing staff."

"Twenty-four-hour care, Frau Koch. That means three to four qualified staff around the clock plus others for therapy, diet, cleaning, medical care. A small hospital for one single patient."

"I have Frau Senn's complete support."

When Simone Koch left the hospital, Dr Wirth had promised to consider the matter and to discuss it with colleagues and the relevant authorities. He had no doubt that the authorities and the management of the home would welcome the offer with open arms. He was just not sure how Rosemarie would react to it. At any rate he would do his best to convince her.

But Elvira thought that Simone's plan to convert the little guest house into a mini nursing home was going a little too far. She wanted to have him under control, certainly, but not at such close quarters as that.

"Don't you think a private hospital would be the most practical solution?"

"He doesn't need a hospital," Simone persisted. "He just needs a little care when he has one of his bad days."

"I saw him here that day and he was completely confused."

"He was having one of his bad days."

"If you bring Koni here your husband will have a fit. Not to mention Thomas. There must be some solution which would be less of a strain on us all."

"You can't always run away from your responsibilities."

"We're not responsible for Konrad Lang."

"He belongs to the family in a way."

Elvira answered her calmly. "What do *you* know about the family?"

"There's no question of it," Rosemarie Haug replied when Felix Wirth told her about Simone Koch's visit at the weekend. They were sitting in the conservatory at the convalescent home on Lake Constance, drinking coffee and looking at the mist over the lake.

"She's got a guilty conscience now. They think they can make up for what they've been doing to him for 60 years by spending money now. They want to use him one last time, to salve their guilty consciences."

"On the other hand," Felix Wirth mused, "it would be the last opportunity for him at least to spend his old age in the style in which he was brought up."

"When I suggested private care for him you persuaded me against it."

"We're talking of four to five hundred thousand francs a year. For a man you hardly know and who doesn't remember you."

"Do you know what his last words to Thomas Koch were? 'Piss off!' I think that deserves some respect."

The mist mingled with the bare fruit trees on the shore.

"I have to get away from here, Felix."

Konrad Lang was sitting in a place where there were lots of people when something interesting happened: Gene Kelly danced out of the television set. At first he danced on a newspaper which he tore into two pieces as he did so, then he danced on one half, which he tore into two pieces again. Then suddenly he was in the room and kept on dancing.

Konrad Lang said to an old woman sitting next to him who was having a conversation with a baby, "Did you see? He's in there now." But the woman carried on talking. And then something else interesting happened: suddenly *she* was in the television set and he saw that the baby was a doll and that the old woman was a witch with a pointed chin and a pointed nose.

It frightened him and he shouted, "Watch out, watch out, a witch, a witch!" Then a tall man came up to him and said, "Shut up or you'll be in trouble."

Then he knew he just had to get out of there right away.

He stood up and went to the lift but it had no button. He walked down the corridor to a door which led to a fire escape.

It was locked. But the key was hanging alongside it in a little glass box. That was locked, too. But next to it was a little hammer also in a glass box. He rammed his elbow into the glass of this box so that he could take the hammer out. Then he hit the glass of the little key box with it, took the key and opened the door. He heard the witch bickering behind him. He stepped on to the top landing of the six-storey fire escape. He began to climb down slowly.

When he reached the landing of the fifth floor he heard Gene Kelly shouting above him, "Herr Lang!"

One of the witch's tricks. He carried on without so much as a glance upwards.

On the third-floor landing he saw them coming: mountain soldiers in winter uniforms. They climbed up the steps slowly and thought he hadn't seen them. He heard footsteps on the metal steps above him too. When he looked up he saw white trouser legs. More mountain soldiers.

He sat on the railings and waited. They wouldn't get him alive.

Rosemarie Haug could see from a distance that all was not well at the Sonnengarten. There were care assistants, nursing staff, firemen and police standing on all the landings of the fire escape on the west façade of the six storey building, apart from on the third, where one lone man was sitting on the railings.

Police cars, ambulances and fire engines were lined up in front of the building. As she approached she saw a three-metre high inflatable air cushion. When she had parked her car she suddenly knew who the lone man was. She started to run.

A policeman stopped her at the barrier.

"I have to get through," she gasped.

"Are you a relative?"

"No. Yes. I'm his lady-friend. Let me up there. I'll speak to him."

Ten minutes later, after the duty doctor had confirmed to the police that Frau Haug was the patient's only relative, Rosemarie began to climb very slowly up the staircase.

"You really gave me a fright there, Konrad," she called out as cheerfully as possible. "If you only knew how it looks from down there. It looks really dangerous: they're all very worried, they don't understand your sense of humour."

She had reached the second landing and was approaching the stairs to the third, past the last outpost of the rescuers.

"I'm coming up now, Konrad, and then we'll go to Des Alpes. I could do with a drink after this, couldn't you?"

Konrad made no reply. Rosemarie had reached the half-landing leading to the last section of staircase before the third landing. She carried on.

"Aren't you coming down to meet me, Konrad? I can hardly make it, and just think, there's a lift inside and it's cool there too. I'm coming now, Konrad. OK?"

She could see him now. He was sitting on the railings with his back to the drop, looking quite unconcerned.

She walked up the last two steps and stood on the landing, not three metres away from him.

"Phew, here I am! Aren't you going to come and say hello? This isn't like you, just sitting there."

Without any sign of recognition Konrad Lang let himself fall backwards over the railings.

He was the only one not to scream.

Konrad Lang fell softly and hurt himself only slightly in the scuffle with the firemen who were trying to free him from the air cushion.

Four men had to restrain him so that the doctor could give him a sedative and the nurses could take him back to his room.

Rosemarie needed a sedative too.

As did the manager of the Sonnengarten. "It had to happen some time," he said to the chief fireman. "What a crazy rule. An emergency key for the fire-escape door in a locked ward! You might as well put in diving boards!"

Rosemarie Haug stayed by Konrad's bed. Before he went to sleep he said, "Goodnight, nurse."

When she phoned Felix Wirth about it that evening he asked whether she was still against the idea of the Kochs taking care of Konrad's future.

"Who am I to dictate to a man who, given the choice between me and jumping from the third floor, chooses to jump?"

Simone had been to see Konrad Lang almost every day since her first visit. In a funny way, she felt a link with him. The Koch family had played a decisive role in his life, although they had never adopted him. They had used him for their own purposes and when he was no longer of any value to them, they had cast him off. The first of these had already happened to her; she was slowly preparing herself for the second.

On the day after the jump she found him cheery and in better spirits than he had been for a long time. No trace of a recollection of the previous day dampened his mood.

"At your service, madame," he said to the pretty unknown woman whose visit obviously meant a lot to him. As he bent over her hand, she saw that he had black bruises on his neck and his left ear was cut.

When she took the ward sister to task, the sister told her the injuries were the result of yesterday's incident. It was obvious to Simone: a suicide attempt.

She went for a long walk with him, in the hope that on the way he would tell her more about what had happened.

Konrad enjoyed the walk like a child. He dragged his feet through the deep leaves, sat on every seat by the edge of the path and watched fascinated as a group of forestry workers cut up a fallen beech tree with a large chainsaw.

He passed over questions about his jump from the third floor with an uncomprehending smile.

It was already growing dark when they went past the Grand Hotel des Alpes. Konrad made a beeline for the entrance, nodded to the doormen as though to old acquaintances and took a surprised Simone straight into the bar.

"Small world," he said to the barmaid who took their coats. She called him Koni and brought him "a Negroni as usual".

Simone ordered a glass of champagne and finally was certain that this man did not belong in a nursing home.

"Gloria von Thurn und Taxis had a birthday cake made for the Prince's sixtieth birthday with 60 marzipan penises on it. He was queer of course. But only a chosen few knew. Did you know that?"

"No, I didn't know that," Simone Koch giggled, pleased to be taken into his confidence.

When the pianist began to play they ordered another round. Suddenly Konrad stood up and went over to two old ladies in large floral-patterned outfits who were sitting at a small table close to the piano. He exchanged a few words with them and when he came back his eyes were filled with tears.

"Are you sad, Herr Lang?" Simone asked.

"No, happy," he answered, "happy that Aunt Sophie and Aunt Klara are still alive."

"Oh, and I thought you had no relatives."

"Whatever made you think that?" he replied.

*

When Simone told Elvira Senn about Konrad's suicide attempt she was not very interested.

But when she asked who Aunt Sophie and Aunt Klara were, Elvira pricked up her ears.

"Did he tell you about Aunt Sophie and Aunt Klara?"

"What do you mean 'tell me about them'? He met them."

"They've both been dead for 60 years," Elvira snorted.

When Simone left a quarter of an hour later Elvira had promised to reconsider the guest-house plan.

The management of the home were quickly convinced. It meant a free place for them and they would be rid of a patient who had caused them a great deal of trouble recently. The day after his jump from the fire escape Konrad had been brought back tipsy by his new visitor and been abusive to little Frau Spörri.

The authorities welcomed the Koch family's private initiative given the current crisis in nursing-home care and their financial considerations. Konrad Lang was penniless, without relatives and in the guardianship of the town.

Thomas Koch was particularly surprised at Elvira's change of heart. "I don't understand you," he said. "Just when you could finally be rid of him, you're bringing him here."

"I feel sorry for him."

"There are other ways of proving that."

"I'll soon be 80. I don't have to prove anything any more."

Thomas found it unpleasant to be reminded of the transience of life by the frailty of his former playmate who was the same age as himself. "Put him in a private home for my sake, but please not here."

"I'll never forget, you know, how you begged me that day, 'Please, Mama, please can he stay?'"

"I was just a child then."

"So was he."

123

Thomas shook his fleshy head. "You've never said things like this before."

"Perhaps we've come full circle." Elvira got up from her armchair as a sign that she regarded the discussion as over.

"I shan't be looking after him," Thomas Koch said.

Things were not so easy with Urs.

"You can't be serious," he laughed.

"I know it must strike you as rather odd."

"Odd, you can say that again. Why do you want to do it?"

"Perhaps for his mother's sake, Anna Lang. She was a good friend to me when I was going through difficult times."

"Before she ran off with a Nazi and abandoned her child."

Elvira raised her shoulders. "So I should abandon the child again?"

"Koni isn't a child. He's a pushy old man who has lived off us all his life and has now gone so gaga that they had to, or rather were able to, certify him."

"He wasn't always a pushy old man. He was also a good playmate and a loyal friend to your father."

"He's been amply compensated for that. He's never lifted a finger all his life."

Elvira was silent. Urs persisted.

"Please don't do this. It's ridiculous. The state should take responsibility. They could look after dozens of Konis with what we pay in taxes. And these nursing homes are good."

"So good that patients in a locked ward can throw themselves off the fire escape."

"My only complaint against them is that they put an air cushion down."

"There's another reason why I want to do this. Simone needs a job."

"Oh, yeah?"

"Just look at her. But then that's exactly what you don't do."

"Simone had a different idea of marriage. It doesn't mean she needs to play Mother Teresa."

"She's felt much better since she's been taking an interest in Koni. Perhaps he appeals to her maternal instincts," Elvira added somewhat suggestively.

Urs was about to object, thought better of it and quickly stood up.

"You can't be dissuaded then."

"I don't think so."

7

THE VILLA RHODODENDRON'S GUEST HOUSE HAD ORIGINALLY been a laundry, with servants' quarters on the top floor. Like the Villa, it was made of red brick and it had a dovecote that matched its tower. Situated to the rear of the Villa, it looked out on the Villa's kitchen and utility rooms in the shady part of the grounds.

It had been converted into a guest house in the fifties. A living room had been furnished with wing chairs and smoker's tables, walnut bookshelves, a built-in bar, a small piano, solid walnut doors with brass handles and coats of arms on the double-glazed windows. Next to the living room there was a bedroom, a bathroom and a toilet, and on the top floor there were four further bedrooms and another bathroom. There was no kitchen.

It had not been a great success. It could hardly compete with the large airy guest rooms in the Villa, with their views of the lake, and since they had converted the roof space in the sixties the family had had enough rooms for the staff.

So the guest house had most of the time lain empty, apart from when it was used by Thomas Koch or his wives as a sulking ground during their various marital crises.

Simone Koch deployed all the talent for organisation with which she had amazed her bosses during her short professional career as a secretary in a film production company. They had employed her with no great enthusiasm in order to curry favour with her father, who held an influential position in one of Switzerland's most important advertising agencies.

In under two weeks she had adapted the guest house to the needs of Konrad Lang and his carers. The bathroom was reduced in size but equipped to hospital standards and in the space saved they built a modern, compact kitchen. The toilet was fitted with supports and handrails, and they bought a multipurpose hospital bed – the most sophisticated model on the market. The living room was redecorated in soft colours: the old furniture was brightened up, the fitted carpets removed, the wooden floor sealed, the walls painted white, the heavy fusty curtains replaced with light airy ones and, on the recommendation of the neurologist, the bar emptied.

On the first floor were two pleasant staff bedrooms, a bathroom, a fitness and therapy room, and a staff room with a cooking alcove, a television set and two monitors connected to cameras in the ground-floor rooms.

All the windows and the main door could be opened only with security codes.

The director of a private home-nursing service had advised Simone on the equipment and had also engaged the nursing staff.

For the day care: Frau Irma Catiric, 46, a Yugoslav, a qualified nurse and geriatric nurse, resident in Switzerland for 22 years.

For the night care: Frau Ranjah Baranaike, 38, a Tamil from Sri Lanka, resident in Switzerland for nine years, five of them as a nursing auxiliary in an old people's home, with diplomas in general and nursery nursing which were not recognised in Switzerland since she had trained in Colombo.

As a relief for the day and night shifts, Jacques Schneider, 33, Swiss, a qualified care assistant who was studying medicine by the alternative route and financing his studies by working nights.

They had also thought of a relief nurse in case someone from the permanent nursing staff was unavailable: Sophie Berger,

44, Swiss, a qualified general and geriatric nurse, mother of two children, back in the profession for a year already.

For the dietary food: Luciana Dotti, 53, Italian, resident in Switzerland for 33 years.

For the physiotherapy: Peter Schaller, 32, Swiss, a qualified physiotherapist specialising in geriatrics and neurology.

For the occupational therapy: Joseline Jobert, 28, Swiss, who had never completed her psychology studies, an occupational therapist in various private old people's homes.

Dr Felix Wirth, 47, had offered his services for the neurological care. The general medical care lay in the hands of Dr Peter Stäubli, 66, Elvira Senn's personal GP.

The cleaning staff consisted of two younger women from Romania and Albania, neither of them very strong in the German language but with experience of hospital work.

On one cold day in late November, Konrad Lang moved into the guest house of the Villa Rhododendron.

When he walked into the living room his first words were "Small world!"

If Simone had needed any more proof that Konrad Lang did not belong on the sixth floor of the Sonnengarten, then the change that took place in him from the very first day would have sufficed. He flourished. He enjoyed his food, complimented the diet cook in Italian, slept without sleeping tablets, shaved himself and dressed himself without any assistance, albeit colourfully.

He took over the little house as if he had always lived there and as early as the second day made suggestions for improvement: he would rather have music than "that". By "that" he meant the television set which was sitting in the wall of bookshelves.

"What sort of music?" Simone asked.

He looked at her in amazement. "Piano music of course."

That very same day Simone bought a stereo unit and all the piano music she could lay her hands on. When she played the first CD in the evening, he said, "Don't you have Horowitz playing that?"

"Playing what?" Simone asked.

"The Nocturne Number 2 in F-sharp major, Opus 15," he answered tolerantly. "This one is Schmalfuss."

After his first visit even Dr Wirth acknowledged to Simone that Konrad was improving. His spells of alertness were longer, his ability to concentrate had improved and, as a result, so had his ability to communicate and to master complex sequences of tasks such as getting up, shaving and dressing.

"Don't get your hopes up too much," Dr Wirth added. "Variations like this, with spontaneous temporary improvement, are, I'm afraid, quite typical." He did not mention that rapid deterioration often followed.

But Simone was optimistic, simply because no one could prove with absolute certainty that Konrad Lang was suffering from Alzheimer's. Even Dr Wirth had to admit that.

Konrad's favourite activity was walking in the grounds. This was not entirely straightforward for Simone because part of the deal was that she kept him away from the family. It was especially difficult when Thomas and Urs were at home. She had to explain to Konrad, who would be waiting for her in his outdoor clothes, why it was not possible to go.

In this respect, Elvira was less of a problem. The Stöckli, where she stayed for most of the time, held no interest for Konrad at all. He regarded it as something that did not belong to the grounds and made a detour round it.

Not so the Villa. After a little while, he always made it into the starting point and the aim of their walks. "It's getting chilly, let's go inside," he said whenever they were near it. Or, "We should go back, Tomi's waiting."

More often than not Simone managed to distract him with the potting shed. This was his favourite place, and he always knew where the gardener kept the key hidden on top of the doorframe. Every time he opened the door he said mysteriously, "Now you have to smell."

They both breathed in the smell of peat, fertilizer and bulbs that filled the shed. Then Simone had to sit down next to Konrad on a crate and after a few seconds he would be far away in a different and, judging by his facial expression, happier age.

After a while, when she had managed to coax him back into the present, he reluctantly allowed himself to be taken back to the guest house. Yet as soon as he walked into the living room he seemed quite at home. He sat down in an armchair and waited for Simone to put on some music. Then he closed his eyes and listened.

After a while Simone tiptoed out. She would have loved to know whether he realised that she was no longer there when he opened his eyes again.

When the music stopped and Konrad opened his eyes, it was often Nurse Ranjah who had taken Simone's place.

In the nursing home, serving the evening meal had been a job for the day nurses. The patients had to eat or be fed as early as half past five, like little children. But here in the guest house even the meal times were civilised. Luciana Dotti brought in the evening meal between seven and half past and it was up to the night nurse to keep Konrad company or to help him with it, whichever was required.

Nurse Ranjah always greeted Konrad in the Hindu manner, with a little bow and her hands pressed together under her chin. Konrad responded in the same way. They spoke English together and her accent took him back to Sri Lanka when the island was still called Ceylon and when the grounds in which the Galle Face Hotel was situated were a golf course.

He had gone there once in the fifties with Thomas Koch at the invitation of the British governor, whose son they knew from St Pierre's.

Ranjah was quite different from the loud, resolute, warm-hearted Nurse Irma Catiric who intimidated him with her motherliness. Ranjah was gentle and reserved, with the natural tenderness with which the Sri Lankans surround their old and sick.

Konrad Lang respected Nurse Irma. But he loved Nurse Ranjah. When she had her night off and Jacques Schneider, the mature medical student, stood in for her there was something missing for him. Even if he could not say what.

Konrad Lang's move into the guest house of the Villa Rhododendron also seemed to have been a fortunate decision for Rosemarie Haug.

In the two weeks it took to prepare the guest house she visited him a few times at the Sonnengarten. He never gave her the slightest sign of recognition.

When she was going down in the lift after her last visit she felt a sudden surge of relief that she would never have to experience that pungent smell again.

Her guilt vanished completely when Felix Wirth told her how well Konrad Lang had adapted to the move, how happy he seemed, what good hands he was in and how wonderfully well he was being cared for.

At the end of the first week after the move, by arrangement with Simone Koch and accompanied by Felix Wirth, she paid Konrad a visit. She loved the guest house's atmosphere of efficiency and homeliness.

Outside the living room she heard Konrad laughing (when had she last heard him laugh?) and when the nurse took her in he was sitting with a young woman, painting at the table in the window. He stopped laughing, looked at her irritably and asked, "Yes?"

"It's me, Rosemarie," she said. "I just wanted to see how you were."

Konrad looked back at the young woman, shrugged his shoulders and carried on painting. Rosemarie stood there hesitantly for a moment. When she was outside she heard his light-hearted laughter again.

She felt a burden lifted from her. Until that moment, she had not realised how heavily it had been weighing upon her. That evening she slept with Felix Wirth for the first time. Rosemarie Haug slipped out of Konrad's life without his even noticing.

Simone Koch found a new lease of life, too. Not, as Elvira thought, because she now had a job to do, but because for the first time since she had joined the Koch family, she had asserted herself. And not in a trivial matter such as choosing the colour of the curtains in the library or the menu for the meal on Epiphany. She had imposed her point of view – against the family consensus – on a delicate question of principle.

In so doing she had achieved more than she could ever have dreamed of. This revolt by a woman whom the family had ridiculed and rejected had not only helped Konrad, it had also improved her standing both with the family and with the staff. All of them, except Urs, treated her with more respect.

Konrad Lang became the most well-cared-for Alzheimer's patient you could imagine. He was permanently surrounded by professional carers and yet everything was done so as to avoid an institutional atmosphere, and so that he felt safe and at home.

Every morning the physiotherapist came, worked with him on his co-ordination and movement and got his circulation going.

Every afternoon the occupational therapist came, helped him solve some easy puzzles and did some memory exercises with him. He was happy to paint watercolours for her and patiently sang songs while she accompanied clumsily on the piano. Now and then he even did her the favour of tinkling away at something on the keyboard himself.

He had a well-balanced diet, rich in vitamins A, C and E, to counteract the cellutoxic atoms. His cerebral blood supply was stimulated by extracts of gingko. His vitamin B_4 and B_{12} levels were closely monitored and adjusted when necessary.

His days were fully occupied and regulated, and no one stopped listening when he told the same story for the umpteenth time. Those around him gave him the feeling that they liked him. No one in the guest house found that difficult. Konrad Lang was a lovable man.

Two Sundays before Christmas Konrad was standing ready in the porch in his coat and fur hat when Simone arrived.

"Herr Lang's been waiting to go out for an hour. He doesn't want to miss the snow," Nurse Irma explained.

As soon as they were outside, Konrad, who otherwise always took the day at a leisurely pace, said "Come on!" and went on ahead. It was an effort for Simone to keep up with him. When they arrived at his goal, the potting shed, they were both rather out of breath.

He leant against the wooden wall of the shed and waited.

"What are we waiting for, Konrad?" Simone asked.

He looked at her as if he had only just at this moment noticed her presence.

"Can't you smell it?" And he looked up at the overcast sky which, in the far distance, was merging with the hills behind the lake.

Suddenly large, thick snowflakes began to float down, falling on to the edge of the water butt, the top of the compost heap, the little flagstone path, the branches of the fir trees, on the rose beds and the black branches of the plum trees.

"It's snowing fazonetli," Konrad said.

"Fazonetli?" Simone asked.

"Little handkerchiefs. From 'fazzoletti'."

The little handkerchiefs fell from the grey sky and cooled down the grass and the branches and the flagstones until the ones that came down after no longer melted. Soon everything was covered with a light grey veil, which quickly turned white and grew thicker.

"It's snowing fazonetli," Konrad shouted and began to dance with outstretched arms in the flurries of snow, his face turned to the sky, his mouth and eyes as wide open as possible.

"It's snowing fazonetli," he sang, flinging his fur hat into the air.

"It's snowing fazonetli," Simone sang.

Both of them danced in the dazzling snow until they could carry on no longer for laughing, crying and happiness.

Konrad and Simone came back to the guest house with wet hair and white coats. Nurse Irma took Konrad away. Simone went into the living room, lit the two candles on the advent wreath, put on Schumann's piano concerto, sat down on the sofa and waited.

When the nurse came back with Konrad he was in dry clothes, his hair had been dried and his cheeks glowed like a happy child's. He sat down in an armchair, ate a little of the Christmas cake on the smoker's table, closed his eyes and listened to the music.

Shortly afterwards he fell asleep.

Simone blew out the candles and tiptoed out of the room.

Outside was a slim, tall, red-haired woman in her mid-forties in a white nurse's apron.

"I'm Sophie Berger, the relief nurse. Sister Ranjah is off-duty and Herr Schneider had an accident in the snow with his car."

"Is he hurt?" Simone asked.

"No. But he ran into a tram. It'll take a while to sort things out."

"Well, you won't have a lot of work to do. I think Herr Lang will sleep very well."

Simone dialled the code for the main door.

"Have you met Herr Lang?"

"Yes, I've already had the pleasure."

Simone draped her wet coat around her shoulders and walked contentedly back to the Villa. The black granite flagstones were beginning to show through again.

*

Konikoni opened his eyes and shut them again immediately.

After a while he opened them again, but this time quite slowly so that people outside would not be able to see. At first just a little light came through his eyelashes, then he could make out the shape of the furniture, and then he saw Mama Anna.

She was wearing a white apron like a nurse and was busy setting the table.

He waited until she went out and he could hear her talking in the kitchen. He got up out of the armchair in a hurry and hid behind the sofa.

He heard Mama Anna come in again, then he saw her shoes and legs.

"Herr Lang?" she called. Then she went back out of the room. He heard her opening the door to the bedroom. "Herr Lang?" Then the bathroom door. "Herr Lang?"

She spoke to someone in the kitchen. He heard footsteps on the stairs.

After a while she came down again. "Herr Lang?" She opened the porch door and the main door. There was silence for a while. Then he heard Mama Anna's voice calling "Herr Lang?" in a low voice outside the window.

Konikoni stood up and crept into the corridor. He could hear sounds from the kitchen. The porch door was open. He went to the main door. It was only pulled to. Smiling, he slipped out into the night. The sky was clear, and a half-moon hung above the pale range of hills.

The Kochs had a few guests in, as they always did on Sundays in Advent. It was a tradition going back to Edgar Senn. He had started to invite managers of the Koch Works to dinner as a special mark of honour on the first Sunday of Advent. As the company prospered and the number of managers increased, these managers' dinners spread to every Sunday in Advent.

The guests this evening came from the textiles and power

divisions, a rather risky mix of younger fashionable managers (textiles) and older more conservative directors (power), all with their respective wives. Twenty-eight people, including Elvira, Simone, Thomas and Urs, were seated around the huge dining table.

The first course had just been served when Simone was called away from the table. Urs got up from his chair briefly as she excused herself; all the other men did the same.

The relief night nurse was waiting outside in the hall.

"Herr Lang has disappeared."

"Disappeared? How could that happen?" Simone asked, already slipping on a coat and hurrying to the door.

Sophie Berger ran after her. "He isn't in the house," she called out, as Simone started out towards the guest house. "I've searched everywhere."

Simone changed direction. The two women walked in silence through the grounds where the wet snow was dripping off the trees.

There was still some snow here and there in front of the potting shed and in the moonlight you could see footprints leading up to it. The door was unlocked. Simone opened it. "Konrad?"

No answer. A patch of moonlight fell through the open door. The crates on which they always sat were there, and the peat, the bulbs, the sacks of fertilizer. But not Konrad. Just as she was about to leave, she saw something on the ground, and picked it up. It was Konrad's slipper. When she looked more closely she found the other one too, and his socks next to it.

"Frau Koch," Sophie Berger cried, "look!"

Simone went outside. The nurse was pointing to the imprints of two bare feet in the settled snow. One toe was missing on the right foot, two on the left.

"I don't think we'll wait for my wife," Urs Koch said with barely disguised anger to Trentini, who was responsible for serving at the larger occasions in the Villa.

"I hope it isn't anything serious," Frau Gubler, the motherly wife of the turbine director said.

"A large house like this is like an ocean liner: it needs a first officer somewhere," her husband added.

"A lovely image," Thomas Koch nodded.

Elvira Senn resolved to speak to Simone about a few ground rules for hostesses.

The staff were just beginning to serve the second course when there was a rapping on the glass of the door onto the verandah.

Thomas exchanged glances with Trentini. Trentini went to the door, pushed the curtain aside slightly and peered outside. Then he went up to Thomas and whispered something to him.

While they were debating what was to be done, the verandah door began to open, pushing the curtain out into the room. Something moved behind the curtain; then it parted.

Konrad Lang walked in, filthy and dripping wet, his trouser legs rolled up and his feet bare. He looked over the dumbfounded company and then went up to Elvira Senn.

He stopped in front of her chair and whispered, "Mama Vira, Mama Anna has to go away. Please!"

It was the way Elvira had reacted that was troubling Thomas. He was sitting on her left and apart from her, he was the only person who had understood what Konrad said. Elvira turned deathly white and he had to take her back to the Stöckli where she lay straight down on the sofa in the drawing room and closed her eyes. He laid a blanket over her. "Shall I call Dr Stäubli?"

She made no reply.

"Where's his number?"

"On the desk in the study."

When Thomas came back he was rather irritable. "His wife says he has already been called out to Koni. I caught him at the guest house and put him in the picture about priorities."

While they were waiting Thomas asked, "What gave you such a fright?"

Elvira said nothing.

"'Mama Vira, Mama Anna has to go away'?"

She shook her head.

"But he did say that, didn't he?"

"I didn't hear it."

The doorbell rang. Thomas Koch got up and let Dr Stäubli in.

Sudden feelings of weakness in diabetics are often signs that there have been changes in their metabolism. After Dr Stäubli had taken Elvira's blood pressure and pulse, he checked her blood sugar and confirmed that her sugar level was rather low, a complication that can frequently be traced back to a mistake in the diet or a mistake in the dose of insulin. But since he knew Elvira Senn to be a disciplined and careful patient and since during his visit to Konrad Lang he had been informed of Konrad's appearance at the Villa, he guessed there was a different reason.

"Did the appearance of our patient affect you so badly?"

"You could say that."

"If you had consulted me about this Konrad Lang business, I would definitely have advised you against it."

"How could I know they were letting him wander around on his own at night?"

"It's not just this. He's a strain in other ways too. And as your doctor I have to warn you against any over-excitement."

"Am I supposed to throw him out? How would that look?"

"At least try to forget him. Let's behave as if he didn't exist."

Elvira smiled. "How is he?"

Dr Stäubli shook his head. "He was agitated and suffering from serious hypothermia. I've given him a sedative. I hope he'll go to sleep now and then if we're lucky he won't get pneumonia."

He offered her a glucose sweet. "Suck that and another one in an hour. I'll be back again tomorrow morning and then we'll see if we have to adjust the insulin dose."

Elvira Senn unwrapped the sweet from the cellophane. "How long is it before people die of Alzheimer's?"

"Between one and six years, according to the course it takes and the care. Konrad Lang could live to 70 but he may not survive to see next Christmas. He could certainly be in the final stages by then."

Dr Stäubli stood up. "That's if he actually survives this little misadventure. I'll look in on him again now. After that you can reach me throughout the night at home."

Elvira sat up on the chaise longue.

"Stay where you are. I'll see myself out." Dr Stäubli shook her hand. "Until tomorrow, about nine."

Elvira Senn stood up nevertheless and saw him to the door. Then she went to the telephone and dialled Schöller's number.

If Schöller had had to describe his feelings towards Elvira he would not have used the word "love". But he might have talked of reverence, affection, and obedience. And – why should he not admit it? – of eroticism. Schöller was a single man in his late fifties who had always felt drawn to older, dominant women. Sensuality was another thread in their complex bond – albeit not the most important one. Elvira might be 80 but she was an attractive and thrillingly powerful woman.

Schöller was the infrequent, but – according to his normally reliable information – the sole lover of Elvira Senn, which made him, to some extent, also one of her trusted friends. In so far as a self-reliant, calculating woman was capable of anything like trust. He knew that she told him only as much as appeared useful to her and that she used him for her own purposes. Where he differed from most people in her circle was that he found her manipulative behaviour arousing.

Schöller hardly played the dominant role in this strange relationship, but Elvira could rely on his protective instinct. What she

139

reported to him in detail late that evening, pale and in a weak voice, ensured his hostility to Konrad Lang and to all those who pressed his case.

It was long past midnight, and the thermometer had fallen well below zero when Schöller left the Stöckli, full of hate: Elvira had carefully wound him up.

The cellars of large houses are no different from any other: they smell of washing powder, mould and heating oil and are full of things that people will never use again. Their light switches glow and the light goes out of its own accord again after a few minutes.

The boiler room for the Villa Rhododendron was not difficult to find. It was situated right next to the cellar steps and a constant, gentle, regular vibration could be heard through the door. It was unlocked. The heating system had been modernised and altered time and again in the 20 years since its installation. It consisted of a large boiler, a burner, a reserve burner, a circulation pump, a reserve circulation pump and a maze of insulated pipes which centrally heated all the buildings on the property. At the point where the pipes left the boiler room they were lined up neatly with safety valves and blue plastic labels, which read "garage", "tower", "Stöckli", "gardener's house", "west wing" or "attic" and so on. The heating was divided up into areas that could be switched on or off as required.

The light in the boiler room went out. Schöller felt his way towards the yellow glow of the light switch. The room lit up again. He went back to the valves and turned one off. It was labelled "guest house".

Sophie Berger was under no illusions about her employment prospects: this mishap was a considerable setback. Even if they made allowances for the escape attempt having been cleverly contrived, the private nursing service would probably not use her again. Dr Wirth, who had been summoned from a restaurant where at this time of year it was necessary to reserve a table four weeks in advance, had not given the impression that he would give her another chance like the one she had enjoyed after the first incident with Konrad Lang.

He had told her quite curtly that she should watch the patient on the monitor and report to him or to Dr Stäubli if he should wake up. Under no circumstances should she go into his room.

She was happy to follow these instructions. She had not the slightest desire to meet the old man again. She held it against him personally that he had caused her so many difficulties. She had always had a good relationship with confused patients before, especially with the male ones. Was it her fault if she reminded him of someone?

And so she sat in the staff room staring at the monitor. Konrad Lang lay on his back sleeping with his mouth wide open. Perhaps she could retrain as a dental nurse? Or leave the medical profession completely, work in a bar, where the old fogies didn't make a run for it whenever they saw her.

And where it was not so cold as it was with rich people. She stood up, fetched a blanket, sat down in the only comfortable armchair, wrapped herself up and kept her eye on the monitor.

She woke up because she was frozen. It was almost six o'clock. On the monitor Konrad Lang was still asleep with his mouth wide open. Only he had kicked off his covers now and his nightshirt had ridden up.

Sophie Berger stood up and walked quietly down to the bedroom. She picked up the cover from the floor and covered Konrad Lang up. He was bathed in sweat although the thermometer in the room read only twelve degrees.

She went back to the staff room and rang Herr Hügli in the gardener's house. It was a while before he answered.

"It's Frau Berger here, the night nurse at the guest house. Is there something wrong with the heating?"

The heating was not really Herr Hügli's department. But at

six o'clock in the morning he felt himself responsible for it too. He went into the boiler room and after a while discovered that the valve on the pipe leading to the guest house was turned off. He turned it on and phoned the night nurse back. "Everything's all right," he reported. He did not want to get anyone into trouble.

When the day nurse Irma Catiric arrived shortly after seven it was slightly warmer in the guest house. Nevertheless her first question was: "Is there something wrong with the heating? It's like a fridge in here."

"Everything's all right. I checked up on it."

Nurse Irma went into the bedroom, came out again a short time later, went to the telephone without a word and dialled Dr Stäubli's number.

"Pneumonia," was all she said. Then hung up again.

"Are you blind?" she hissed at Sophie Berger as she walked past.

"They forbade me to go in there," she was about to say. But Nurse Irma had already disappeared back into Konrad Lang's room.

Although Konrad was not in a bad condition physically, the pneumonia set him back a long way.

He became more confused owing to the lack of oxygen, the antibiotics weakened him, he was not eating and he had to spend all day on the drip. He could be lifted out of bed only with a combined effort, and he remained passive and unresponsive during physiotherapy. Only when Nurse Ranjah came did he place his hands together under his chin and smile.

Dr Stäubli came every day, examined him and encouraged him. "Start eating again, Herr Lang, get up, move around. If you can't get yourself fit again, I'm sure I can't." He had to report to Elvira after every visit to Konrad, and explained, "If he survives then it will be at a high price. This is typical of Alzheimer's patients: it goes in stages, either in a lot of little ones, or, as in his case, in a few big ones."

"Is he saying anything?" she wanted to know every time. When he said no she appeared relieved.

She also asked Simone, "Is he saying anything? Do you talk to each other?"

Simone shook her head. "Perhaps you should visit him some time. You could try to talk to him about the past. I don't know anything about it."

"The past is all over," Elvira said.

"Not with this illness," Simone said.

Konrad Lang might well have died had it not been for Nurse Ranjah. When the diet cook had given up in despair after another unsuccessful attempt to tempt him with one of his favourite meals she began to feed him secretly with tasty titbits which she brought from home: almonds soaked in honey, little spicy balls of coriander-flavoured rice, small pieces of cold roast beef with lemon and onions – all popped straight into his mouth with her long slim fingers. She chatted away to him at the same time in a mish-mash of Tamil, Singhalese and English and cuddled and kissed him like a baby.

Sister Ranjah told no one about the success of her therapy. There had been unfortunate consequences in previous cases because her methods almost always offended against hospital regulations.

So it was only by chance that Simone came to find out about it. She had a full day of duties and so, unusually, was only able to visit Konrad after dark. As she went into the guest house she heard the chattering coming from Konrad's bedroom. She opened the door quietly and saw Nurse Ranjah feeding a very happy Konrad.

When Konrad saw her and took fright Ranjah stroked his hair and said, "Don't worry, Mama Anna isn't here."

Only then did she see Simone standing in the doorway.

*

"Who's Mama Anna?" Simone asked Urs that evening. "She is someone Konrad is afraid of."

Urs had no idea.

Her father-in-law was more help. "His mother was called Anna. But why should he be afraid of her?"

"Didn't she dump him on some farmer when he was a child?"

"You could hate someone for that. But be frightened?"

"Perhaps we don't know the whole story."

Thomas Koch shrugged his shoulders, stood up and excused himself. An ageing playboy between marriages.

Simone couldn't sleep. In the middle of the night she had an idea. She got up, went down to the hall and waited until her father-in-law came home. When he finally staggered in with glazed eyes she had fallen asleep in the armchair. She awoke with a start and asked, "Did she have red hair?"

"Blonde or brown curls, I just love girls," he sang.

"Konrad's mother, I meant."

It took Thomas a while to catch on. Then he laughed. "Fiery red."

"Old photographs? I don't have any old photographs. They only show us how old we are." Elvira was sitting in her breakfast room and gave Simone to understand that she was disturbing her. "What do you want them for?"

"I want to show them to Konrad. Sometimes they can help break through an Alzheimer's patient's apathy."

"I don't have any."

"Everyone has some photos."

"I don't."

Simone gave up. "Do you have any idea why he's frightened of his mother?"

"Perhaps because he hasn't got anywhere in life," Elvira smiled.

"What sort of a woman was she?"

"The sort of woman who keeps her child a secret from a Nazi diplomat so that he'll marry her."

"But she was your best friend once."

"Anna's been dead for a long time. I don't want to talk about her."

"How did she die?"

"In an air attack on a train, as far as I know."

"And she had red hair."

"What does it matter, what colour hair she had?"

"Konrad was frightened of the relief nurse, and she has red hair."

"Anna was fair."

"Thomas said her hair was fiery red."

"Thomas has become a little forgetful himself."

Montserrat had been working at the Villa for only four weeks. She was a niece of Candelaria, who had got into the habit of placing members of her large family in service at the Kochs'. Montserrat was employed as a chambermaid.

"The señora was in the don's office today," she told Candelaria over lunch. "She was looking for something in his desk."

"Did you knock?"

"I thought there was no one there: I saw him leave."

"You should always knock."

"Even when you're sure the room's empty?"

"Even when there's nothing left of the house but the door."

Montserrat was 19 and still had a lot to learn.

Urs was not much help either. Simone broached the subject over lunch, which for once he was taking at the Villa.

"Why do you need old photos?" he asked irritably. He suspected that once again it had something to do with Konrad Lang, her hobby-horse.

"The specialists have recommended we look at photographs from the past with him, to connect him with the present. But there doesn't seem to be anything like that in your family."

"Elvira has shelves full of photograph albums."

145

"She won't give me any. She says she doesn't know where they are."

He laughed in disbelief. "In her study, on the bookshelves. Loads of them."

Simone waited until three o'clock in the afternoon, when Elvira usually did her correspondence. She went to the Stöckli and knocked on the study door.

"Yes?" Elvira answered in a surly voice. Simone had broken one of the taboos of the house. When Elvira was in her study she was not available to speak to anyone.

Simone went in. "Urs tells me that you keep your photos in here. Perhaps I could borrow a few."

Elvira took off her spectacles. "It's obvious that Urs hasn't been in here for a long time. Or can you see photographs anywhere here?" She pointed to the bookcase next to her.

There were a few files, a series of business reports on Koch Industries, its diversified companies and other business ventures, arranged by year, an 18-volume dictionary and two framed photographs of Elvira, one with her first husband and one with her second.

Other than that, not one photograph, not one photograph album.

"Perhaps no one is supposed to see how she keeps getting younger," Thomas Koch laughed when Simone told him about it.

She found him in the best of spirits. He had just this very moment decided to spend the holiday season on the *Why Not?*, the Barenboims' yacht which was cruising in the Caribbean with a fun crowd. He would still spend Christmas in the Villa – an unwritten law – and fly to Curaçao the following morning and board the yacht there. Accompanied by Salomé Winter, 23.

As a result he was extremely helpful and immediately agreed to obtain some photographs for Simone, "by the box-load" if that was what she wanted.

146

But when he confidently opened the photograph drawer it was empty. Although he could have sworn that they were there.

He even took some time to look in other likely places. The photos were nowhere to be found.

Christmas Eve was celebrated in the Villa Rhododendron with the immediate family. A huge Christmas tree stood in the library with decorations dating back to Wilhelm Koch's first marriage: transparent glass balls that shimmered like bubbles, glassy icicles and angels which had been fashionable at the turn of the century, with faces like dolls. The branches were weighed down with red apples on silk ribbons and hung with lametta and angel's hair. All the candles were red. On the top of the tree a golden angel blessed all people of good will with outstretched arms.

It was a family tradition that the oldest man present read the story of the Nativity. For many years that had been Thomas Koch.

"And lo, the angel of the Lord came upon them," he read solemnly, "and the glory of the Lord shone round about them: and they were sore afraid. And the angel said unto them: Fear not: for behold, I bring you good tidings of great joy, which shall be to all people. For unto you is born this day in the city of David a Saviour, which is Christ the Lord."

Afterwards Thomas sat down at the piano and played his rusty Christmas medley.

Elvira listened full of emotion, Urs thought about the capital gains due in the electronics division, Thomas about Salomé Winter, 23, and Simone about Konrad Lang.

Konrad Lang sat with Nurse Ranjah in the living room at the guest house. No one could guess what he was thinking.

On Christmas morning Simone knocked at her father-in-law's door, absolutely determined to bring about a Christmas miracle.

Thomas Koch turned round, made a thousand excuses, protested and pleaded. But Simone would not give up.

Perhaps it was the anticipation of the Caribbean, perhaps the 1875 Armagnac of which he had partaken in honour of the anniversary of his father's birth, perhaps his inability to refuse any request from pretty young women, or perhaps it was simply the emotion that swept over him at the idea of being capable of such a magnanimous gesture; at any rate he turned up to see Konrad Lang in the guest house before he left.

When he went into the room and saw Konrad sitting motionless in the window and staring at him vacantly he immediately regretted his decision. Nevertheless he sat down next to him. Simone left them alone.

"Urs is lucky to have a wife like that," Thomas said.

Konrad didn't understand.

"Simone, the one who's just gone out."

Konrad didn't remember.

"I'm joining the *Why Not?* tomorrow."

Konrad didn't react.

"The Barenboims' yacht," Thomas said helpfully.

"Oh, right," Konrad said.

"Do you need anything? Can I get you anything?"

"What?"

"Anything at all."

Konrad thought about it. He tried to organise his thoughts so that he could make some kind of reply. But then just when he had the feeling that he might be able to, he no longer knew what he was supposed to be replying to.

"I see," he said finally.

Thomas Koch was not a patient man. "Enfin bref: if you think of anything, let me know."

"D'accord," Konrad answered.

Thomas sat down again. "Tu préfères parler français?"

"Si c'est plus facile pour toi."

They spoke in French about Paris. Koni explained to Thomas

148

where the best oysters could be eaten at the moment at Les Halles and wanted to know if he was running Eclair this season at Longchamp.

Les Halles was pulled down in 1971 and Thomas had not owned a racehorse since 1962.

The trick with French did not work for Simone. It was as if for Konrad this language, which gave him access to a certain part of his memory, was connected only with Thomas Koch.

But in the evening she experienced her second Christmas miracle.

Simone had furnished a room in the Villa to her own taste: floral patterns on the armchairs, chaise longue, curtains and cushions; great quantities of lace and dried flower arrangements; and an artificial scent of summer afternoons wafting from the various bowls of potpourri. Urs mockingly called it the "Laura Ashley room" and made no secret of the fact that he thought it ghastly. But for Simone it was her only refuge in this huge house with its mix of gloomy late 19th-century and severe Bauhaus styles.

When Simone went into the Laura Ashley room that evening there was a yellow envelope on her small desk.

"I *did* manage to find a few photos after all. God, how we've aged! Good luck. Thomas," he had scribbled hurriedly on a piece of paper.

The photos all resembled each other: carefree young people in fifties ski outfits at a long table in a ski hut; carefree young people in fifties swimming costumes by the rails of a yacht; carefree young people in fifties evening dress with New Year party hats and paper streamers at a long table; carefree young people in fifties casual wear in an open convertible. You could recognise a young Thomas Koch in all the photos, and a young Konrad Lang in most of them.

Konrad Lang reacted to the photos as Simone had hoped.

"That was New Year," he said when she showed him the picture of the happy crowd. "At the Palace."

"What year?" Simone asked.

"Last year."

On the photograph with the convertible he pointed to the driver: "That one there is Peter Court. In 1955 not far out of Dover he collided head on with a cattle truck. He was returning after three months in Europe and experiencing problems driving on the left. Twenty-six."

At the photo of the ski hut he shook his head in amazement: "Serge Payot! He's still alive."

Then he picked up the group photo on the yacht and smiled. "The *Tesoro*. Claudio Piedrini and his brother Nunzio. And . . ."

He tore the photograph into tiny shreds and muttered, "The bastard. The bastard. The damned bastard."

Then he closed his mouth and did not open it for the rest of the visit.

When Simone stuck the photo back together later nothing particularly attracted her attention. Thomas had his arm around a girl, as he did on all the other photographs. Konrad was not there.

Konrad woke in the middle of the night and knew that he hated Tomi. True, he did not know why; but he was brimming with hate. He knew that it was directed at Tomi because he could think of all the people in his life – Elvira, Edgar Senn, her husband, Joseph Zellweger from the Zellweger farm and his skinny wife, Jacques Latour, the piano teacher – without feeling anything more than a certain dislike or some fear. With the Piedrinis it was certainly rather more than dislike, more like abhorrence, but nothing in comparison to Tomi.

Whenever he thought of Tomi, his heart stopped beating for a moment. He felt as if the blood were rushing to his cheeks and he had only one desire: to destroy the bastard.

He sat up and climbed out of bed. The door opened immediately and Nurse Ranjah's sing-song voice emerged from the bright crack of light: "Mama Anna isn't here."

"I'll kill the pig," Konrad gasped.

Nurse Ranjah put the light on and was alarmed at his facial expression. She went up to him and put her arm around him.

"Which pig?"

Konrad thought about it. Which pig? He didn't know any more.

The next day Simone came with the photos again. "That was New Year in the Palace. 1959," he said. And: "Peter Court! I thought he'd been in a crash." And: "Oh, Serge Payot. And Tomi, the bastard."

"Why is Tomi a bastard?" Simone asked.

"Everybody knows why," he replied.

The following day, out of guilt, Simone travelled to Bad Zürs to ski with Urs ("Remember me? I'm Urs, your husband!" he had shouted to her a while ago on her way back from the guest house) and to celebrate New Year. She gave Nurse Ranjah the photos so that she could look at them with Konrad.

When she returned, his lethargy had given way to something new. It seemed like anger.

Nurse Ranjah confirmed the impression. She told her how he had been more restless during the night, how he had nightmares and sometimes woke up full of hate.

"Then we'll not show him the photos any more," Simone said.

Nurse Ranjah looked at her in surprise: "But then you'll be depriving him of one of his feelings."

And so Simone continued to show him the photos.

"What sort of photos?" Elvira Senn wanted to know.

In Dr Stäubli's report to her about Konrad's condition, he had said as an aside, "He appears to be regressing. He hardly reacts to the photos any more."

Dr Stäubli described to her the photographs that Simone had looked at over and over again with Konrad. First with some notable success, but recently it was increasingly clear that they no longer made sense to him.

"What do you mean, 'success'?"

"It stimulated him. He started to talk. He got the dates muddled up, but that's part of the disease."

"What did he talk about?"

"About the people in the photos, the places where they were taken. Quite amazing some of them. Forty-year-old photos, all the same."

"And he isn't reacting to them any more?"

"Hardly at all. The part of his brain where he stores these memories appears to be affected now, too."

Dr Stäubli would have loved to know why that seemed to reassure Elvira.

8

A LITTLE MORE THAN A YEAR AFTER FAUSTO BERTINI, THE sleigh-driver, had found him in a snow hole in the Stazerwald, it seemed as if Konrad Lang was going to withdraw into himself completely. The only people who could still gain access to at least a part of him were Nurse Ranjah, whom he beamed at as soon as she entered the room and whom he spoke to in grammatical, very correct English, and Joseline Jobert, the occupational therapist, for whom he painted his watercolours with clear, economical brush strokes.

It was a miserable January: hardly a day when you could see down to the lake below, hardly a day without monotonous icy-cold rain.

Simone was experiencing her seventh marital crisis. On their skiing trip Urs had made the acquaintance of Theresia Palmers, a floozie from Vienna, whom Erwin Gubler, one of the most important property dealers in the country, had arranged to have flown in for the holiday period. Urs had now installed her in the tower suite of the Des Alpes, according to family tradition. Simone had found out because amongst the telephone messages was one that said, "Would Herr Urs Koch please call Frau Theresia Palmers at the Grand Hotel des Alpes, tower suite." And underneath was a telephone number.

But it was not the affair itself that worried Simone. It was more the timing. She was pregnant. True, Urs was not yet aware of this: she had found the message on the day she was going to surprise him with the news. But she doubted whether he would have behaved any differently had he known.

The melancholy January and the feeling of despair that was slowly spreading through the guest house added to her unhappiness. For the first time since she had taken Konrad Lang under her wing she was overwhelmed by depression.

She still forced herself to visit Konrad at the usual times, but they were demoralising moments spent in mutual silence, each one sunk in a personal hopelessness.

Increasingly often Simone left early and increasingly frequently after a visit like this she escaped to her Laura Ashley room and sobbed her heart out. Rather more for herself as the days went on and rather less for Konrad Lang.

It seemed as though Simone Koch would be the second woman to vanish unnoticed from Konrad Lang's life.

Elvira Senn waited for a few more days. When the news from the guest house promised no improvement in Konrad Lang's condition, she yielded to Dr Stäubli's pressure and went to Gstaad, where she was going to spend her traditional winter holiday in the Kochs' chalet.

"Getting away will do you good," he said, promising to hold the fort. "If anything happens, I'll give you a call."

"Even in the middle of the night."

"Even in the middle of the night," he lied.

Elvira in Gstaad, Thomas in the Caribbean, Urs preoccupied with his affair – social life at the Villa Rhododendron had come to a standstill and Simone, in her condition, was not likely to do much. She was happy not to have any duties, staying in bed or in her room until the late afternoon and only dressing for the visits to Konrad Lang which her sense of duty required.

One misty Saturday – when a cold continuous rain was beating on the window panes, the cluster of beech trees by the pavilion was hardly visible, Urs was in Paris for the weekend, "on business", and Simone's limbs were as heavy as the wet branches of the old fir tree by her window – she did not go to Konrad.

Nor did she leave her room the next day. And the day after that she had managed not to think about Konrad until, late in the afternoon, there was a knock at the door of her room.

It was Nurse Ranjah, who had heard she was not feeling well and wanted to know if she needed anything. She had brought one of Konrad's watercolours with her.

It looked like a colourful garden on the edge of which was a short tree trunk. Next to it Konrad had painted the word "tree".

It was not so much the picture that moved her but what he had written in clumsy letters on the bottom edge: "Konrad Lang. I really wanted to write about it."

What did he want to write? And about what? About the strange garden with its red, green, yellow and blue wavy lines, circles, dots and ribbons, which could perhaps be hedges, paths, ponds, bushes, flowers and flower beds? Or about the large word "tree" alongside the small pitiful trunk?

Did he also want to write that a trunk is still a tree?

"I really wanted to write about it." And what was preventing him? That he had already forgotten what he wanted to write? Or that there was no one who would understand what he meant?

The watercolour was proof to her of how much was still going on in this brain, which the doctors said would soon no longer be able to control even the simplest bodily functions.

Simone Koch did not vanish from Konrad's life. On the contrary, she resolved to do everything she could to make sure he did not disappear out of hers.

Dr Wirth had been somewhat surprised when he was given a message during his visit to Konrad, asking him if he would please see Frau Simone Koch briefly afterwards.

Now he was sitting in this strange young girl's room, which did not fit in with the house at all, trying to make it clear that there was at present no cure for Alzheimer's.

"As things stand we can do no more than we are already doing: gingko, vitamins, physiotherapy, occupational therapy, memory training. We've actually been pretty successful. What we are seeing now is a new phase. It is unstoppable, Frau Koch."

"There's no chance of halting the disease?"

"There are people who talk about that happening in the foreseeable future."

"What sort of people?"

"Alzheimer's is a big problem, so there is a great deal of money to be made from finding a cure. There can't be many pharmaceutical companies that are not doing research into it."

"And are they getting results, would you say?"

"New ones every month, some of them very promising."

"Then why aren't you trying something? What has Herr Lang to lose?"

"Not much in his case, but a great deal in mine. These medicines are not yet licensed."

"Don't they sometimes do trials on volunteers?"

"At this stage of the illness patients aren't capable of volunteering any more."

"Then they can never do trials with Alzheimer's patients."

"Yes, they can. If the patient gives his consent in the early stages. Pre-emptively, as it were."

"Who does he give this consent to?"

"To the doctor treating him, normally."

"Has he given it to you?"

"No."

"Why not?"

"It was never discussed."

"Meaning, that you never suggested it to him?"

"It isn't a part of normal practice". Dr Wirth was beginning to

156

feel uncomfortable. "Is there anything else I can do for you? I'm expected back at the hospital."

"Can they do trials without the consent of the patient?"

Dr Wirth stood up. "Very difficult."

"But not impossible."

"There are ways."

"Then I should be glad if you would investigate them."

"I'll happily do that," Dr Wirth promised. "Try again with some photographs from a different period. Sometimes you can get things moving that way."

She heard nothing from Dr Wirth for a week, then she saw him by chance in a smart restaurant. Urs had taken her there in a bid to dispel any suspicions he felt she might have.

Dr Wirth was sitting with a *menu surprise* a few tables away opposite an attractive woman in her mid-fifties. It was not a business meal; that was obvious just from looking at them.

The woman seemed familiar to her. But she recognised her only when the two of them went out arm in arm: Rosemarie Haug, Konrad Lang's lady-friend, who never showed her face these days.

Perhaps she was doing Dr Wirth an injustice, but she decided there and then to change Konrad's neurologist.

This decision and the wonderful Bordeaux made her so elated that she allowed herself the cruelty of confessing to Urs that she was pregnant.

That put a sudden end to the affair with Theresia Palmers of the Grand Hotel des Alpes, tower suite.

"Do you know a good neurologist?" she asked her gynaecologist, Dr Spörri, during her check-up.

"You don't need a neurologist. It's quite normal to be slightly depressed in the early stages of pregnancy."

"I've been spending some time looking after an Alzheimer's patient," she explained.

"As an introduction to looking after a baby?" Simone's gynaecologist asked, rather tactlessly.

After the check-up, he wrote down the address of a neurologist and arranged an appointment for her.

"Don't become too involved with the Alzheimer's patient. It'll make you depressed."

The neurologist's name was Dr Beat Steiner. He listened to Simone in silence. Then he said, "There are some promising signs of a breakthrough, it's true. Some drugs are very close to being licensed. Dr Wirth is one of a handful of doctors who are doing clinical trials on some of them. If he is not doing them on this patient then he must have his reasons."

Simone did not mention Rosemarie Haug. "He didn't ask for his agreement earlier on. And at the stage he is at now it would be very difficult to obtain consent."

Something in Dr Steiner's reaction made her ask, "Do you have a different opinion?"

"It's a rather tricky situation going against a colleague, Frau Koch. You can see that. Especially when one is as ill-informed about a case as I am here." He thought about it for a moment. "But let me give you a theoretical answer: it is possible to test chemical compounds that have proved successful in preclinical trials and that have also not shown any side effects on healthy volunteers in clinical trials. To do this the consent of the patient is required or, if that is no longer possible, that of his relatives. And the agreement of the ethics committee."

"And if there are no relatives?"

"Then the legal guardian is responsible."

"And the agreement of the ethics committee, would we get that?"

"If the trial is sensible and the risk calculable, you would obtain permission for a single application."

"Do you do trials like this?"

Dr Steiner shook his head. "Professors and external lecturers with research contracts from pharmaceutical firms and hospital doctors do them."

"So who would that be?"

"Dr Wirth."

"Apart from Dr Wirth?"

"In your case the patient is in private care. That's a problem. It would be easier if he were in a hospital. Would that be a possibility?"

Simone had no need to think about it. "No, there's no question of that."

"Then it will be difficult."

"Will you enquire about it anyway?"

Dr Steiner hesitated.

"Please."

"I'll be in touch."

When Simone walked into the living room of the guest house Konrad Lang was sitting at the table. His hand was on a large plastic ball with coloured stripes.

She sat down next to him. After a while he took his eyes off the ball and looked at her. "Just look how that goes behind like that," he said pointing at the ball.

"You mean how the colours go round the ball?"

He looked at her in the way a teacher looks at a hopeless schoolchild. He shook his head, laughed and studied the ball again.

"Yes, I can see it now," Simone said.

Konrad looked up in surprise. "How did you get in here?"

Immediately after this visit to Konrad Lang, Simone decided to do something daring.

She got hold of the key to the Stöckli that hung in the kitchen porch in the Villa and waited until the security men had finished their round and left the property. Then she set off.

It was a gloomy day. The lights had to be on in the houses and the mist was so thick that it was dripping off the fir trees. Simone's raincoat was damp from the short walk down to the Stöckli. She strode into the entrance hall as if it was her perfect right.

The house was warm and well aired. There were fresh flowers on the chest of drawers next to the coat-stand, as there were every day. Elvira loved the idea that she could come home at any moment unannounced and would find everything just as if she had been out for only a few hours.

Simone stood in the hall for a moment, undecided, wondering where she should begin. Then she turned towards the breakfast room.

Fresh flowers here too. And today's untouched papers on the table in the window. The only likely piece of furniture was a small sideboard made of chrome and cherry wood. She opened the sliding doors. All she found was a Meissen tea service with twelve place settings, some breakfast crockery, a few glasses and some bottles of liqueur.

In the breakfast room, next to the door into the hall, there was another door leading into the dressing room. Simone opened it and had a fright when at the same moment another door opened on the opposite wall to reveal the silhouette of a woman in the door frame. Then she noticed that the wall was a mirror. On both sides of the room there were tall sliding doors. When Simone opened one the light went on in the walk-in cupboard behind it.

She searched fruitlessly through four such cupboards full of clothes, laundry, blouses, shoes, furs and suits without success. Then she discovered a door handle in the mirrored wall and opened another door, which led into an elegant bathroom in emerald-green marble.

Simone opened a few cupboards with mirrors, some drawers full of cosmetics and a small fridge for insulin cartridges, then went through the next door.

Elvira Senn's bedroom had nothing of the cool understatement, clear-cut lines and co-ordinated colours of the other rooms. Here reigned a riotous mix of art nouveau, baroque, Biedermeier and Beverly Hills.

A Biedermeier bureau with exquisite marquetry in maple root veneer stood next to a bed of amazing dimensions for a woman of her age; opposite the bed was an opulent Empire chest of drawers, and between the two windows, with their full curtains made of dusky pink crêpe de Chine, stood a simple walnut display cabinet filled with the knick-knacks of an eighty-year life. On the wall by the bathroom, there was an art deco dressing table in black, red and gold lacquer.

The whole room smelt of powder and heavy perfume and was already half obscured in the early dusk of the gloomy day.

Simone closed the curtains, put on the light and made a start on the Biedermeier bureau.

As part of their service, the Kochs' security firm carried out additional patrols whose frequency and times were determined randomly by a computer in the company's control centre. On this day the order caught the patrol just as they were about to knock off work. "Additional patrol Rhododendron," the radio announced as they turned into the underground garage of the control centre.

"That bloody computer," cursed Armin Frei, who was driving the car.

"We might have already left," Karl Welti suggested. He had a date with a pretty dental nurse.

"But we haven't left, have we?" responded Frei, whose only date was with the regulars at his usual watering hole, where later on he would be able to say, "Do you know what trick that bloody computer played on me today?"

He turned the vehicle round and drove back to the Villa Rhododendron.

"At least stop at a phone box for a minute, Mr Jobsworth."

"I'm not a jobsworth just because I don't want to rip off my employer."

"There's a phone box just here, Mr J."

By the time they got back to the Villa it was dark. They unlocked the gate and announced to the intercom, "Security service, additional patrol." Then in a bad temper they followed the beams of their flashlights through the dripping wet grounds.

When they came to the Stöckli they saw a strip of light coming from the bedroom and glistening on the wet leaves of a rhododendron bush.

"It's down as unoccupied at the moment," Armin Frei said.

"That's all we need," groaned Karl Welti.

Simone was disheartened. Nothing in the bedroom either. She made sure that she had not disturbed anything and put off the light. Standing in the dark, she still had the image of the bureau before her eyes. There was something not right about it. She put the light back on and saw what it was: the flap had been up when she had come into the room, and now it was down. She put it up and turned the key but it wouldn't close. She tried the key a few times and then, when it still refused to budge, turned it in the wrong direction. The key turned and the desk was locked.

She put the light out again, and once again she could see the image of the bureau before her. There was something not right about it. When she put on the light she saw that the side panel of the top half of the piece of furniture was now sticking out. She went closer and discovered that the side panel could be opened like a door. It must have sprung open when she had turned the key the wrong way.

The door concealed a hollow space between the false and the real back of the bureau. Inside were nine photograph albums in various covers.

Simone took them out, allowed the secret door to snap shut and switched off the light.

When she opened the door into the corridor she was blinded by two strong flashlights.

"Security service, don't move," ordered an agitated voice.

The two security men knew Simone and apologised.

Simone dismissed the apology. "It's good to know that you're so vigilant. Can I get you something?"

Armin Frei was not averse to the idea. But Karl Welti said curtly, "No thank you, not on duty." If they hurried he would still be in time for the dental nurse.

Armin Frei retaliated by taking his time in getting out the report pad from his breast pocket. "Then the only thing we need is your signature."

"Oh, come on! Surely that isn't necessary for family."

"We have the house listed as temporarily unoccupied." Armin Frei laboriously began to enter the facts: place: bedroom Stöckli, time: 18.35.

"I'd rather you didn't make a report. It's a surprise for Frau Senn's eightieth birthday." She pointed to the photograph albums.

Armin Frei caught on. "Oh, right. We did that for my father's sixtieth. With old photos."

"That's it," Simone said.

"That's it," Karl Welti urged.

The nine albums came from various periods, most of them from the late fifties and early sixties, showing the massive, rather casually dressed Edgar Senn, next to whom Elvira looked delicate, elegant and aloof, like the Demoiselle alongside Babar the King. Thomas Koch was in a few of the photos and Konrad Lang in none at all.

There was one album from the years immediately after the war. Thomas was in most of these photographs: Thomas in school uniform, Thomas in tennis gear, Thomas in a ski suit, Thomas on horseback, Thomas being confirmed. In some of the pictures there was also a rather awkward-looking boy who could have been Konrad.

The second-oldest album was from before the war. It was full of photographs of famous places all over the world. In almost all of them you could see a young Elvira, sometimes with one small boy, sometimes with two.

The oldest album was from the thirties. Most of the photos were taken in the Villa Rhododendron or in its grounds. They showed a childlike Elvira and an elderly Wilhelm Koch.

And there were empty spaces where only scraps of paper remained from photographs that had been torn out.

The following day Simone had copies made of the three albums in which Konrad appeared. Also — but she did not know why — of those with the torn-out photos. Afterwards she went back to the Stöckli and replaced all nine albums in their hiding place.

When she visited Konrad around midday she was met by an irritable Nurse Irma Catiric. "Won't eat," she sighed reproachfully as if Simone were responsible for it.

She found Konrad sitting in front of an untouched plate of vegetable cannelloni, a glass of fresh carrot juice, celery and apples and a bowl of salad.

Nurse Irma picked his napkin up from the floor and tucked it into his collar. "Come along now, let's show your visitor how nicely we can eat." When she was harassed, slip ups like this had been known to creep into Nurse Irma's nurse's jargon.

Konrad tore his napkin from his neck and hurled it on to the floor. "You're in for it now," he snarled.

Nurse Irma threw a look up at the ceiling and walked out.

"I need your help," Simone said. Konrad looked at her in surprise.

"I've brought a few photos with me and I don't know what's in them."

She helped him to get up (since the pneumonia he was sometimes unsteady on his feet) and they sat down together on the sofa. Simone had brought the album with the photos in which the awkward-looking boy whom she presumed to be Konrad sometimes appeared.

"This one here, for example. Can you tell me who the people are?" The photo was taken on a paddle steamer. It showed a few boys of the same age with rucksacks and a man with a rucksack and white peaked cap.

Konrad had no need to think about it. "That's Baumgartner, our class teacher, of course. On the school outing to the Rütli. That's Heinz Albrecht, that's Joseph Bindschedler, that's Manuel Eichholzer, that's Niklaus Fritschi, that one there is Richard Marthaler, Marteli we call him, and the fat one is Marcel von Gunten. Tomi's the one without a rucksack."

"Why doesn't Tomi have a rucksack?"

"We share one."

"And how was the school outing?"

"When Furrer took this photograph it had stopped raining for once."

"Who's Furrer?"

"The geography teacher. This one here is Tomi on the Lanigiro ski-slope in St Moritz. 'Lanigiro' is 'original' written backwards, a famous orchestra. They often played in St Moritz. I took the photo."

Konrad leafed through the album animatedly. He could comment in detail on all the photos in which he appeared. If someone's name did not immediately come to mind he would get annoyed, as if he was not someone who normally had that trouble. "It's right on the tip of my tongue," he kept repeating.

He could also comment on some of the photos in which he did not appear. "This one here is Tomi on Relampago, that means 'lightning' in Spanish. I was still at the Zellweger farm then. The stallion was already sold when I came back to the Rhododendron."

On a photograph with Thomas and two young men in cricket

sweaters holding tennis rackets, he commented: "That's Thomas with our room mates at St Pierre's, Jean Luc de Rivière and Peter Court. I have 'retenue' because they caught me in the village."

"What's 'retenue'?"

"Detention."

Nurse Irma, who had come back into the room, scolded, "You'll get 'retenue' here too if you don't eat up."

Koni stood up obediently, sat down at the table and began to eat.

Koni had gone into the village and bought four bottles of wine in the Auberge du Lac.

It was roast beef for supper that evening and de Rivière had said, "A glass of red wine wouldn't go amiss," and scored some points for the laughter that followed.

So after the meal Konrad went to the nursery, leant a ladder against the wall, climbed up it and tried in vain to pull the ladder up and let it down on the other side. For a moment he was about to abandon his mission but the image of himself entering the room like a returning hero with his trophy of red wine was too sweet. He jumped down and decided to worry about how to get back in again later.

He acquired four bottles of house wine in the Auberge du Lac without a hitch. But climbing back into St Pierre's proved to be impossible. He walked up and down in front of the wall and had to stand by and watch the first lights going out in the bedrooms. He had the choice of being absent at the roll call or trying to persuade the porter to let him in without reporting him. Finally he rang at the porter's lodge. After a while the porter shuffled up, opened the little window in the huge gate, recognised Konrad and let him in. Konrad was hardly inside before he held out two bottles of red wine to him. The porter put on his glasses and read the label sceptically. Konrad pulled the third bottle out of his coat and when he saw the old man start to shake his head, the fourth one too.

Then they went into the porter's lodge together and the man informed the "surveillant" on duty.

He received four weeks' "retenue": house arrest outside class times, meals in his room, and 15 times round the sports field at the double as his only kind of sport. And the disgrace of knowing so little about wine that he thought he could bribe old Fournier with four bottles of house wine from the Du Lac.

Now he was sitting in his room waiting until Tomi, Jean Luc de Rivière and Peter Court came up. They would be in the middle of a conversation they had started in the games room and they would not take the trouble to explain to him what it was about. Then they would make allusions to events in which he had not been involved and laugh at jokes that had been cracked in his absence.

When they came in they had a girl with them.

"Hey! How did you smuggle her in?" asked Koni, laughing as he stood up.

She said, "Konrad, may I introduce you to Dr Kundert and Dr O'Neill."

Konrad winked at them both and shook hands with them.

"Delighted, Herr Doktor. Delighted, Herr Doktor." Then he waited, smiling, to see how the game would go on.

"Both these gentlemen would like to examine you, if you have no objection."

A game of doctors and nurses! "Not at all, Mademoiselle." He winked at the other two again.

The girl now went to the door and opened it. "I'm over in the Villa if you need me."

"Stop, stop, not so fast. Aren't you joining in?"

"Perhaps another time," she answered and closed the door.

"Why are you letting her go?" he asked de Rivière and Court. But they were at their little game again. They were talking about things which made no sense to him, referring to events that had taken place without him and talking of people he had never heard of in his life.

"Where's Tomi then?" he asked. They both pretended that they had no idea what he was talking about.

Then he twigged. "I'm over in the Villa," the girl had said. Three guesses who with.

Dr Peter Kundert was a 38-year-old neuropsychologist. He had studied medicine and psychology and, with his MD and PhD, had specialised in neuropsychology. He was participating in a clinical trial as part of Professor Klein's team at the Magdalena Hospital. He personally regarded it as a waste of time.

Dr Ian O'Neill was a biochemist of roughly the same age. He came from Dublin and was participating in the same project as a member of a research team in a pharmaceutical company in Basel. He shared Kundert's opinion.

They had met through their work and become friends. They had admitted their doubts over a drink. Later on O'Neill told Kundert about another compound, POM 55, which he considered would have incomparably greater chances of success. Not only because he was much more closely involved in it.

The next day Kundert made the mistake of telling his boss about O'Neill's comments. Klein took it as a criticism of his own work and so any possibility that O'Neill's project might be given a chance at the Magdalena Hospital was lost.

Meanwhile the preclinical trials of POM 55 were completed and had gone off so satisfactorily that it was time for the clinical trials, which O'Neill was to co-ordinate. That would mean the end of any collaboration between Kundert and O'Neill. So they were both immediately very interested when they heard from Dr Steiner that there was an Alzheimer's patient in exclusive private care on whose behalf great interest had been expressed in using an experimental drug as part of a clinical trial. It would be a chance for Kundert to participate in the project nevertheless, outside his work at the Magdalena Hospital, albeit not in an official capacity.

Kundert and O'Neill were very pleased by the condition of the patient. A loss or any great impairment of the faculty of speech would have been a sign that the illness was too far advanced, the damage irreversible: no ethics commission would have given them consent for the trial.

They were sitting in Simone's room like two little boys who would be given a new toy if they behaved themselves.

Kundert was tall and walked with a slight stoop, as if he were trying to make himself shorter. His face seemed always to be smiling and he wore glasses, which he took off and held in his hand whenever he was speaking. His thick black hair was already streaked with some white. It hung down the nape of his neck in little tight curls.

O'Neill was short and stocky. His brown hair was dull from all the lacquer he used to prevent it sticking out in all directions like a dried flower arrangement. His expression was that of a stray dog ready to join in a free-for-all at any moment.

It was Kundert who spoke.

"Herr Lang is confused and disoriented, undoubtedly, but surprisingly alert, even if his sense of place and time is unclear. He called us de Rivière and Court."

"His room mates at St Pierre's in the forties," Simone explained.

"He speaks unusually fluently and he has an amazing vocabulary at his disposal. He even spoke in French and English. That means that what we call aphasia, when the faculty of speech is affected, has not yet set in or is still not very far advanced."

"It wasn't always like that: there were spells when he didn't speak at all. It's only since I found some photographs from his youth that he has become so interested and articulate."

"It's important you continue to look at these photos with him during any possible treatment."

"Do you really think there's a chance of curing him?" Simone asked.

They looked at each other. Dr O'Neill took over. He spoke a polished High German but with an English accent and the

169

strange Irish lilt that makes every sentence end in a question.

"There are three key features of the brain of an Alzheimer's patient: first, the plaques, which are deposited between the brain cells and consist mainly of toxic fibrillary amyloid; second, the inflamed nerve cells around them; third, the neurofibrils, the skeletons of the cells that are over-phosphorised and cease to function as a result. How these three factors are inter-related we do not know."

Simone must have looked at O'Neill helplessly. He felt himself compelled to add, "Three important pathological changes and we don't know if one conditions another and, if so, which one does what to which. So we have a choice of tactics. We can try to make the amyloid non-toxic or stop the inflammation of the cells or the over-phosphorisation of the neurofibrils."

"But tell her what our assumptions are," Kundert urged.

"Our hypothesis is: the toxic amyloid is the cause of the inflammation of the surrounding nerves and of the hyperphosphorisation." O'Neill waited for the effect his theory would have on Simone. But she nodded and waited for him to go on.

"We know that the amyloid becomes toxic when it becomes fibrillary. Therefore we have to prevent that."

"And can you?"

Dr Kundert and Dr O'Neill exchanged glances. O'Neill answered, "I maintain that we can, yes."

Dr Kundert added enthusiastically, "The results so far are impressive. It works in a cell culture, it works in rats and the pre-clinical trials in healthy volunteers have not shown any side effects."

"But you've never tried it out on an Alzheimer's patient?"

"Herr Lang would be one of the first."

"What are the risks?"

"That the illness will advance."

"That's a risk he's taking anyway," Simone answered.

An afternoon in October. Koni was standing in front of the greenhouse by the compost heap. There was a musty smell from the

170

damp, moss-covered brickwork of the foundations and base of the building. He had a view from here over the path covered with slippery leaves that led back to the gardener's house and the main building.

The agreement was that he was to knock twice on the glass behind him whenever danger threatened. And that he had to stand with his back to the greenhouse and never, under any circumstances, turn round.

Koni kept to this part of the bargain on one secret condition. He hid a small round pocket mirror in his right hand by means of which he peeped under his left armpit into the greenhouse.

There was not a lot to see. It was gloomy in the greenhouse and his view was interrupted by the flowerpots and fan-like leaves of the potted palms kept under glass for the winter. But from a certain angle he could sometimes faintly make out in the greeny black of the hothouse the gleaming white flesh of Geneviève, the amenable gardener's daughter – a breast perhaps, or could it be a buttock?

Everyone said that Geneviève would let you do anything. This idea transformed any rendezvous with her into a hectic, tangled encounter of inexperienced lovers getting themselves into a hopeless muddle.

But Koni was not one of the lovers. His role was to keep watch for the young romantics. The boys all considered this the natural division of labour, as did Koni, at first.

But recently, since he had hit upon the trick with the handbag mirror, he had gradually transferred himself into the other role and imagined he was the one who was tearing down those pink knickers – or was it a bra? – and baring that bottom – or was it a breast?

Koni stood in front of the greenhouse next to the compost heap. In the little mirror, Tomi was wrestling with Geneviève's unresisting limbs. Koni tried to make out something definite in the ever-changing reflection.

Suddenly there was a smell of stale cheroot. He looked up and stared right into the suspicious face of the head gardener. Koni panicked and knocked twice on the glass.

Now he was sitting in his room in his armchair awaiting the consequences.

Suddenly the door opened and Geneviève came in with a vacuum cleaner. She smiled at him, plugged it in and began to vacuum. He watched her manoeuvring the cleaning nozzle between the table and the chair legs and, as she did so, she gradually came nearer. She pushed aside the little coffee table between his armchair and the sofa and vacuumed the carpet in front of his feet.

Now she pushed the nozzle under the sofa. When the tube hit the bottom edge of the sofa she bent down so that her behind was now exactly at Konrad's eye-level. She was wearing a lime-green overall which reached just above the hollow of her knee.

Konrad knew that Geneviève would have no objection if he grabbed hold of the hem of her overall with both hands and lifted it up.

This he did. For a fraction of a second he was gazing at a disappointing jumble of underwear stuffed into creamy tights, then he heard a shriek and felt the sting of a slap on his cheek.

He immediately started to cry.

"Sorry, sorry, but not to pull skirt up, Herr Lang," Svaja Romanescu wailed as Nurse Irma came in, having seen the incident on the monitor.

"We don't hit patients – even when they're dirty old men."

They were now recording the video monitoring – one of Dr Kundert's innovations. There were two sets of tapes for each 24 hours, which were reused alternately if nothing untoward had happened. In this way Kundert could study any observations the care staff had made during his absence. This was especially important as they prepared for the treatment with POM 55, in which they had placed so much hope. His visiting times were very irregular because he was doing his work at the Magdalena Hospital as before. He was waiting for the pharmaceutical company to agree to the trial under these circumstances and with this team. Not until then would he tell his professor and tender his resignation.

Dr Wirth had also not been informed. But since his visits took place at set times it was easy to avoid him meeting the two neurologists.

At Simone's request, Kundert was staying out of Dr Stäubli's way for a while. She did not want to rely on his discretion given his long-standing relationship with Elvira. And she took care that he did not get to learn of her photo sessions with Konrad.

Simone and Dr Kundert watched the recording of the scene on the monitor with Nurse Ranjah: how Konrad Lang, sitting still in the armchair raised his head and smiled; how Svaja Romanescu came into view with the vacuum cleaner at the left-hand side of the screen; how she pushed the coffee table away and bent down to clean under the sofa; and how Koni quite casually lifted her skirt and got a slap for it.

"It's quite out of character," Simone said in surprise.

"It isn't unusual for a patient's character to change with Alzheimer's."

"It's the photos," Nurse Ranjah said. "The photographs you were looking at with him, they were from the time when boys are like that."

"Might that explain it?" Simone asked.

"Patients often live very much in the past. If Konrad Lang is reliving his puberty then it's not such a far-fetched idea. May I see the photos again?" Dr Kundert asked.

Nurse Ranjah looked inquiringly at Simone. When she nodded Nurse Ranjah went out of the room and came back with the pile of copies from the album from the St Pierre days. Simone kept the others in her room.

Kundert looked at the pictures. "Not the worst time in a man's life," he remarked finally. "If all goes well we shall have some success before he loses his memory of that too."

*

Simone was not so confident they would succeed. Over the next few days she thought she saw signs that Konrad's interest in the pictures was waning. Even the names of his school friends and the circumstances in which the photos had been taken were no longer so easy to recall. Many of Konrad's reactions – the way he lost his thread when he was in the middle of one of his favourite subjects, or when she wanted to turn his attention towards one particular picture – seemed familiar to her. It had been exactly the same when he had begun to lose interest in Thomas's photos from the fifties and sixties.

As if she did not already have enough problems with other people, she began to experience some of her own. The first three months of her pregnancy had passed without any of the side effects that other women often complained of: nausea, morning sickness, sudden dizzy attacks during the day. But now, in the fourth month, when these symptoms were normally disappearing, for Simone they were only just beginning.

"Don't worry about it," her gynaecologist said to her.

"Tell that to my husband," she replied.

In the beginning Urs Koch had touched her with his excessive solicitousness, but now he was getting on her nerves. Every time she got up at night he asked, "Are you OK, sweetheart?" and when she spent a long time in the toilet, he knocked at the door and whispered, "Do you need anything, sweetheart?" He had never called her "sweetheart" before.

The morning sickness was difficult for her to conceal from him and it was not long before he used it as a means of putting pressure on her about Konrad Lang.

"I admire your commitment, but it's time to start thinking about yourself. Leave him to the experts!"

Then Elvira returned.

During her absence Simone had repeatedly asked herself whether she had left things exactly as she had found them, whether perhaps the albums in the secret compartment of the bureau had been in a certain order or whether the people at the photo-copying service had left any tell-tale marks or notes between the pages.

When she and Urs had Elvira round for a small welcome-home meal her nerves were jangling.

As Elvira bestowed her two cold kisses on Simone, she showed no signs of having noticed anything. She looked rested. Her face had a discreet and even tan, nicely set off by the subtly lighter tone of her hair.

She told them a little about the mutual friends she had met up there, spent a short time on Thomas's decision to round off his Christmas cruise, as he put it on the telephone, with three weeks in Acapulco, and then got to the point:

"How's our patient?

"As well as can be expected."

"Sitting there staring ahead of him?"

"No, talking."

"What about?"

"About the old days."

"What?"

"At the moment, about his days at St Pierre's."

"That must be more than 50 years ago."

"He's going backwards. Further and further back into his memory."

"She's making herself ill with Koni. She should look after herself too." Urs smiled at Simone, "Shall we tell her?"

Simone stood up and walked out of the room.

Urs sat there flabbergasted.

"Go on, go after her!"

"Sorry, it's . . . Simone . . ."

"I'd already worked it out. I'm very pleased for you."

Urs was hardly outside when Elvira stood up too.

*

Dr Stäubli had received another late-night call. Shortly after ten o'clock he arrived at the gate of the Villa Rhododendron and met a tall young man who was just pressing number four, the bell for the guest house, on the panel of unlabelled buttons. The two men nodded to each other. Simone's voice came over the intercom. "Dr Kundert?"

"Yes, it's me."

The door release buzzed.

"May I come in with you?" Dr Stäubli said.

Kundert hesitated. "I don't know. They're very strict here about security. Are you expected at the Villa?"

"No, at the Stöckli. But I'm often at the guest house as well with our patient Konrad Lang. I'm Dr Stäubli."

On the way he inquired of Kundert, "Have you just joined us?"

"Yes, quite recently."

"Psychiatry?"

"Neuropsychology."

"And Dr Wirth?"

They had reached the turn off to the guest house. Stäubli stopped and waited for an answer.

"Pleasure to meet you," Kundert said hurriedly and left Stäubli standing there.

Stäubli was met in the Stöckli by an uneasy Elvira.

"You don't look like an emergency," he smiled.

"The tan's hiding the pallor. My sugar's too high. And sometimes the ground sways."

"You're 80 and have only just come down from fifteen hundred metres."

"I'm not 80 yet."

He followed her into the bedroom. Even as he was taking her blood pressure she wanted to know, "How is he?"

"No different from the day before yesterday when we last spoke on the phone."

"You didn't mention anything about any detailed memories of 50 years ago then."

"No, I didn't because it isn't true. A lot of people would envy you your blood pressure. Me for instance."

"Simone says he's telling stories about his time at St Pierre's."

"It's true he is talking again but it's rubbish. If she can understand it then there's something wrong with her."

"She's pregnant."

"Then she shouldn't be playing at nurses with young doctors in the middle of the night."

"Is that what she's doing?"

"At this very moment. I came in with him: Dr Kundert, a neuropsychologist."

"And what's wrong with Dr Wirth?"

"I asked myself the same question."

"And?"

Stäubli shrugged his shoulders. "And the sugar readings?"

Elvira pointed to the dressing table. The charts for her blood sugar, urine sugar and ketone body readings were there. Stäubli studied them.

"The fluctuations are within the tolerance levels."

"I can only say how I feel," Elvira retorted coolly. "You always say yourself that readings taken by the patient are inaccurate."

Dr Stäubli began to rummage about in his doctor's bag.

"What's wrong with Dr Wirth?"

"I'll ask him myself."

"Keep me informed." Elvira turned her face away as Dr Stäubli pricked her on her fingertip and spread a drop of blood on the test strip.

Two days later Dr Kundert was out of work.

Stäubli had made inquiries with Wirth as to what exactly Kundert was up to with Konrad Lang. Wirth had already heard of Kundert. He was a talented member of the team led by Professor

177

Klein, the head of geriatrics at the Magdalena Hospital.

Klein reacted in surprise to Wirth's inquiry and summoned Kundert.

Kundert stood his ground with some courage and gave a more or less honest account of himself. The conversation lasted ten minutes and then Kundert received his letter of instant dismissal. The reason: gross breach of his contract of employment. Against which, legally, there was no argument.

Now, even more stooped than usual, he was sitting with Simone. "There's nothing else for me to do but to find another post and as far away as possible. Professor Klein is very influential."

"Could you imagine being permanently employed as a member of the care team?" Simone inquired. "Or at least for the time being. Until you can sort things out."

"O'Neill's boss won't give me the trial. He probably has a furious Professor Klein on the phone to him right at this very moment. He'll have to stop the trial. Klein will insist."

"All the same."

"What advantage is it to you if we're not able to carry out the trial?"

"I won't have to look at Wirth's face any more."

Kundert smiled. "That's reason enough, admittedly."

A hospital doctor doesn't earn a fortune, certainly, but too much for the budget Simone had at her disposal for Konrad Lang. There was nothing else for it but to speak to Urs.

"Are you sure it will take some of the pressure off you?"

"Quite definitely. The man would be available 24 hours a day."

"What does Elvira think about it? It's all her money in the end."

"I'd be pleased if we didn't have to discuss every aspect of my pregnancy with her."

The surprising prospect that difficulties with his wife's pregnancy might be resolved by employing a neuropsychologist for an unloved family friend convinced Urs Koch. Dr Peter Kundert was taken on with immediate effect. For accountancy purposes, as a company doctor for Koch Industries, but privately, one hundred per cent for the care of the patient Konrad Lang.

It was precisely this accountancy dodge that authorised the research team managers at the pharmaceutical company in which Ian O'Neill worked to include Dr Kundert, the company neuro-psychologist of a Swiss conglomerate, in the clinical trials of POM 55.

The arguments of the aggressive Dr O'Neill and the head of research's aversion towards the pretentious and conceited Professor Klein, which had been growing for several years, clinched the matter.

9

"SEE HOW THAT'S PULLING US ALONG," KONRAD LANG
said. Simone Koch tried to understand him. They were sitting in
the back of Dr Kundert's car, in a line of cars driving up the road
through the woods to the hospital.

Konrad explained it to her. "If that one goes, we go too. And
when it stops, we stop too." He pointed to the cars ahead of them.

Simone understood now. "You mean like a train."

Konrad shook his head. "I mean this here. See how it's pulling
us along."

Simone had grown accustomed to Konrad seeing things that
she was unable to see. Or seeing things quite differently from her.
He could look at the window and say, "There used to be a different
one hanging there." Which meant therefore that he saw the
window as a picture on the wall.

But when he was telling her about a photograph he could also
describe what was in it at the top and the bottom and in the
foreground and background with his hands and feet. Because he
thought she would not understand the three dimensions. This was
happening more often of late and it was worrying them all. Twice
now he had described the photograph on the paddle steamer in
this way, where previously he would have rattled off the names
of everyone in the picture. "That one there is here, that one there
is there."

They were on their way to the university hospital where various clinical tests had been performed on Konrad over the past few days; a diagnostic appraisal, as a basis for the ethics commission's decision, and to obtain some comparative results for the treatment.

They had carried out the psychological tests in the guest house. Konrad had had the electroencephalography, and the tests on the blood flow in the different parts of his brain.

Today they were completing the last test, the CAT scan.

Konrad had submitted to all the examinations with either indifference or amusement. Even now he allowed himself to be helped on to the bed uncomplainingly and to be pushed into the cylinder of the CAT scanner.

As it turned round, first of all slowly, then faster, and faster still, Konrad fell asleep.

He was still asleep when they pulled the bed out of the scanner.

"Herr Lang?" the assistant called.

"Herr Lang?" Dr Kundert called.

No response from Konrad. Kundert shook him gently, then rather harder.

"Good morning, Herr Lang," he said quite loudly now.

Konrad opened his eyes. Then he tore the cover off and looked at his bare feet. "I just knew it," he gasped. "Three toes."

He jumped off the bed and landed so awkwardly that he broke his left tibia and fibula.

"That's really bad luck. Poor fellow!" Elvira Senn said when Dr Stäubli told her about Konrad Lang's accident as he examined her. Her tone sounded more interested than sympathetic. "Is it bad?"

"The fracture in itself isn't too serious. But it's a bad setback for an Alzheimer's patient if he becomes bed-ridden. He won't be able to do any exercises, his mobility and co-ordination will suffer, there will be an increased danger of complications such as circulatory problems, embolisms, muscle loss and bone decalcification."

"Will it speed up the course of the illness?"

"There's a significant danger of that." He wrote something in her medical records.

"It's probably better for him this way."

Dr Stäubli looked up. "Why do you think that?"

"It's no life."

He thought about this for a moment. "I don't know. Perhaps it only seems like that to us. Perhaps he's living in a world that we know nothing about. Perhaps that's the real life."

"You don't seriously believe that?"

Dr Stäubli shrugged his shoulders. "It's something I wouldn't like to have to decide, at any rate."

As a precaution, Kundert and O'Neill decided not to mention the accident to the ethics commission that in two days time was to make a decision on Dr Kundert's application, amongst other things.

The incident in the scanner had a positive side to it, too: Konrad Lang's medical history, which Dr Wirth had handed over reluctantly and in three stages, mentioned a similar incident during the first CAT scan just over a year ago. There too the patient had connected the event with the loss of his three toes.

"That means in the first place that he learnt something new a year ago," Dr Kundert explained to Simone Koch, "and in the second that it's stored in the episodic memory and could be recalled by the same episode."

"And is that a good sign?"

"It possibly means that this area of the brain is not so badly damaged that it can't be stimulated again."

Kundert and O'Neill decided to emphasise this aspect of the incident to the ethics commission.

When Simone visited Konrad the day before the commission's decision she took some new photographs with her.

He was lying in his hospital bed staring at his leg in plaster which was hanging from a bar above the bed on a sort of block and tackle. When she showed him the photos of the two boys with Elvira on holiday he did not seem particularly interested.

There was Konrad as a child standing next to Thomas and Elvira in a deserted St Mark's Square in Venice, surrounded by dozens of pigeons. From the short shadows it must have been midday. In the background empty tables stood in front of the colonnade cafés whose sun-blinds were all lowered so that the more sensible people could eat, untroubled by the midday sun.

Konrad knew where some of the pictures were taken. "Venice," he said, or "Milan." And in all of them he recognised "Tomi, Koni and Mama Vira."

"Mama Vira?"

"Mama Vira."

There was Konrad with Tomi on a deserted beach, building a sandcastle in the shadow of a striped awning. In the background a row of similarly striped beach huts. Just where the shadow of the awning ended, Elvira was lying on a lounger in a modest bathing costume. Next to her was a second empty chair.

"Tomi, Koni and Mama Vira."

"Where?"

"At the seaside."

There were three photographs on the last page. One showed in detail the belly of a dark ship, two rows of port holes and the pattern of the rough bolts on the outside surface. A white gang-way with the inscription "Dover" went up into the interior of the ship where, in the semi-darkness, the white shirt front of a man obviously in uniform could be made out.

The second photograph showed the same gangway again from closer up. In the background was the man in uniform, in the fore-ground were Elvira and Thomas, their backs to the ship, waving into the camera.

It was the third photo which had a profound effect on Konrad. It showed the gangway from the opposite angle. Part of a harbour building in the background, a few people in hats and coats waving, and in the foreground, on the gangway, a woman and a man. You could see his thin, smiling lips, his eyes shaded by the brim of a soft felt hat with a wide band. He was wearing an open tweed coat over a three-piece woollen suit, a pale shirt and a striped tie. His coat collar was turned up, and his left hand was in his pocket, which was placed so high up that he had to bend his arm.

It was impossible to see whether his right arm was hanging at his side or around the waist of the woman next to him. She was the same height as him and was smiling provocatively into the camera. A small fur hat sat jauntily on her page-boy haircut. She was wearing a coarse tweed suit with a fur collar that matched the hat, a sweater with fine diagonal stripes and a long Paisley-patterned scarf. A bag with a long strap was slung over her right shoulder.

"Mama Anna," Konrad gasped contemptuously, and with a violent movement swept the photocopies off the bed.

When Simone studied the picture later she thought she could detected a certain resemblance between the woman and Sophie Berger, the red-haired relief nurse.

Koni had to lie in bed in the dark although he was afraid of the dark. He was not allowed to call out and not allowed to get up either.

Otherwise the noisy black men with the white eyes who brought the coal would take him away. They came into the cellar at the hotel with full black sacks and went out again with empty black sacks. Once he saw one of them going out again with a sack that was still half full. He asked Mama Anna what was in the sack.
"People like you who don't do as they're told."
"What do they do with them?"
"What do you think they do with them?"
Koni had no idea but he imagined the worst.
The worst would be if he had to stay in that black sack for ever. In the dark for ever.

Koni had never been afraid of the dark before. Not until they were in London. Sometimes sirens suddenly sounded in London and then it went dark. They were practising for the war, people said, and he saw from the people that they were afraid as well.

It was really the sirens he was afraid of but because the dark was connected with the sirens, he was afraid of the dark too.

And so Koni had a choice between a fear of the dark or a fear that he would be caught with the lights on. There had been times when he had opted for the latter and put the light on. As a result Mama Anna had tied him by his leg to the bed.

He could hear her in the next room with the man who was not to see him. If the man saw him Koni went into the sack.

Men had come and stayed before, too. But they were allowed to see him. He was allowed to say goodnight to them and then go to bed. Sometimes they brought something for him. But this one was not to see him.

And so he was tied up in the dark.

Nurse Ranjah sat in the staff room and watched Konrad's bedroom on the monitor. The room was in darkness and Konrad could only be seen as an outline against the lighter background of the bed. He was not moving, but she knew he was awake. With the plaster, Konrad could sleep only on his back, and when he slept on his back, he snored. But there was no snoring coming over the intercom, only the shallow breathing and deep sighs of someone lying awake at night.

Nurse Ranjah got up from her chair, crept down the stairs and carefully pressed down the handle of his bedroom door. When she was in the room she noticed him holding his breath.

"Herr Lang?" she whispered. No reaction. She went up to his bed.

"Herr Lang?"

Konrad Lang did not stir. Nurse Ranjah was worried now. She felt for the switch that hung on the rail by the bell and put on the light.

Konrad put his hands in front of his eyes.

"I didn't put the light on, Mama Anna," he pleaded.

"Mama Anna isn't here," Nurse Ranjah said and took him into her arms.

At the staff handover the next morning Nurse Ranjah reported the incident to Nurse Irma. "Tell the doctor that the devils of the past are not letting him sleep."

Later on Dr Kundert and Simone watched the recording of the incident.

"Why would he be frightened of the light?" Simone asked.

"He wasn't frightened of the light. Only of putting on the light. Because Mama Anna had forbidden him to. He wasn't afraid of the light. He was afraid of Mama Anna." Dr Kundert wound the video back to the place where Konrad Lang kept his eyes closed and pleaded, "I didn't put the light on, Mama Anna."

"'Mama Anna'," Simone repeated. "Have you any idea why he calls them 'Mama Anna' and 'Mama Vira'?"

"Baby talk," Kundert suggested.

"Or perhaps there are two children of the same age and both call their mother 'Mama', which leads to constant confusion. Hence 'Mama Anna' and 'Mama Vira'."

One week later the consent arrived from the ethics commission for the admission of the patient Konrad Lang, 67, to a single trial application of POM 55. Dr Kundert could hardly wait to tell Simone.

But Simone had just had a bad night. Urs had insisted on phoning Dr Spörri. The doctor had called round before his surgery opened and ordered her to stay in bed. She was in the eighteenth week and the morning sickness was worse than ever. It was starting in the middle of the night now and the bed was beginning to spin round. Sometimes she had to get up at three o'clock to be sick.

186

"But there must be something wrong," Urs kept on saying. He was used to people taking his objections seriously.

Dr Spörri reassured him: "Sickness and dizziness are part and parcel of a healthy pregnancy. We know from studies that the babies of women who have these symptoms generally weigh more and are more likely to be born on time."

Nevertheless he ordered Simone to stay in bed, more to reassure her husband than out of medical necessity.

Candelaria, the housekeeper, had strict instructions from Urs to keep all phone calls and visitors away from his wife.

"But it's very important," Dr Kundert insisted.

"If doctor says no, is no," Candelaria answered. "You should know, you doctor too."

Thus he had to wait patiently until the afternoon when Simone felt better and went over to the guest house in spite of Candelaria's protests.

"We can make a start," Kundert remarked casually when she went into the staff room, which was becoming more and more like an observation room.

Simone thought at first that he was referring to the monitor on which the physiotherapist could be seen struggling with an apathetic, prostrate Konrad. Only when she noticed how he was smilingly waiting for her reaction did she understand.

"They've given us the green light?"

"O'Neill's coming tomorrow with the POM 55. We can do it the day after."

"As soon as that?"

"With each day we delay, more cells are being lost."

Simone sat down at the table on which there were coffee cups and a thermos flask. She had changed over the last months. She used less make-up and did not dress so smartly. Her style had become more practical, her clothes more classical. Her features had become more feminine. Her figure hardly showed any trace of her pregnancy, but she was rather pale and her make-up could not disguise the shadows under her eyes.

"Are you feeling better?" Dr Kundert asked.

Simone nodded.

"Can we count on you?"

In the event of them obtaining the consent, they had planned a whole series of tests to record the effect of the treatment. Alongside the examinations with technical equipment, the laboratory diagnoses and the psychological tests they also wanted to check Konrad's powers of recollection with the photos from his past. Simone had declared herself willing to collaborate with them on this part of the programme. She was to carry on showing him the photos and, as she did so, to stick to a certain pattern of questions in the hope that they would be able to establish from his answers whether his memory had deteriorated or remained the same.

"Of course you can count on me. But perhaps it's better if you put me down for the afternoons."

Konrad's favourite photograph showed a Mercedes convertible in a meadow on the edge of a wood. Elvira, all dressed in white, was leaning on the chrome cover of the spare wheel, which fitted neatly on to the elegantly curved front wing. She was wearing a tight calf-length skirt, a short double-breasted jacket with wide lapels, gloves, and a beret pulled down towards her right ear. Only her stockings and shoes were black.

Tucked under her left arm she had a crocodile-skin handbag without a handle; her right elbow was leaning nonchalantly on the open window. At first sight it looked as if she was on her own in the picture. But when Konrad saw the photo for the first time he had pointed out to Simone a tuft of hair behind the rear left wing: "Koni." On closer observation you could make out a half-hidden forehead and an eye peeping out.

Then Konrad pointed to the front left mudguard: "Tomi." There too you could see a boy hiding, peeking out in the gap between the headlights and the radiator. "The Mercedes does a hundred and ten."

From then on, every time this photo came round he waited in amusement to see whether anything attracted her attention about it. When she did him the favour of not finding anything special about the picture, he took a childlike pleasure in showing her the two hidden boys. "Koni. Tomi." And added in a businesslike manner, "The Mercedes does a hundred and ten."

Whenever he was apathetic and depressed and pushed the photos away she could always bring him round with this trick photograph. It would work, if necessary, several times in succession.

Simone was playing this little game with Konrad when Nurse Irma came in and gave her the news that Dr O'Neill was in the next room and would like to have a word with her for a second.

O'Neill and Kundert were standing by the table in the living room round a small square appliance with a mask attached. It looked like one of the oxygen masks that cabin staff demonstrate to passengers before a flight.

O'Neill did not waste time on the hellos. "We should try it out to see how he reacts to it."

"What's that?"

"An aerosol appliance. We're going to administer the POM 55 with it. It's inhaled."

"Inhaled? I'd imagined it would be injected or swallowed."

"That would be better. But we're not so advanced yet. He has to inhale it. The best way of overcoming the blood-brain barrier."

Simone nodded. "What should I do?"

Dr Kundert intervened. "The atomiser is already filled with water and a few drops of essential oil. All I would like you to do is to go back in and look at some more photographs with him. Then we'll come in and you'll ask him to inhale for a short time and we'll watch whether there are any problems, whether the mask fits, and so on. He should be as relaxed as possible."

When Simone went back into Konrad's room he was day-dreaming. She had some trouble in focusing his attention on the photographs. Only when the Mercedes came round did he show any interest.

"Oh, and this one here, is that Elvira in front of a car?"

He smiled for a moment and said nothing. Then he pointed to the back mudguard. "Koni." And then to the front. "Tomi."

Then he laughed and added, "The Mercedes does a hundred and ten."

He hardly paid any attention to Dr Kundert and Nurse Irma when they came into the room with the appliance and put it on the mobile swivel tray on which Konrad's meals were now served.

He became aware of the appliance only when they manoeuvred the tray over his bed and Simone took the photocopies off his bedclothes and said, "Oh, yes, let's just do this quickly in the meantime."

"What's that?" he asked Nurse Irma.

"An inhaler. For inhaling."

"Oh, right," he nodded. But they could see that he had no idea what he was supposed to do with it.

"We'll put the mask on you and then you take a few deep breaths. That's all."

"Oh, right," he nodded. Then he looked at Simone, grinned and shrugged his shoulders.

"It'll do you good," she said. Konrad happily allowed them to put the mask on him.

Dr Kundert ordered, "Breathe in – breathe out – breathe in – breathe out." Konrad Lang obeyed. At the fifth inhalation Kundert pressed the plunger on the nebuliser and let it go when Konrad exhaled. Konrad kept breathing quietly.

After seven inhalations Kundert stopped pressing the plunger, let Konrad take a few more deep breaths and then took the mask off him.

"All finished," he smiled. "How do you feel?"

Konrad smiled at Simone again and shrugged his shoulders.

The nurse moved the tray away. Simone put the photographs back on the bedcover. As Kundert and the nurse were leaving the room they heard Konrad say, "The Mercedes does a hundred and ten."

The boat glided slowly down the river. The jungle reached into the river from both banks. Koni dipped the paddle in, pulled, took it out, brought it forward, dipped it in, pulled, took it out, brought it forward, dipped it in. Faster and faster moved the boat, flowed the river, moved the boat, flowed the river.

Now Koni heard a voice. It said, "Row, row."

Koni dipped the paddle in, pulled, took it out, brought it forward, dipped it in, pulled.

"Row, row, row," said the voice.

But I am rowing, Koni thought.

"Breathe, breathe," said the voice.

Koni opened his eyes. A face was looking down at him, its mouth, nose and hair covered by a white cloth. He could see only the eyes.

"Breathe, breathe," said the face.

Koni breathed. Suddenly he was gripped by a terrible pain. He wanted to clutch his stomach but he couldn't. His hands were tied.

He screamed. Someone pressed a mask up to his mouth and nose.

Koni tried to turn his head away.

Someone held his head firmly. His stomach was hurting.

"Breathe, breathe," said the voice.

Koni held his breath.

"Breathe, breathe."

Koni breathed.

The pain went away.

"Row, row," said the voice.

Koni dipped the paddle in, pulled, took it out, brought it forward, dipped it in, pulled. Faster and faster moved the boat, flowed the river, moved the boat.

"Row, row."

"Breathe, breathe."

"Breathe."

"Breathe!"

Koni opened his eyes. It was dark. He screamed and screamed and screamed.

The door flew open and the light went on. Nurse Ranjah ran to Koni's bed.

He had pushed the bedclothes off and was clutching his stomach.

"There there, there there," Nurse Ranjah said, stroking his face.

"It hurts," Koni whimpered.

"Let's see." Ranjah gently took his hand away. Underneath was Konrad's old appendix scar.

Simone had a bad night. She slept restlessly and awoke shortly after two. For a long time she tried to keep breathing regularly so that Urs, who was a light sleeper, would not notice that she was lying awake and begin to pester her. "What's wrong? Aren't you well? Can I get you something? Shall I call the doctor? Something's wrong. It isn't normal. Perhaps we should change doctors. You don't take enough care of yourself. It's all this nonsense with Koni. You said it would be better with the new doctor. You're responsible for two now. It isn't only your child, it's mine too. Can I get you something? Do you have to go to the bathroom, sweetheart?"

She was unaware that she was alone in bed until she saw the strip of light under the door leading to the "boudoir". She put on the light.

The room slowly began to spin round and the saliva collected in her mouth. She sat on the edge of the bed and tried to concentrate on something else. Suddenly it seemed she could hear Urs's voice in the boudoir. She stood up slowly, walked to the door and opened it.

Urs was perched on the little desk, smiling and holding the telephone receiver close up to his face. When Simone came into the room he looked so guilty that it was pointless trying to fool her. He remained seated, lowered the receiver and watched as she closed the door behind her in disgust.

Simone just made it to the bathroom. Then she threw up as she had never done before in her life.

She did not know how long she knelt in front of the toilet bowl. But when she came out of the bathroom, pale and exhausted, Dr Spörri was waiting for her. She took him into her Laura Ashley room without deigning to look at Urs standing next to him. She closed the door and lay down on the chaise longue. The doctor took her pulse and blood pressure.

"You'll have to go into hospital until you improve."

"I won't get better in hospital."

"But we can feed you artificially there. You're not putting on any weight, you're dehydrated. It's bad for your baby."

"I can be artificially fed here."

"You need care and monitoring, which can be done only in hospital."

"I have a hospital here, too."

Shortly after sunrise Simone was attached to a drip in one of the two staff bedrooms on the first floor of the guest house. Urs had made a weak, vain attempt to protest.

"Be quiet," was all she said and he immediately backed down.

After his initial scepticism Dr Spörri appeared impressed by the standard of the guest house, its staff and equipment.

Nurse Ranjah expertly prepared the infusion, and when Dr Spörri had set it up she deftly inserted the cannula and the drip tubing.

Shortly afterwards Simone fell asleep.

*

Simone was woken by a rather artificial cough. She opened her eyes and saw Nurse Irma standing by her bed, changing the infusion bottle.

"Your husband was here," she smiled. "I said you were not to be disturbed."

"Good. Tell him that the next time too. What time is it?"

"Just after two."

Simone was shocked. She had slept for eight hours. "And Herr Lang?"

"All ready to start."

"Why didn't you wake me up?" Simone pushed the cover back and tried to get up. Nurse Irma put her hand on her shoulder. "Dr Kundert said I was not to wake you, but that when you were awake I was to call him. I'll do that now. You must wait."

Shortly afterwards Kundert came in.

"I thought I was needed for the tests." Simone said.

"We wanted to wait until you woke up when they changed the drip."

"And if I hadn't woken up, would you have started without me?"

Kundert smiled. "But you did wake up."

"Come on, take this off me." She held out her arm to him.

"Do you really feel up to it? I don't think there'll be a problem. Nurse Ranjah is there too. She has a calming effect on the patient."

"He's not calm?"

"He had a restless night. So Nurse Ranjah came. Just in case, she says."

"Please take this off."

Kundert stood up, fetched the disinfectant and a plaster, clamped the infusion apparatus, removed the cannula, disinfected the area and put a plaster on. Then he went out. "We'll wait for you downstairs."

In Konrad's bedroom the aerosol apparatus was set up on the mobile table, which was waiting behind the bed, out of his sight. Kundert, O'Neill and Nurse Irma stood next to it and nodded to Simone as she went into the room.

O'Neill's hair showed signs of a restless night.

Nurse Ranjah was sitting on Konrad's bed looking at photographs with him. When Simone came in he looked up briefly and greeted her with a bewildered smile that said, "Who are you, lovely stranger?"

"Don't let me disturb you, I only wanted to look at the photos with you for a little while."

Konrad was delighted to have such a large audience. He continued his commentary on the pictures. He was more alert than the previous day and also stopped at pictures that had not particularly interested him before: Venice, a sandy beach, Milan Cathedral.

Dr O'Neill opened a cool box in the background, took out a small ampoule, disinfected its rubber stopper, stuck a filling needle in and drew up its contents. He injected this into the nebuliser and nodded to Simone.

Nurse Ranjah was leafing through Konrad's favourite photographs. "This one here would be interesting for us. Can you tell us anything about it?" She nodded to O'Neill.

The compressor of the aerosol appliance began to buzz. Nurse Irma pushed the mobile tray towards the bed.

Konrad Lang was enjoying the game. Just as he was about to begin, Simone said, "Oh, but let's do the inhaling quickly first."

She lifted the photos up off the bedcovers, and Nurse Irma pushed the appliance under his nose.

"What's that?"

"It's inhaling time again."

Konrad was reluctant to reveal his ignorance. "Of course," he nodded and allowed the mask to be strapped on without resisting. Simone and Nurse Ranjah smiled at him. Then they made room for Dr Kundert.

"Breathe in – breathe out – breathe in – breathe out," he ordered. Konrad obeyed. Kundert adapted himself to his rhythm. Then he pressed the plunger, let it go, pressed it, let it go. With every intake of breath Konrad was now inhaling drops of POM 55 as a fine spray.

"Breathe in — breathe out — breathe in."

"Breathe, breathe."

Konrad Lang closed his eyes.

The level in the atomiser dropped.

"Breathe, breathe."

"Row, row."

Konrad opened his eyes wide, grabbed the inhalation mask and tore it off his face.

No one was expecting it, no one had the presence of mind to stop him. Kundert was just able to rescue the appliance from destruction in Konrad Lang's wildly flailing arms.

Konrad Lang could not to be persuaded to put the mask on again. And so O'Neill and Kundert reluctantly decided to leave it at that. O'Neill's measurement of the remaining POM 55 revealed that they had administered around 80 per cent of the dose before the incident.

"That should be enough," he said. It did not sound very convincing.

It had taken some time for Konrad to calm down. Simone had tried and failed to distract him with the photographs. He gradually relaxed only when they had all left the room and Nurse Ranjah came with her honeyed almonds and chattered her tender nonsense to him.

Kundert, O'Neill and Simone were now sitting in the staff room.

"If it doesn't work we shall never know whether it was simply because the dose was too small," Kundert said in annoyance.

"The dosages of experimental drugs are a matter of luck anyway," O'Neill said consolingly.

"What happens now?" Simone asked.

"We just have to wait," Kundert answered.

"For how long?"

"Until something happens."

10

"THEY'VE BEEN TRYING *WHAT*?" ELVIRA SENN ASKED, dumbfounded.

"Konrad Lang has been given the drug as part of a clinical trial," Dr Stäubli explained.

"Can they do that?"

"If the doctor makes an application and all the participants agree."

"I wasn't asked."

"You aren't involved in that sense. The people involved are the doctor, the pharmaceutical company, an ethics commission and the patient. In this case, the official guardians."

"And they all agreed?"

"Obviously."

Elvira Senn shook her head. "I thought it was incurable."

"It is. So far."

"And Koni might be the first person to be cured?"

"At best he'll make a scientific contribution to Alzheimer's research."

"Without knowing it."

"Without even suspecting it."

Over the next days in the guest house they concentrated on getting the two patients back on their feet.

Konrad Lang was fitted with a plaster cast on his leg. The

therapist and Nurse Irma tried to get him to take a few steps every day.

Simone Koch spent most of each day on the drip. But in the afternoons she looked at photographs with Konrad for about an hour, or for as long as she was able to engage his interest. She asked him her precise pre-set questions; Dr Kundert evaluated the answers over the monitor.

For the moment, apart from the usual fluctuations, there was no sign of any deterioration. But after such a short time this gave no real grounds for optimism.

The only surprise in the guest house during these days was a visit from Thomas Koch.

There he was suddenly standing at the door, tanned, full of energy and demanding to be let in. Nurse Irma, who had never seen him before, made the mistake of asking him who he was and what he wanted. And he made the mistake of replying, "What the hell's that got to do with you? Let me in."

Dr Kundert heard the loud voices coming from in the porch, went to see what was going on and saved the situation.

Shortly afterwards Thomas was standing irritably in the room where his daughter-in-law was attached to a drip, counting each drop.

The sight of her – a pretty woman and the mother-to-be of his first grandchild – immediately calmed him down. Instead of complaining about his reception by Nurse Irma, which he had fully intended to do, he said, " I hope you'll soon be feeling better."

"I hope so too," Simone sighed. "How was it?"

"Where?"

"I don't know. Wherever you've just been."

Thomas Koch thought about it for a moment. "Jamaica."

"Perhaps you go away too much."

"Why?"

"If you have to think so long about where you've just been."

"It's old age." He laughed rather too loudly and sat down on the chair by the bed. Then he became serious. He took her hand in a fatherly manner.

"Urs has confessed to me that you aren't sleeping over here solely because of your health."

Simone made no reply.

"I've given him a good talking to."

She wished he would let go of her hand.

"I'm afraid he's got that from me. A leopard doesn't change its spots. But you can rely on one thing with the Kochs: when the going gets tough we stand by our women. What else matters? Nothing."

She pulled her hand away.

"I can understand of course. It just isn't done and particularly not when the woman's expecting. There's no excuse for it." He came to the point. "Nevertheless, I think you should move out of here. Doctors, nurses and an old man who is on the way out: it's a depressing environment for a mother-to-be. We'll get a room ready for you in the house and employ a nurse. You'll be amazed at how quickly we'll have you back on your feet."

"I have everything I need here and I am very well looked after. An unfaithful husband isn't really an ideal environment for a mother-to-be either."

"It won't happen again."

"It's happened too often already."

"It'll sort itself out."

"No."

It sounded as if Simone had been thinking everything over for a long time. Yet it had only become clear to her just now, at this very moment. Never again. It was time for her to think about how things would proceed.

"What does that mean?"

"I don't know yet."

"Don't do anything foolish."

"Certainly not."

Thomas stood up. "Can I give Urs a message?"

Simone shook her head.

"Get well soon," Thomas said, squeezing her arm.

"Did you go to see Konrad?"

"No."

"Why not?"

"I wouldn't know what to talk to him about."

"About old times."

"Old times make us old," Thomas said with a grin, and walked out of the room.

Simone began to feel better from that moment on. That evening the smells penetrating from the dietary kitchen made her feel hungry instead of nauseous. She asked a surprised Nurse Ranjah to bring her something to eat and devoured two large salami sandwiches. She had a wonderful night's sleep. The dizziness and morning sickness disappeared. She tucked into a huge breakfast.

The sudden certainty that she did not love Urs and did not want to spend the rest of her life with him had made Simone well again.

She no longer had any need of the drip, but planned to keep this news from the Koch family until she had considered her next move. For the time being it would be better to stay in the guest house.

As abruptly as Simone's condition improved, so Konrad's deteriorated.

He had tried to get up several times in the night. Each time Nurse Ranjah, who never let the monitor out of her sight, had appeared in his room and prevented the worst.

Each time he insisted on getting dressed. Ranjah, who was born and brought up in the tradition of respect for the elderly and their wishes helped him to the wardrobe and helped him to dress.

Then when Konrad was standing in the room, dressed in a

bizarre outfit – Ranjah let him have his way in that too – he no longer knew what his plans had been.

Then Ranjah patiently helped him to undress again and put him back to bed, brought him some tea, stayed with him until he had gone to sleep and went back to the monitor in the staff room. Until the next time.

What worried Dr Kundert as he analysed the recording of this night was that Konrad's English had become worse. He was spending a long time searching for words and mixing up his English with French and a bit of Spanish.

It was also a bad sign that he had wet the bed. Konrad's occasional incontinence had previously been related to his apraxia, the inability of patients in an advanced stage of Alzheimer's to perform complex sequences of actions. But with the support of the nursing staff this had not been a great problem for him until now.

Now there was a fear that his brain was beginning to lose control over his bodily functions.

Dr Kundert was reckoning on the patient's condition deteriorating. When Simone had her photo session with Konrad at the usual time this afternoon, he watched the monitor particularly closely.

After a few minutes he knew that his fears had been confirmed. Konrad was certainly interested in the photographs Simone showed him, but it was the interest of a person seeing them for the first time. He could hardly answer any of the standard questions and few of his usual explanations were forthcoming. Again and again Simone had to offer him the back-up prompt they had pre-arranged. And more and more frequently Simone shot a helpless glance towards the hidden lens.

When she came to the photograph with the convertible, Kundert was unable to sit on his chair any longer. He stood up and moved as close to the monitor as possible.

She asked her usual question, "And is this Elvira here?"

Konrad hesitated as always. But this time it was obviously not to keep Simone in suspense but because he really had to think about it.

Then he nodded and smiled. Simone smiled with relief, too, as did Kundert in front of the monitor.

Konrad Lang pointed to Koni's tuft of hair behind the rear left wing and said, "Tomikoni."

Then he pointed to Tomi in the gap between the left headlamp on the front wing and the radiator and grinned. "Konitomi."

Simone improvised. She pointed to the hidden boy who Konrad up until now had always referred to as "Koni" and asked, "Koni?"

Konrad shook his head in amusement and said emphatically, "Tomi."

"And how quickly does the Mercedes go?" she asked.

"No idea."

Kundert and Simone looked at the photographs together. "When you pointed to Koni, he said 'Tomikoni'?"

"And when I pointed to Tomi, he said 'Konitomi'."

"He wanted to hide the fact that he didn't know which of the boys was hiding where."

"So why did he continue to mix up the names when I pressed him?"

"By then he had already forgotten the trick with Tomikoni and Konitomi."

Simone was disheartened. "Does that mean the treatment isn't working?"

"It can't have worked yet. It means only that the illness is taking its course. But it doesn't say anything about POM 55. Another connection from nerve cell to nerve cell has been cut off before the drug was able to work. We've just been unlucky."

"Konrad most of all."

"Yes, him most of all."

Both of them fell silent. Then Simone said, "Imagine it's worked and there's nothing more there."

The idea had crossed his mind.

*

Koni saw all the faces in the room. They were watching him from the wallpaper and the curtains. Most of them were nasty. Some were nice and nasty. Very few were only nice.

If he didn't move they didn't see him and couldn't do anything to him.

It was no good to put on the light. Then other faces came. Ones that pulled faces in the wind. And then animals came too which lay in wait on his chair. So it was better not to put the light on. Then you could keep your eye on the faces. And then there were only his clothes on the chair.

The hope that the change in Konrad was merely a temporary setback died in the days that followed.

Dr Kundert's tests showed a clear deterioration in virtually every result. His physiological condition had got worse as well, as the physiotherapist was able to confirm.

The report by Joseline Jobert, the occupational therapist, was less disappointing. Konrad was still devoted to his watercolour painting. The results were even more abstract, and the spelling of the legends that he always gave his pictures had suffered. There were repetitions of letters or syllables in almost every other word because he forgot that he had already written them. "Eueurope", he wrote, or "appleletreetree".

He hummed along with her as always to hiking songs, Christmas carols and student songs, which she sang aloud to him in broken German.

But he was still only reacting passively to the photographs which Simone showed him. He no longer said, "Venice", "Milan" or "at the seaside" when she asked him where a place was. When she suggested, "Is that at the seaside?" or "Is that in Venice?", he nodded at most.

She could also show him the photograph of St Mark's Square and ask, "Is that in Paris?" and he would nod then, too.

He was no longer able to distinguish between Thomas and

himself. He confused himself and Thomas or called them both "Tomikoni" and "Konitomi". On the other hand he identified Elvira Senn on every picture as "Mama Vira".

Simone was depressed when she went back to her room after the final photograph session and put the copies down on the table.

"I'm pleased you're feeling better," said a voice behind her.

It was Thomas Koch. He had sat down on the edge of the bed and stood up now. Simone looked at him and waited.

"The nurse let me in. Probably remembered that it was my house."

"I'm not coming back to the Villa if that's what's brought you here."

"That's a matter for you and Urs."

Simone waited.

"How's Koni?"

Simone raised her shoulders. "Not so good today."

"And the miracle drug?"

"No result," she said. "Yet," she added quickly.

Simone Koch had never seen Thomas Koch like this. His self-confidence was gone. He stood in her small, simple room looking embarrassed, not knowing what to do with his hands. He actually seemed to be concerned.

"Sit down then."

"I haven't much time." He picked up the photos from the table and leafed through them absent-mindedly. Simone panicked. But Thomas appeared quite uninterested in their origin.

"So many memories," he murmured thoughtfully.

"He has fewer every day." Simone pointed to one of the boys under the awning on the beach: a square head, close-set eyes.

"That's you, isn't it?"

"Yes, you can see that."

"Koni can't distinguish between the two of you any more. Sometimes he calls you Koni, sometimes he calls himself Tomi and sometimes he calls you Tomikoni and Konitomi."

"It's a dreadful illness." Thomas continued to leaf through the photos. "How did it begin?"

"The same as for most people: minor lapses of memory, slight absent-mindedness, things going missing, forgetting names, having difficulties with menus, losing your sense of direction, then not recognising close friends any more, forgetting the names of household objects, no longer knowing what they're used for any more and remembering only things from far back in the past."

"What do you mean, difficulties with menus?"

"People who once needed a minute to study a menu just sit there and look through it and can't decide."

Thomas nodded. As if he knew what she was talking about.

"Would you like to see him?"

"No," he said quickly. "No, perhaps another time. You must understand."

Simone understood. Thomas Koch was genuinely concerned. But about himself, not about Konrad Lang.

Konitomi would have liked to go to sleep. He was tired. But he didn't want to. If he went to sleep they came and stuck a needle in him.

He couldn't put his arms behind his head if he lay on his back. Then they stabbed him in the armpits. With long needles.

Tomikoni didn't know which was better: if he didn't put the light on they wouldn't see him, but if he put the light on he would see them coming.

But if he went to sleep he wouldn't notice when they put the light on. Then he would notice they were there only when it was too late.

If he hid perhaps they might go away again.

Konitomi quietly pushed his cover back and drew up his legs. It was not very easy. They had fixed something heavy to his left leg so that he couldn't run away.

Now he would put his feet down over the edge of the bed. First the right one, then the heavy one.

He let himself down from the edge of the bed. He stood next to the bed.

Where should he hide?

Too late. The light went on.

"Don't stab me," Tomikoni pleaded.

"There now, there now," Nurse Ranjah said soothingly.

Since the day when he had been fobbed off at the door of the guest house with the information that Simone was not to be disturbed, Urs Koch had allowed almost four weeks to elapse. During this time he had been forced to keep up to date about his wife's condition through a third party. Until now he had always found that the "don't run after women, and they'll come back by themselves" tactic had worked well.

He had come to know and value Simone's compliant nature and in spite of her current revolt — no doubt just a side effect of her pregnancy — he was sure his tactic would work.

When his father said, "You'll have to behave yourself for once, otherwise she'll get some silly ideas," he had asked, "suicide?"

When Thomas replied "divorce," Urs grinned and thought no more about it. He waited a while longer. Then, when she still did not get in touch he changed his tactics.

He went to the guest house with a large bouquet of camellias, Simone's favourite flowers, rang the bell and let her know, via Nurse Irma, that he would not go away until he was let in. Even if he had to wait all night.

It did the trick. Shortly afterwards he was led into Simone's room.

"I would like to apologise and ask you to come back to me again," he said, opening the conversation. Another part of his new tactics.

Even when Simone replied, "No, Urs, there's no point," he did not say the wrong thing, which, God knows, was not easy for him. "I'm conscious of the fact that I can never make up for what I've done."

Not until Simone answered, "No. So it's better if you don't even try," did he stray from his lines and flare up.

"Do you want me to shoot myself?"

Simone stayed calm. "It's all the same to me what you do. I'm getting a divorce."

For a moment she thought he was going to scream. But then he burst out laughing.

"You're joking. Just look at yourself. You'll soon be six months gone."

"I don't need to look at myself to know that."

"How do you imagine we're going to do it? Have a child and get divorced all at the same time?"

"Would you prefer it was one after the other, in the right order?"

"Neither. I don't want a divorce at all. There's no question of it. I'm not even going to discuss it."

"Fine. Neither am I." Simone went to the door and put her hand on the door handle.

"You're not going to throw me out of my own guest house."

"Please, just go."

Urs sat down on the bed. "I'll never agree to a divorce."

"I shall file for one."

"On what grounds?"

"Adultery, seven times over. If that's what you want."

Urs raised his eyebrows. "Your proof?"

"I'll move heaven and earth to find witnesses and proof."

Simone was still standing at the door with her hand on the door handle. She looked very determined.

Urs stood up and stepped closer to her. "That doesn't happen to me, my pregnant wife divorcing me after two years. Do you understand? It's as simple as that. It doesn't happen to me and it isn't going to happen to us. It doesn't happen to the Kochs."

"I couldn't care less what happens to the Kochs," Simone said and opened the door.

"Because it happened when you were pregnant, is that it?"

Simone shook her head.

"Why then?"

"Because I don't want to spend the rest of my life with you."

On one deceptive spring day – the föhn wind had swept the sky blue and left the gardeners scratching their heads – Koni painted "House for Snowsnowballs in May".

Simone had arrived a little too early for the photograph session. The occupational therapist was still with Konrad who was sitting at the table engrossed in his painting.

When Simone said hello he nodded briefly and turned back to his sheet of paper. He dipped the brush into the glass of muddied water and worked on a sheet of watercolour paper with it.

Simone sat down and waited. When the therapist said, "Good, Herr Lang, wonderful, I really like that. May I show it to Frau Koch?" she stood up and went over to the table.

The paper was still wet and crinkly. A watery, cloudy blue-grey on a white background. A wide brush stroke surrounded by browny yellow brush strokes of the same thickness radiating outwards. Underneath he had written in large bold capital letters, "KoniTomi Lang – House for Snowsnowballs in May."

"That's really very nice," Simone said. She sat next to Konrad and put the photographs in front of him on the table, while the occupational therapist tidied up her equipment. In all the activity arising from this Simone had not heard Dr Stäubli come into the room.

Not until she looked up at the camera, disheartened by the third "Tomikoni, Konitomi," did she see him standing by the table.

The windows in Elvira's breakfast room were open. The afternoon sun shone right into the room, as far as the little sofa where she was sitting with Dr Stäubli.

He had just come back from the guest house and had reported a further deterioration in Konrad's condition.

"Still no miracle cure then," she established.

"It doesn't look like it. When I came in he didn't even recognise himself on the old photographs. 'Konitomi' and 'Tomikoni' was all he said."

"What old photographs?"

"Simone was showing him the photographs of you and Thomas and Konrad, on some trip around Europe. The boys are probably about six."

Elvira stood up without speaking and disappeared through the door into the dressing room. Dr Stäubli remained seated and wondered what he might have said wrong.

After a short time Elvira returned with a photograph album. "These photographs?"

Stäubli took the album, leafed through it and nodded. "These are the very ones. Photocopied."

Elvira had to sit down. She suddenly looked almost as old as she really was. Dr Stäubli took hold of her wrist, looked at his watch and began to take her pulse.

Elvira jerked her hand out of his grip.

Dr O'Neill, Dr Kundert and Simone were in the staff room drinking coffee. They could see Konrad Lang sitting in an armchair on the living room monitor. His leg with the plaster was strung up and he was dozing. He had eaten nothing for breakfast or lunch.

Simone asked the question that had been troubling her for some time: "Is it completely impossible for the treatment to have accelerated the process?"

Kundert and O'Neill exchanged glances. "Yes. In so far as a scientist can rule anything out completely, yes," O'Neill answered.

"So it isn't completely impossible?"

"In cell cultures and in experiments on animals the process was halted after two to three weeks. In no case was it only slowed down and in no case was it accelerated. I would always concede that we are not sure whether the same thing happens with people, but

I am 100 per cent convinced that it couldn't have the opposite effect. But I can't prove that to you scientifically."

O'Neill poured himself some coffee. Simone and Kundert could not help thinking that his short speech was, as much as anything, an attempt to convince himself.

"It's been five weeks now with Konrad," Simone remarked.

"Thank you for reminding me," O'Neill grumbled.

"Perhaps it's the missing 20 per cent of the compound. Perhaps we should do a second application."

"We have permission for a single application."

They looked at the monitor. Konrad Lang moved. He opened his eyes, looked around the room in surprise, closed them again and carried on dozing.

"I still think it's working," O'Neill declared.

"If it isn't too late now," Simone said doubtfully.

"A person can continue to function with only parts of his brain," Dr Kundert said.

"They have to be the right parts of course," warned O'Neill.

"And if the wrong ones survive?" Simone wanted to know.

"One research team has shown that nerve cells can regenerate themselves under certain conditions. And we also know that in cell cultures we can treat cells in a number of ways that result in new contacts being established. Only we don't know whether that's good or bad news, because as a rule new contacts are established when the cells learn something. It's a very controlled process. If we trigger that process in an uncontrolled manner it may be that contacts are established that we don't really want."

"Which means that until we can solve that problem, the cells remain damaged."

O'Neill did not want to commit himself. Kundert carried on. "Neurology knows of many cases in which patients lose large parts of the brain after a head injury or operation. Sometimes they have to learn many things again right from the beginning, sometimes they have forgotten whole areas of their life. But more often than not they regain the functions that allow them to lead a normal life again."

"Do you believe that would be possible in Konrad Lang's case?"

"If the treatment is successful in stopping the deterioration, then, as long as he can still speak and understand language, there is a chance that we could stimulate the remaining cells into forming new contacts. He would probably have very large gaps in his memory and we would have to correct the organisation of his knowledge – with painstaking attention to detail. We are assuming this is possible otherwise we wouldn't be here."

"You're trying to encourage me," Simone smiled.

"Have I managed it?"

"A little bit."

Elvira had summoned Thomas and Urs to her study, where the informal board meetings of the company used to take place. She came straight to the point.

"Urs, your wife has been stealing from me."

Urs was flabbergasted. He had presumed it was about a business matter.

"I don't know how and with whose help, I only know that she is in possession of some photographs that I keep in a safe place." She pointed to the albums lying on the table. Urs picked one up and began to leaf through it.

"She must have forced her way in here and had copies made. Dr Stäubli has seen her looking at them with Koni."

Thomas also picked up an album and began to leaf through it.

"Why would she do a thing like that?"

"She wants to stimulate him with them, or something like that. It's supposed to re-establish his link with reality. Reality!"

"Are you just presuming that or do you know?"

"She was continually pestering me to give her some old photos. And Thomas, too. Wasn't she, Thomas?"

Thomas was absorbed in the photograph album. He looked up. "What?"

Elvira waved him aside and turned to Urs again. "I want the photos back, and right now."

"But you have them anyway. You said she only had copies made."

"I don't want her rooting around in the past with Konrad."

Urs shook his head and flicked through one of the albums. "Why have so many photographs been torn out?"

Elvira took the album from him. "Get me the photos back."

Thomas laughed out loud and held his album right up to Urs. "What do you see here?"

"Elvira in front of a convertible."

"And can't you see me and Koni?" he grinned.

Elvira snatched the album from his hands.

Thomas looked at her, stunned. Then he bent down to his son. "The Mercedes does a hundred and ten."

"Bring me the photos!" Elvira ordered and stood up.

"Is there something in the past that we're not supposed to know about?" Urs asked suspiciously.

"Bring me the photos!"

Urs stood up angrily. "And I thought it was about the company."

"It is about that, too." Elvira walked out of the room.

"She's getting old," Thomas explained to his son.

Konrad Lang was still on strike. He wouldn't eat, he couldn't be persuaded to paint a stroke, and he had hit the therapist when he had tried to put gentle pressure on him to do some harmless exercise. Dr Kundert had given instructions that Konrad would have to be fed intravenously that night if he also refused his evening meal.

They had decided that Simone would show him the photos from the oldest album today in the hope that this would rouse him from his apathy.

Koni sat in his dressing gown in his armchair in the living room. It had not been possible to dress him. He did not react when

Simone came into the room, nor when she pulled up a chair and sat down next to him.

"Koni," she began, "I have a few new pictures here. I need your help with them." She opened the album.

The first photo showed a young Elvira in the conservatory at the Villa Rhododendron. She was wearing a calf-length skirt and a sleeveless, high-necked pullover with a round white collar peeping out above the neckline. She was sitting on a lounger, knitting. In the foreground you could see the back of a Biedermeier armchair, which was now in the boudoir in the Villa with different upholstery.

"This lady here, who's she?"

Konrad was not looking.

Simone held the album up to his face. "This lady here."

Koni sighed. "Fräulein Berg," he answered, as if to a difficult child.

"Oh, and I thought it was Elvira."

Koni shook his head at such stupidity.

Next to the picture of Elvira was an area of white where a photograph had been removed from the album. Simone leafed through.

The next one was taken from the south of the Villa. It showed the steps up to the large terrace where Wilhelm Koch was standing. He was wearing pale trousers, a white shirt and tie and a dark waistcoat, but no jacket. He had a round, bald head and was smiling artificially into the camera.

"And this man?"

Koni had resigned himself to the fact that he had to explain even the most obvious things to this woman with all her questions. "Papa Direktor," he answered patiently.

"Whose papa is he?"

"Tomitomi's."

On the opposite page, alongside the white spaces that marked a torn-out photograph, you could see the pavilion. The rhododendrons were still small bushes and the spruce trees in the background were no longer there today. Two old ladies in broad-brimmed hats and shapeless, wide, almost full-length dresses were standing by the iron railings.

"Aunt Sophie and Aunt Klara," Koni explained, unasked. His interest was aroused now. A relieved Dr Kundert took note of it at the monitor.

Simone and Konrad went through the album together page by page. There were pictures of the grounds, of "Papa Direktor", of "Fräulein Berg" and of "Aunt Sophie" and "Aunt Klara". And pictures now marked only by an area of white.

One of the last shots showed Elvira in a short-sleeved floral, two-piece summer dress standing by the balustrade on the terrace. Next to her stood Wilhelm Koch. He had his arm round her possessively, a gesture not in any of the other photos. In the background you could see the lake at the bottom of the valley and the range of hills on the other side, which at that time had hardly been built on.

"Papa Direktor and Mama," Konrad commented.

"Whose mama?"

"Tomitomi's," Konrad Lang sighed.

"Is Fräulein Berg Tomitomi's mama?"

"She is now."

With the last photograph, around which all the others had been torn out, something strange happened. The photograph showed a border in front of a hedge and a tub with an oleander bush in flower which the photographer had probably been trying to capture. Koni studied it closely for a long time. Finally he said, "Papa Direktor and Tomitomi."

Simone glanced up at the hidden lens.

"Papa Direktor" – Koni pointed to a spot in the oleander bush – "and Tomitomi." He pointed to a place right underneath it.

Not until Simone looked more closely did she notice that the photographer had forgotten to wind on the film and that the photograph was a double exposure. In the blur of the hedge she could pick out Wilhlem Koch's bald head. And the outline of a child on his knee. Dr Kundert and Simone sat for a long time with the photos and tried to make sense of Konrad's answers. It was no secret that Elvira's maiden name had been Berg. But if this name was familiar to Konrad he must already have known her, before his mother Anna Lang took up her post at the Villa Rhododendron. By that time Elvira was already Frau Direktor Koch.

Of course it was not improbable that the young Elvira, as the wife of a man so much older than herself, had engaged somebody she already knew for company.

Much more curious was the double exposure. The more she trained her eyes to see the weaker of the two pictures, the clearer it became. There was no question that the man was Willhelm Koch. But the child did not look like Thomas. He had neither the characteristically shaped head nor the close-set eyes. If the little boy resembled anyone, he looked more like the childhood photos of Konrad Lang.

"Why is there not one single photograph of Thomas in the whole album?" Dr Kundert asked.

"Perhaps they are the ones that are missing."

"Why would anyone tear them out?"

Simone spoke aloud what they had both been thinking. "Because the child in the photos is not Thomas Koch."

That same night Urs phoned Simone from the Villa. "I have to speak to you. Now. I'm coming over."

"There's nothing to talk about."

"And what about the photos you stole from Elvira?"

"I only borrowed them and had copies made."

"You broke into her house."

"I used the key."

"You forced your way into her private accommodation. There's no excuse for what you did. You'll have to apologise."

"I'm not apologising."

"Give her the photos back right away."

"She's afraid of those photographs. And it's slowly dawning on me why."

"Why?"

"There's something odd about their past. She's frightened that Konrad might expose something."

"What on earth could a sick addle-brained man possibly expose?"

"Ask Elvira! Ask her who was in the photos she's torn out!"

Tomi lay in the peat in the potting shed, warm under his jute sacks. He stayed absolutely quiet. There was snow outside and it was snowing fazonetli. She was looking for him.

When she found him she would stab him. Like Papa Direktor.

He had seen it.

He had woken up because Papa Direktor was talking in a strange loud voice, the voice he used when he had been drinking schnapps. He heard him coming up the stairs and staggering into the room where he and mama slept.

Tomi stood up and looked through the crack in the door, which they always left open until they went to bed. His mama and Koni's helped Papa Direktor into the room and put him on the bed. Koni's mama gave him some schnapps. They undressed him and laid him down on the bed.

Then Koni's mama stuck a needle in him. She covered him up, switched off the light and went out of the room. Tomi opened the door wider and went up to Papa Direktor. He smelt of schnapps.

Suddenly the light went on and Koni's mama came back. She took him by the hand and put him to bed.

"Why did you stick a needle in Papa Direktor?" he asked.

"If you say that again I'll stick one in you too," she replied.

Early in the morning he heard voices in the next room. He climbed out of bed to see what was wrong. There was a crowd of people there, including his mama and Koni's. Papa Direktor was lying absolutely still in the bed.

Then Koni's mama saw him and led him away. "What's wrong with Papa Direktor?" he asked.

"He's dead," she answered.

It was snowing outside, getting deeper and deeper, rising up over the roof and the trees.

Tomi closed his eyes. They wouldn't find him here.

But when he woke up his arm was sore. He looked down: his arm was bandaged and there was a needle stuck in it. So they had found him after all.

He tore the needle out. The light went on. He closed his eyes. "Don't stab me!"

There was a light on in the Stöckli as well. It was late when Urs arrived at Elvira's. They sat in the drawing room. The remains of a fire glowed in the hearth.

"She says you're afraid of the photos because of something odd in the past. You're afraid Koni might remember it."

"What do you mean 'odd'?"

Urs could not tell whether Elvira was worried.

"She said to ask you who was in the photographs that have been torn out."

Yes, she was worried now. "I don't know what she means."

"I do. I saw the album here, the one with the torn-out photos."

"I don't remember. Probably I didn't like myself in them."

Elvira looked at Urs. He was different from his father. He didn't run away from problems. He wanted to know what lay ahead of him, so that he could take the right course of action. Urs Koch was the right man for Koch Industries. He would preserve it as Elvira had built it to be: big, healthy and beyond suspicion.

"If there's something I ought to know then you should tell me."

Elvira nodded. She would not let things get to the stage that he had to know.

*

The next morning Elvira went to the guest house. Simone and Dr Kundert were with Konrad. Simone was trying to persuade Konrad to eat some breakfast, but he was just staring at the ceiling.

Nurse Irma came in. "Frau Senn's outside and says she wants to speak to Frau Koch."

Simone and Kundert exchanged glances. "Bring her in," Simone said.

Shortly afterwards Nurse Irma came back. "She doesn't want to come in. She says you have to come out. She's quite angry."

"If she wants to speak to me she can talk to me in here."

"Do I have to say that? She'll kill me."

"You're stronger than she is."

Nurse Irma went out and was gone for quite a while. When she came back Elvira was with her. She was pale and finding it difficult to stay calm. She ignored Konrad and Dr Kundert and stood in front of Simone. She had to pull herself together before she could speak.

"Give me the photos!"

Simone was just as pale. "No. They're needed for therapeutic purposes."

"Give me the photos now!"

The two women stared at each other, neither of them prepared to yield.

Then Konrad's voice rang out from the bed. "Mama, why did you stick a needle in Papa Direktor?"

Elvira did not look at Konrad. Her gaze wandered from Nurse Irma to Dr Kundert to Simone.

Then she turned and walked out of the room.

Simone went up to Konrad's bed. "Did she stick a needle in Papa Direktor?"

Konrad put his index finger to his lips. Ssh.

Since Simone was no longer being fed intravenously and Konrad Lang was no longer eating, Luciana Dotti concentrated on Simone.

She was a qualified diet cook certainly, but she did not hold with diets for pregnant women. She cooked her *fettuccine al prosciutto e asparagi, pizzoccheri della valtellina, penne ai quattro formaggi,* and every time Simone came near the kitchen between meal times she tried to pop a little roll of Parma ham or a slice of salami into her mouth. *Per il bambino.*

Today lunch was *conchiglie alla salsiccia e panna* and Simone had had two large portions pressed on her. Even as she was clearing the table in the staff room Luciana announced, "This evening I'm making *maccheroni al forno alla rustica,* baked with a topping of aubergines and smoked mozzarella. It's pure poetry."

Simone was quick to react. "Oh, didn't I tell you? I've been invited out for a meal tonight."

Luciana bore this with some dignity. "Have a nice time," she wished her curtly and cleared away. Nurse Irma helped her.

Dr Kundert looked at Simone. She felt his eyes on her and looked up. "Aubergines with smoked mozzarella. I didn't know what else I could do."

"You haven't been invited out?"

She shook her head.

"And how will you solve that one?"

She shrugged her shoulders.

"May I offer you my assistance?"

Elvira Senn spent the whole day in her bedroom and did not allow anyone in to see her. In the evening when it was time for her insulin she went to the little fridge in the bathroom, took out her insulin pen, held it over the washbasin and pressed the plunger. Then she turned on both taps and let the water run for a long time.

Tomi lay in bed crying. But only quietly. When Koni's mama heard him she would come and stick a needle in him. She had said so herself.

Koni's mama was sleeping in the next room, which made it quite likely that she would hear him. She was called Mama Anna now. And mama was called Mama Elvira. Otherwise no one knew which mama they meant because Koni's mama and his mama were both called Mama.

Tomi was crying because he had to sleep in Koni's little bed in Koni's room.

It was a game. Sometimes Tomi played Koni and Koni Tomi. Then Koni was allowed to sleep in Tomi's bed and Tomi in Koni's.

But Tomi didn't like the game. Koni's room was in the house behind the Villa where Koni's mama slept. Mama Anna. He was frightened of her.

He heard voices arguing in the stairwell. The door opened and the light went on.

"Don't stab me," Tomikoni said.

"No one's going to hurt you, child," the voice said. "We're going to take you to bed."

Tomi was pleased. It wasn't Mama Anna. It was Aunt Sophie and Aunt Klara.

Elvira was sitting up high in her enormous bed. The föhn wind had died down, March was showing itself in its true colours again. The dusky pink crêpe de Chine curtains were drawn, admitting only a little light from the grey afternoon.

On the Biedermeier bureau next to the bed and on the wide Empire chest were two lamps with silk shades, which bathed the room in a pearly light.

Urs sat on a small upholstered armchair by the side of the bed. Elvira had begged him to come to her as she had some important things to say to him.

"You asked me yesterday if there were things in the past that you should know about. There are."

Two hours later, when Urs looked out over the guest house from one of the Villa's windows, he was not so untroubled as he had led Elvira to believe. He returned Dr Stäubli's wave perfunctorily as the doctor passed by on his way to the Stöckli.

Elvira had telephoned Stäubli and told him her blood sugar level. "There's something wrong there," he had said and set out immediately.

When he took her readings he frowned and took out a capsule of old insulin, a type of insulin that works quickly but is effective only for a short time and which is used for an initial dose when there is no insulin present at all.

He picked up a syringe and injected her in the top of her thigh. "You definitely haven't eaten a pound of chocolates?"

Elvira waved him aside. She hated sweet things.

"And you're sure you've given yourself all your injections?"

"I think so. But perhaps it's better if you check the fridge in the bathroom. I am an old woman."

Dr Stäubli went into the bathroom. Elvira leant out of bed and delved into his bag. When he came back a little later he was puzzled. "It all seems to be fine. The records and the actual consumption tally. I'll send the opened cartridge to the lab."

Dr Stäubli promised to have a look at her again the next day.

When she was alone Elvira felt under the bedclothes, brought out a capsule of insulin and put it on the bureau.

Simone and Dr Kundert had reserved a table at Fresco, one of the many old local bars, which the new owners had completely gutted and turned into a trendy restaurant with white paint, paper tablecloths, good-humoured staff and unpretentious international cuisine.

They ordered a Greek salad, and tacos as a main course. The waitress was friendly and informal. "I think we're the only people in this room not on first-name terms," Simone remarked to Dr Kundert. From then on they were.

"I've wanted to ask you this for a long time. Why are you doing this for him? You don't really know him."

"I don't know." She thought about it. "I'm just sorry for him. He's like a worn-out teddy bear, brought out now and then when you're bored and the rest of the time totally neglected. It can't have been any life."

Kundert nodded. Simone's eyes filled with tears. She took a handkerchief out of her handbag and wiped them away. "Sorry. This has been happening more often since I've been pregnant." She recovered herself. "Who do you think is on the missing photos?"

"Konrad Lang," Kundert answered, without hesitation.

"I think so too." Kundert poured some wine as Simone continued speaking: "That would also explain why he confuses Koni and Tomi on the old photos."

"They told him he was Koni, but he's Tomi."

"How can something like that be possible?"

"It isn't impossible in four-year-olds: Tomikoni, Konitomi, Mama Vira, Mama Anna." Kundert was becoming agitated. "Both the women confused the boys to such an extent, they played with their identities for so long, that the boys no longer knew who they were. And then they swapped them round."

"And now, with the illness, Koni's old identity is reappearing?"

"It's conceivable that in his case his understanding is so confused that this information has been given a higher priority. Or perhaps his ability to remember has been liberated by the illness, so his old memories have come back to the surface."

"But why should the two women swap the children round?"

"For Anna Lang's child to inherit the company."

The whole thing made no sense to Simone. "Why should Elvira do that for Anna Lang?"

The Fresco had filled up. The babble of voices and laughter of carefree people and the background noise of tangos, bel cantos and rock classics absorbed the enormity of what Simone now said in a low voice: "In that case, Koni would be the true heir to Koch Industries."

*

Even at this late aperitif-hour the bar at Des Alpes was not exactly crowded. A few hotel guests, a few businessmen, a couple whose relationship was not yet so firmly established that they wanted to be seen in more crowded bars and the Hurni sisters, who were using the pianist's break to signal for their bill.

Charlotte, the afternoon barmaid, had been relieved by Evi, who would also not see 50 again and was obviously one of the few regular clients at the hotel's own solarium.

Dean Martin was singing "You're Nobody Till Somebody Loves You" on tape during the interval.

Urs Koch sat in a corner with Alfred Zeller. Each had a glass of whisky in front of him, Urs's with ice, Alfred's with ice and water. They had known each other since their youth. They had been at St Pierre's together, as had their fathers. After boarding school Alfred had studied law and joined his father's well-known practice, whose most important client was Koch Industries. Alongside his work for Koch Industries, he had become Urs's personal legal adviser and, in so far as was possible in such a situation, also his friend.

Urs had telephoned him and asked whether he was by any chance free that evening. "Yes, by chance, I am," Alfred had answered, deciding to give the theatre premiere a miss.

Urs did not know how to begin.

"Pity about the old place," Alfred remarked so as to say something. When Urs failed to understand what he meant, he explained: "The Des Alpes. In the red for years. The mortgage company has called in its loan. Apparently they want to take it over and turn it into an education centre. I'll miss the bar. Quiet enough to be able to discuss something. Noisy enough not to be overheard doing it. You can be by yourselves."

That was sufficient cue for Urs. "What I want to ask you has to be kept to ourselves too. It'll strike you as odd and it could lead you to draw the wrong conclusions. Just regard it as a purely theoretical discussion. I can't tell you any more about the background apart from that it isn't what you think."

"OK."

"Here's the scenario: in the thirties, a young woman marries a well-to-do factory owner, a widower with a five-year-old son; his only heirs are his wife and his son. She exchanges the son for the son of a friend and no one notices. What happens if the matter comes to light today?"

"Why should it do that?"

"It just does. It's a hypothesis. So what happens?"

Alfred thought about it for a moment. "Nothing."

"Nothing?"

"Fraud is statute-barred after ten years."

"Are you sure of that?"

"I do know the limitation period for fraud."

Urs stirred his drink with a plastic giraffe. The ice cubes rattled. "Another question, even more hypothetical: say the man did not die a natural death, but the wife helped it along a bit without anyone noticing."

"Murder becomes statute-barred after twenty years, fraud after ten. If nothing has come to light in this time then that's the end of the matter."

"And the inheritance?"

"The woman as a murderer is disqualified from inheriting for life. That is, if the matter came out today, she would automatically lose all claims to the inheritance."

"And have to return it to the rightful heir?"

"Legally, yes."

Urs nodded. "That's what I thought."

"But if she doesn't do that, there's nothing he can do about it now. The action for the recovery of an inheritance lapses after 30 years."

"And the substitute son?"

"It's even less time for that. For him it lapses after ten. And because there is nothing he can do about having been swapped as a child, he is not even disqualified from inheriting."

"Are you sure?" Urs beckoned to the barmaid.

Alfred Zeller grinned. "Our inheritance laws protect the property better than the heirs."

"Same again?" Evi asked.

At around the same time Elvira Senn was standing in the bathroom dressed to go out and was putting the whole contents of the ampoule she had stolen from Dr Stäubli into three syringes.

She wrapped them in a dry face flannel and put it into her handbag. Then she went into the hall, took the bunch of spring flowers out of the vase next to the hat-stand and went outside. The lamps bordering the path through the rhododendrons had yellow halos of drizzle.

Konitomi was lying in bed. Tomikoni was in the bunk above him. Their mothers were sleeping next door.

The bunks rattled and shook. They were travelling through the night on a train. They were on a long journey.

It was dark; the blind at the window was pulled down. When the train stopped they heard noises and voices by the window, then footsteps and people by the door, talking heatedly in foreign languages.

After a while the bunks jolted. The train creaked and screeched and rattled on, slowly at first, then faster and faster. Rattling on, rattling on, rattling on.

Tomikoni and he each had two mamas now: Mama Anna and Mama Vira. So that they were not so sad at having no papa and no aunts.

He was sad all the same. Tomikoni wasn't.

Nurse Ranjah was surprised when she opened the door to the elderly lady with the large bunch of flowers.

"I'm Elvira Senn. I wanted to bring Herr Lang a few flowers. Is he still up?"

"He's in bed but I think he's still awake. He'll be very pleased to see you."

She let Elvira Senn in, took the flowers from her and helped her out of her raincoat. Then she knocked on Konrad's door and opened it: "Surprise for you, Herr Lang."

Konrad had closed his eyes. When he heard Ranjah's voice he opened them. As soon as he saw Elvira he closed them again.

"He's very tired because he isn't eating anything," Ranjah whispered.

"I'll just sit here for a little while, if you don't mind."

When Ranjah came back into the room with the flowers in a vase, Elvira was sitting on the chair by the side of the bed, watching Koni sleeping.

Ranjah was touched. The old lady had finally found it in her to visit him. When she was outside again she resisted the impulse to watch them on the monitor in the staff room and decided to wait discreetly in the living room until Koni's visitor left.

Simone Koch and Peter Kundert were on their third coffee. The paper tablecloth was covered with scribbled signs and words. There was Konitomi → Tomikoni and Tomi → Koni and Mama Vira → Mama Anna. Kundert found it easier to think if he made notes.

The longer they talked about it the more sense the whole thing made.

"That explains the long journey. So that the children could be re-programmed undisturbed," Simone said.

"And Elvira could dismiss the staff and employ new ones on their return," Kundert suggested.

"And she would have had to keep the boys away from the two old aunts. They would certainly have noticed something."

"So why didn't they notice anything when the children came back?"

"Maybe they were already dead. They look very old in the photos."

Kundert jotted down "When Aunts †", tore the note out of the tablecloth and put it with the others in the breast pocket of his shirt.

The Fresco had emptied. But now the cinemas were out and the restaurant was filling up again. Simone Koch and Peter Kundert did not seem any different from all the people sitting at tables trying to fathom out the film they had just seen.

"Only something doesn't fit," Kundert said, brooding. "Anna Lang. Or rather, what induced Elvira to go along with the swap?"

"He called her Mama. 'Mama, why did you stick a needle in Papa Direktor?'"

Kundert hesitated for a moment. "Perhaps she injected Wilhelm Koch with something."

"She killed him," Simone said bluntly.

"I suppose we can't rule that out." He wrote, "Cause of Koch's death??", tore off the paper and put it with the others.

"I think it would be better if we went back now," Simone said.

Two hours after Elvira Senn had left, Nurse Ranjah noticed that all was not well with Konrad Lang.

When she did her routine check on the patient he was bathed in sweat, deathly white, his heart was racing and his whole body was trembling. His lips were moving as if he were trying to say something.

She put her ear right up to his mouth but the muttering and mumbling made no sense.

"What's the matter, baby, tell me, tell me!" She tried to read his lips.

"Angry? Why are you angry, baby?"

Konrad shook his head. Again his lips tried to form the word.

"Hungry? You're hungry?"

Konrad Lang nodded.

Nurse Ranjah ran out and came back with a jar. She unscrewed it, fished out an almond dripping in honey and popped it into his mouth. And then another, and another.

Konrad swallowed the almonds with a craving such as she had never seen in a sick person before, apart from in diabetics whose blood sugar level had suddenly dropped. But Konrad Lang was not a diabetic.

The strange thing was: the more honeyed almonds he ate, the better he became. His pulse returned to normal, the sweating eased off and he regained some colour.

Nurse Ranjah had just put the last almond in his mouth when the door opened and Dr Kundert and Simone came in. They were both relieved.

"Nurse Ranjah's magic has worked again," Simone said. "Konrad's eating."

Nurse Ranjah told them what had happened. The symptoms indicated hypoglycaemia. Dr Kundert measured Konrad's blood sugar level and confirmed that it was still at its lowest possible level. Nurse Ranjah had probably saved his life with her honeyed almonds. When Kundert injected some glucose into the rubber connecting piece of Konrad's drip he found some small puncture holes. He had not injected any medicines himself in the last 24 hours.

"When Herr Lang tore the drip off last night I renewed the whole apparatus."

Dr Kundert searched for an explanation. A patient with normal blood sugar levels does not go into a hypoglycaemic coma out of the blue. "You didn't notice anything unusual about him during the evening?"

"Only that he was very tired. Even when Frau Senn came, he went on sleeping."

"Frau Senn was here?" Simone asked.

"Yes. She was with him for over an hour."

"Did you notice anything unusual then?"

"I wasn't in the room."

"And on the monitor?"

"I wasn't watching that either. There was someone with him."

Kundert and Simone were already on the stairs.

Thomas arrived at the guest house at two o'clock in the morning looking dishevelled and bloated. Simone had got him out of bed.

"If this isn't a matter of life and death you'll be in real trouble," he had threatened when she insisted he should bring his glasses and come at once.

"That's exactly what it is," she answered. "Life and death."

She phoned Urs too. A sleepy Candelaria assured her that he was still not back.

She took Thomas into the staff room, where she introduced him to Dr Kundert and Nurse Ranjah. He acknowledged their greetings gruffly and declined a chair. He did not intend to stay long, he said. Kundert played the tape from the point when Nurse Ranjah came in with the flowers and then left Elvira alone with Konrad.

"She visited Koni?" Thomas said in surprise. "When was that?"

Simone looked at her watch. "Seven hours ago."

The picture stayed the same. Konrad Lang was lying on his back with his eyes closed. Elvira Senn sat next to him.

Dr Kundert fast-forwarded the tape on to the place where Elvira leapt up from her armchair for a short time and jumped back again. He stopped the tape, rewound it a little and let it run at normal speed.

Now they watched how Elvira carefully got up, bent over Konrad and sat down again. This scene was repeated twice.

When Elvira jumped up for the fourth time during the fast-forwarding, she stayed up and fiddled around by his bed. Kundert played the action at normal speed.

Elvira stood up. She bent over Konrad. She straightened up. She opened her handbag and took out a piece of brightly coloured cloth. She put it on the bedside table. She opened it up. She took something in her right hand. She went to the drip tube with it.

She held the tube in her left hand. What she did next was hidden by her right shoulder.

She went back to the bedside table. She laid the object on the bright cloth. She picked up a second object. She went back to the drip tube. When she held the object up to the light it showed up clearly for a moment against the blanket. It was a syringe.

What she did next was hidden by her shoulder again.

It was only absolutely clear the third time. It was a syringe and she was sticking it into the rubber connecting piece in the drip tube.

Elvira packed the cloth back into her bag and left the room without so much as casting a single glance at Konrad.

"What was that?" Thomas asked flabbergasted.

"Attempted murder. Insulin. Herr Lang was meant to die of a hypoglycaemic coma. Not provable. He survived only thanks to Nurse Ranjah."

Thomas Koch sat down. For a long time he looked as if he had been hit. Then he turned to Simone. "Why did she do it?"

"Ask her yourself."

"Perhaps she's gone mad."

"Let's hope she can prove it," Dr Kundert said.

The next morning Elvira Senn felt marvellous; she had had a wonderful sleep. She woke up in the early morning light with a feeling of immense relief, got up immediately and ran a bath.

When she went into her breakfast room three quarters of an hour later she saw that something must be wrong. Thomas was lying fully dressed on the little sofa with his mouth wide open. He was fast asleep. She shook him. He sat up and tried to work out where he was.

"What are you doing here?"

Thomas thought about it for a moment. "I've been waiting for you."

"Why?"

"I have to talk to you."

"What about?"

He'd forgotten.

Elvira assisted him. "Is it something to do with Koni?"

Thomas thought about it. Suddenly the memories of the previous night came flooding back. "You tried to kill him."

"Who says so?"

"I saw it. It's all recorded on tape."

This jolted her. "Konrad's room is filmed?"

"Only the best was good enough for you."

"What does it show?"

"You injecting something into the drip three times."

"And is he alive?"

"The night nurse saved him. With honey, as far as I can gather."

Elvira went quiet.

"Why did you do it?"

No reply.

"Why did you do it?"

"He's dangerous."

"Koni? Dangerous? To whom?"

"To us: you and Urs and me. Koch Industries."

"I don't understand."

"His sick mind has remembered things that mustn't be allowed to come out."

"What sort of things?"

Outside the window a new day was dawning, overcast like the last. Elvira no longer had the strength to be silent.

"Do you know how old I was when I came to Wilhelm Koch as a nanny? Nineteen. And he was 56. A very old man, to a 19-year-old. He was aggressive and drunk and 56."

"But you married him."

"People make mistakes at 19, especially when they have no money and no qualifications."

There was a knock at the door. Montserrat came in with a tray. When she saw Thomas she took a second place setting from the sideboard. Elvira and Thomas were silent until they were alone again.

"I took Anna into the house so that I wasn't alone and entirely at his mercy. Then she had the idea," – Elvira paused – "then she had the idea of killing him."

Thomas put out his hand for his coffee cup. But it was trembling so much that he abandoned the attempt. She waited for him to say something. Thomas was trying to understand her confession, in all its gross horror.

"Anna had started training to be a nurse. She knew how to do it without it being discovered: a large dose of insulin. They die of shock. The insulin is impossible to detect. Only the puncture is detectable. If someone looks for it."

"You killed my father?" Thomas Koch said now.

Elvira reached for her glass of orange juice. Her hand was steady. She held it for a moment and then put it down, without having drunk from it. "Wilhelm Koch only became your father after his death."

Thomas didn't understand.

"After his death we switched you. Wilhelm Koch was Konrad's father."

While she was giving Thomas time to formulate his next question she reached for her glass again. But now her hand was trembling too. She put it down again.

"Why did you do that?" Thomas managed to ask.

"We wanted you to get everything, not Konrad."

Thomas needed some time to digest this. "But why?" he asked eventually. "Why me?"

"I felt nothing for Konrad. He reminded me of Wilhelm Koch."

"And with me? What ties did you have to me?"

"Anna and I were half-sisters."

Thomas stood up and went over to the window. A monotonous steady rain had set in. "Anna Lang is my mother," Thomas murmured. "And you . . . are my aunt."

Elvira said nothing.

For a few minutes Thomas just stood there, staring at the wet rhododendrons. Then he shook his head. "How could a mother just leave her child in the care of her half-sister like that?"

"It wasn't the plan for her to stay in London. She had fallen in love. And then the war started."

"And who is my father?" he finally asked.

"He isn't important."

Thomas turned away from the window. "What happens when this all comes out?"

"It isn't going to come out."

"They'll call in the authorities."

"You and Urs, talk to Simone. Try to dissuade her. At all costs."

Thomas nodded. "And what about you?"

"I'd better go away for a few days."

He shook his head and made to go out, but remembered, gave her a hug and kissed her on both cheeks.

"Go on now," she answered, giving him a tight squeeze. When he had gone, she had tears in her eyes. "You fool," she muttered and then went into the bathroom.

When his father woke him shortly after seven o'clock, Urs was hungover. It had been a late night. He had celebrated the favourable information from Fredi Zeller rather too well and had ended up around two a.m. in a club that was really no longer appropriate for him since his appointment to the board of directors. At four o'clock in the morning he had found himself in a hotel room in the old town with a delightful Brazilian girl, who, as it turned out later, had a penis. Which at the time had not particularly disturbed him. Quite the opposite, as he was forced to admit to himself afterwards, to his horror.

He had been home for only two hours. He had set the alarm clock for ten o'clock and wanted to have lunch with Elvira to reassure her about the past.

He realised from his father's halting explanation that it was too late for that now.

All he could do was to get his head as clear as possible and make a start on the damage limitation.

He rang Fredi Zeller before he got out of bed. He only hoped Fredi was not so hungover.

Meanwhile in the guest house they were looking after the patient. One thing was worrying Dr Kundert: the nerve cells of the brain are exclusively dependent on glucose for gaining energy. Its sugar reserves last for ten to fifteen minutes at the most. According to the length and severity of a low sugar level it can lead to serious damage, and to personality changes, even in a healthy brain.

In a brain like Konrad Lang's the results could be catastrophic.

The psychological tests that Kundert carried out before Simone's return (she had gone to her lawyer to deposit the video-tape with him) had reassured him a little. Konrad Lang's readings were no worse. Considering his experiences the previous night he was amazingly alert.

But now, as Simone looked through the photos with Konrad, the doctor's spirits sank.

Konrad did not recognise anything or anyone in any of the pictures. None of the prompts produced a reaction. "Papa Direktor" was a foreign term to him, "Konitomi" and "Tomikoni" elicited a polite smile and "Mama Vira" a shrug of the shoulders.

Simone persisted. Three times she started again from the beginning, three times with the same result.

The fourth time, when she showed the young Elvira in the conservatory and asked, "And this, is this Fräulein Berg?" he answered slightly irritably, "As I said, I don't know."

As I said?

*

234

The swishing of the rainwater thrown up by the tyres of the heavy car could hardly be heard inside the black Daimler.

Elvira Senn was staring out of the window at the small bleak towns of eastern Switzerland and the few warmly wrapped-up people who had ventured out into the sleet.

Schöller was not really Elvira's chauffeur, but it often happened that she would summon him at short notice for one of her spur-of-the-moment excursions. It was part of the game that she did not tell him where they were going. Sometimes because she wanted to surprise him, sometimes because she did not know the destination herself.

But this time she seemed to know exactly. She knew the little places well: Aesch by Neftenbach, Hengart, Andelfingen, Trüllikon. Elvira Senn directed Schöller with brief instructions. After leaving Basadingen, a godforsaken place whose name Schöller knew from warnings to walkers and joggers to beware of ticks, she asked him to turn off into a country lane.

After a few detached houses and farms the asphalt stopped. Twice the Daimler's silencer scraped on bumps in the worn-down road. An electricity substation, a fenced-in pumping station, then woods. Schöller looked in the mirror. Elvira was waving him on.

Stacks of neatly labelled wood sawn to precise lengths lined the roadside. She asked him to stop at a pile of newly felled tree trunks. Schöller switched off the engine. Heavy raindrops dripped from the branches of the fir trees on to the roof of the car.

"Where are we now?" Schöller asked.

"At the beginning," Elvira answered.

One beautiful Sunday morning in March 1932 an ill-matched couple were walking through the Geisswald. The man was about 40, well-built, with thin blond hair and a curly moustache. His face was flushed from an early morning drink with the churchgoers in the village pub. He wore a coarse Sunday suit and buried his hands deep in his trouser pockets.

His partner was a 14-year-old girl, blond, with a round, pretty, baby face. She was wearing a calf-length skirt, woollen stockings, knee-length lace-up boots and a cardigan. Her hands were in a muff made of worn rabbit skin.

The girl lived with her parents and half-sister in a yellow pebble-dashed house on the edge of the village of Basadingen. Her mother worked at home sewing shoulder pads for a clothing factory in St Gall. Her father was a sawmill worker. One of the few with ten fingers, as he liked to emphasise.

The man was one of her father's workmates. He was in and out of their house all the time. No one made any objection, as he was a real comedian and they did not have much to laugh about. On his right hand he had only a thumb and index finger. The band-saw had taken the other three. When it had happened, a deathly pale apprentice had brought him the three fingers. "Throw 'em to the dog," he had said. Or so the anecdote went.

This right hand had something obscene about it that fascinated the girl. Once, when he noticed her staring at his fingers, he said, "This can do anything you'd want from a hand." She blushed. From then on he would arrange to be alone with her and then embarrass her with all kinds of suggestive remarks.

She was an inquisitive girl. It did not need much to persuade her to meet him in the Geisswald one Sunday after church. He wanted to show her something she had never seen before. She was not so naive as to believe it was a rare mushroom.

But now as he dragged her into a logging path that led away from the road through the woods her heart was beating fast. And when they came to a clearing covered with fresh sawdust and he asked her to sit down next to him on the trunk of a fir tree she said, "I'd rather go back."

But she offered no resistance when he began to touch her with his callused claw. She made no sound either when he fell on top of her. She closed her eyes and waited for it to be over.

When she had straightened her clothes and stopped crying he

accompanied her to the edge of the wood. Then he packed her off home. "Don't you dare say a word to anyone about this," he said for the hundredth time. It was not necessary. Elvira Berg would not have dreamt of telling a living soul.

She had only recently started her periods so when she was late she never gave it a second thought. In May she began to suffer from dizziness, then nausea. In June her mother took her to a doctor in Constance whom she knew from the days of her first marriage. Elvira was four months pregnant.

She went into a home in the canton of Freiburg run by nuns who were experienced in such cases. In November Elvira gave birth to a healthy boy. The nuns baptised him Konrad, after Saint Konrad, who was Bishop of Constance in the ninth century.

In January 1933 Elvira began her year in western Switzerland. She went to a family in Lausanne for whom she kept house in return for pocket money. She left Konrad in the care of her mother, who passed him off as the illegitimate child of Anna, Elvira's half-sister. The village gossips of Basadingen knew no mercy.

Anna was the daughter from her mother's first marriage to a barber from Constance who had fallen at the Marne in July 1918. Her name was Lang like her father; she was 19 and went to the nurse's training college in Zürich. Not until Christmas Eve in 1933, on her first visit to Basadingen that year, did she learn that Konrad, who was now over a year old, was regarded in the village as her own illegitimate child. She left that same night, but did not carry out her threat to tell the whole world the truth.

Two years later Elvira was pregnant again, this time by "monsieur", the father of the family she was working for. She was familiar with the signs by now and was absolutely determined not to let things advance as far again. She went to her sister, who was in her last year of training to be a nurse. When it became clear to Anna what Elvira was asking her to do, she was shocked and refused. But over the preceding years Elvira had discovered and developed her talent at getting what she had set her mind on.

On the second day of her visit her sister agreed to help her.

During her training, Anna had been present twice at the termination of a pregnancy. She was confident of performing the operation herself. She smuggled out of the hospital the instruments which, as far as she could remember, she needed. On the interior-sprung mattress in her attic room she set to work on Elvira, who had anaesthetised herself with half a bottle of plum schnapps.

It was a disaster. Elvira lost an enormous amount of blood and would not have survived had Anna not sent for an ambulance at the last moment.

Elvira Berg spent four weeks in hospital. "Thank God for that," she sighed, when they told her she would never be able to have any more children.

Anna Lang lost her training place and was given a suspended prison sentence.

Christmas 1935 and the two half-sisters were back in Basadingen in the small, draughty house. They did not know which looked more bleak: their present or their future.

But shortly after New Year their fates took a different turn. Elvira answered an advertisement from an employment agency looking for a nanny for a widower "of considerable means". She was put on the shortlist and was to present herself to Wilhelm Koch, a rich factory owner. When she was offered the job she had little doubt that her success was due solely to the enthusiastic reference that her "monsieur" had written for her.

Thomas Koch was four, an easy-going, placid child who did not make any great demands on her: quite the opposite of his father. But this time Elvira was dictating the terms. In less than a year she was Wilhelm Koch's wife, and shortly afterwards Anna Lang moved into the staff quarters as a maid. She brought little Konrad with her, who was still regarded as Anna's son.

Elvira had been sitting in the back of the Daimler for a long time, deep in thought. The windows had steamed up and the rain was still dripping on to the roof in an irregular rhythm. As she made a move to open the door, Schöller got out, opened an umbrella and helped her out of the car.

"Leave me alone for a moment," she asked. Schöller handed her the umbrella and his eyes followed the frail figure with the large handbag as she moved away uncertainly down the sodden track and finally disappeared round the bend behind a group of young fir trees. He sat down again behind the wheel and waited.

Twenty minutes later, just when he had decided to drive to meet her and had started up the engine, she came back into view. He drove the few metres up to her and helped her into the car. She looked as if she had re-applied her make-up. Only her court shoes were in a sorry state.

When he commented on them, she smiled and said, "Drive me to the sun!"

Schöller drove at the statutory 130. It was not unusual for Elvira not to speak. But for her to nod off was something new.

In the Gotthard tunnel, just under two hours after they had left Basadingen for the south, he noticed in his rear mirror that her eyes kept closing over. "Wake me in Rome," she said when she sensed that he was watching her. Then she fell asleep.

Even when he had to brake rather sharply at the end of the tunnel because the heavy rain on the south side had taken him by surprise, she did not wake from her normal light sleep.

The windscreen wiper struggled hopelessly against the waves of rain and spray as he drove almost at walking pace through the Leventina in a long line of traffic. Elvira Senn went on sleeping.

Shortly after Biasca he was struck by how pale she had become. Her mouth was slightly open.

"Frau Senn," he called quietly. Then louder, "Frau Senn!" And finally almost shouting, "Elvira!"

She didn't react. At the next rest area he braked and turned in, surprising the driver behind, whose long-drawn-out hooting was still audible as Schöller stood in the rain and tore open the back door.

The sweat had melted Elvira's make-up. She was unconscious but Schöller could feel her pulse. He shook her, first of all gently, then violently. When she showed no sign of life he got back behind the wheel and drove off. This time without observing the speed limit. Shortly after Claro he finally reached the exit, found out the number of the hospital in Bellinzona and got the doctor in the casualty department on the phone. He was driving in the outside lane at furious speed. Just as he was relaying the details of the symptoms over the car-phone and informing the doctor of the patient's importance, the last sign for Bellinzona South flew past him. He stepped on the brake, wrenched the steering wheel to the right, noticed that he was cutting off a lorry in the right-hand lane and turned the wheel in the opposite direction. The Daimler careered out of control, crashed into the central reservation, broke through the two crash-barriers, turned over several times, missed a van coming towards it by centimetres and came to a halt on the hard shoulder of the opposite carriageway, radiator facing the direction of the traffic, wheels to the sky.

Two hours after the deaths were confirmed, Urs Koch explained to his wife Simone the legal position as Fredi Zeller had explained it to him. He had refused to conduct the discussion in the guest house. She had finally agreed to come to the Villa but had insisted on her Laura Ashley room.

His manner was extremely decisive and dynamic but she knew him well enough to know that his bloodshot eyes had not been caused by tears for Elvira.

She listened to his spiel quietly and let him sum up in his business-like way. Only when he said, "So you see, from the legal point of view the case is cut and dried," did she ask, "And from the human?"

"Of course from the human point of view it's tragic. For all those involved."

"You won't know just how tragic until I've finished with you."

Urs pinched the bridge of his nose. His head hurt. "What are you threatening now?"

"Publicity." Simone stood up. "You'll be reading and hearing every detail of this shabby story in every newspaper and every radio station in Switzerland and half the rest of the world. You'll hear it so often that even you will be disgusted with yourself."

"What do you want?"

Simone sat down again.

The funeral service did not take place until a week after Elvira Senn's death. The delay was necessary to accommodate the busy schedules of the big names in commerce, politics and culture whose presence would give the funeral service the appropriate atmosphere.

Grave-looking people in sober clothes thronged the square in front of the cathedral. Most of them were acquainted and acknowledged each other silently. When they shook hands they did it sombrely so that people would not think that Elvira Senn's fate had left them cold.

They stood together in small groups chatting in hushed voices. A few officers from the municipal police force saw to it that the guests were not disturbed by members of the public.

In the midst of all this awkwardness the heavy cathedral bells began to toll. Slowly the mourners started to drift towards the church. They gathered for a short time at the door and then fanned out over the hard seats, a whispering, coughing, snuffling congregation calmly bracing itself for the next one and a half hours.

The rows filled up from two directions: from the front with family, friends and acquaintances; from the back with business contacts, society, politics, commerce and press. The two groups met and mingled in the middle rows of the nave. The aisles started to fill up with the particularly busy people who wanted to stay close to the doors.

As they all, with great form and dignity, remembered the deceased woman and did not forget Schöller, who had sacrificed his own life in attempting to save Elvira, the people sitting towards the front stared at the carpet of flowers and tried to decipher the inscriptions on the silk ribbons. The others gave way to their own thoughts.

No one except Dr Stäubli knew of the six capsules of U 100 insulin which were missing from Elvira's fridge.

To the mighty, heartening sounds of the organ and under the sympathetic gaze of the congregation, the bereaved left the cathedral by the central aisle. It took around an hour for the slow-moving stream of mourners to offer their condolences to Thomas, Urs and Simone Koch.

When Simone finally left the cathedral square the sun broke through the clouds. Spring made its presence felt, and the world set about forgetting Elvira Senn.

When Simone returned from the funeral meal (her presence at it was also part of her agreement with the Kochs), the occupational therapist had a surprise waiting for her.

"Come and see, Herr Lang has a present for you."

Simone took off her coat and went into the living room where Konrad had been spending part of his time again and where he had been taking his meals since Nurse Ranjah's life-saving action with the honeyed almonds. Now he was sitting at the table painting.

The therapist picked up a sheet of paper from the table and held it out to Simone.

It was the grey-blue watercolour bearing the title "House for Snowsnowballs in May". But now at the bottom it said, "For Simone".

Simone was touched. Less by Konrad, than by the therapist

who had obviously dictated her name to him to cheer her up a little after the funeral.

"Thank you very much, Koni, that's wonderful. Who's Simone?"

Koni gave her his pitying look. "Why, you are of course."

The following day O'Neill was there. He studied the videotape of this therapy session with Kundert; then he too was convinced that the occupational therapist had not been cheating.

Which meant that Konrad Lang had learnt a new name and remembered it.

In the afternoon at the usual time Simone had a photograph session with Konrad, this time with all four albums, even the three to which he had not reacted for a long time.

All his memory of the scenes from his life portrayed there were gone.

But when she came to the last album and pointed to the first picture – the young Elvira in the conservatory – he said reproach-fully, "Fräulein Berg. You knew that yesterday."

That evening the staff of the guest house had a party to celebrate. Luciana Dotti cooked six different pasta dishes, and Simone went down into the Villa's wine cellar and came back with eight bottles of Château d'Yquem 1959, a rare wine that Edgar Senn himself had cellared.

"To POM 55," Ian O'Neill called out whenever Luciana topped up his glass.

"If it wasn't the insulin," Peter Kundert grinned each time.

"Or the honeyed almonds," Nurse Ranjah added.

Peter Kundert was the last to leave. When Simone took him to the door they kissed.

Whole sections of Konrad Lang's life were lost to him, but with intensive training they managed to reorganise his old knowledge bit by bit and to re-establish his link with reality.

He had to re-learn how to follow sequences of events, simple ones at first, then more complicated ones.

After a few months he could get up without help, wash, shave and dress, though when doing the latter his outfit did not always quite match.

The more he learnt, the more came back by itself. It was all that O'Neill and Kundert could have hoped for in their wildest dreams: simply because the disease was halted, the brain cells were stimulated and stimulated each other. They formed new contacts with long disused parts of the brain and so suddenly re-awakened them.

Much remained blocked, but memories kept popping up to the surface like corks that had been tangled deep in the web of his memory.

The guest house of the Villa Rhododendron became a focus of international interest among researchers into Alzheimer's, and Konrad Lang was its uncontested star.

In June Simone and Urs Koch's marriage was dissolved.

In July Simone gave birth to a healthy little girl whom she baptised Lisa.

In September, on one of the last beautiful evenings of summer – there was a smell of freshly mown grass and down by the lake the lights of the suburbs twinkled busily – Konrad Lang sat down spontaneously at the piano in the living room of the guest house. He opened the lid and stroked the keys with his right hand. He played a few chords and then, very quietly, the right-hand melody of Nocturne Number 2 in F-sharp major, Opus 15, by Frédéric Chopin. Uncertainly at first, then with increasing courage and fluency.

When Nurse Ranjah came into the room quietly he smiled at her.

Then he brought in the left hand to help.

And the left accompanied the right. It stopped for a moment, paused for a few bars, came in again, picked up the melody from the right, continued it alone, then threw it back again. In short, it behaved like an independent being with a will of its own.

I I

TWO YEARS LATER POM 55 WAS LICENSED AND MARKETED
internationally under the name of Amildetox (R). The drug was
the first breakthrough in the treatment of Alzheimer's. In most
cases it was successful in halting the disease's advance or, as Dr
O'Neill put it, in infinitely slowing it down.

The big problem remained early recognition. Intensive research
all over the world had still not succeeded in devising a reliable way
of diagnosing Alzheimer's in the early stages. So Amildetox (R)
was an effective drug, but one that was doomed always to be used
too late.

Research concentrated on the regeneration of lost nerve cells.

O'Neill and Kundert's hopes that simply stopping the inflammation would provide sufficient growth-stimulant for the cells were
only partly fulfilled. Certainly the two doctors had some pleasing
results in the rehabilitation centre. After treatment with Amildetox
(R) patients regained many of their capabilities and were able, to
some extent, to lead an independent life. But results as sensational
as with Konrad Lang had, to date, failed to materialise.

Konrad Lang suffered from total amnesia of the greater part of
his past but he seemed able to cope with that quite well. He had
more or less complete memories only for the last two and a half
years, that is, from the time when his therapy began to show some
success. This had the advantage that no unpleasant memories
troubled him, making him into a well-balanced, contented old man.

He had control over his bodily functions, was mentally and financially independent and, with a childlike wonder, made short and then longer journeys to places that he had often visited in his earlier life, always in the company of an attractive Asian woman, a former nurse from Sri Lanka, who must have been many years his junior.

His speech centre had almost completely recovered, his sense of direction was back to normal and if anyone wanted to hear anything about his co-ordination they had only to listen to him playing Chopin with a gentle touch.

Dr O'Neill and Dr Kundert were inclined to the view that the crucial factor in Lang's amazing recovery might have been the hypoglycaemia, the low sugar level in the brain cells, triggered by Elvira Senn's attempt on his life with insulin. They sometimes regretted that they were unable to repeat this experiment.

Elvira Senn's portrait hung in a prominent place in the hall of the Clinique des Alpes rehabilitation centre, the Elvira Senn Alzheimer's Foundation, where Konrad Lang occupied the tower suite. A pleasant abode, so long as he managed to keep out of the way of the patient with the square head and close-set eyes in the room beneath him, who addressed him as "Koni", which no one else ever did, and bored him with his completely fictitious – and supposedly shared – memories of their youth.

The Des Alpes was full of strange guests who sometimes dressed rather flamboyantly or came into the dining room with dolls and talked to them. But which large houses have no eccentric guests?

The clinic was under the management of Dr Peter Kundert and his wife Simone, with whose little daughter, Lisa, Konrad had formed a very warm relationship. Sometimes he played the "Mosquitoes' Wedding" for her, an amusing song from Bohemia that had come easily to him one day out of a maze of forgotten memories.

When he was in the mood, during cocktail hour in the bar at

the Clinique des Alpes, he would play the bizarre guests a few old tunes from a time he could not remember.

The Hurni sisters felt that things had really livened up since the arrival of the new pianist.